The
Paris
Connection

The Paris Connection

Lorraine Brown

G. P. Putnam's Sons
New York

PUTNAM
— EST. 1838 —
G. P. PUTNAM'S SONS
Publishers Since 1838
An imprint of Penguin Random House LLC
penguinrandomhouse.com

First published in Great Britain, as *Uncoupling,* by Orion Publishing Group Ltd.,
a Hachette UK company, 2021
Copyright © 2021 by Lorraine Brown

Library of Congress Cataloging-in-Publication Data

Names: Brown, Lorraine, author.
Title: The Paris connection / Lorraine Brown.
Other titles: Uncoupling
Description: New York : G. P. Putnam's Sons, 2021. |
First published in Great Britain, as Uncoupling, by Orion Publishing Group Ltd.,
a Hachette UK company, 2021.
Identifiers: LCCN 2021023451 (print) | LCCN 2021023452 (ebook) |
ISBN 9780593190562 (trade paperback) | ISBN 9780593190579 (ebook)
Subjects: LCSH: Paris (France)—Fiction. | GSAFD: Love stories. |
LCGFT: Romance fiction.
Classification: LCC PR6102.R69175 U53 2021 (print) |
LCC PR6102.R69175 (ebook) | DDC 823/.92—dc23
LC record available at https://lccn.loc.gov/2021023451
LC ebook record available at https://lccn.loc.gov/2021023452
p.   cm.

Printed in the United States of America
1st Printing

Interior art: Paris sketch © Zoom Team / Shutterstock
Book design by Alison Cnockaert

For my dad, who would have loved this

The
Paris
Connection

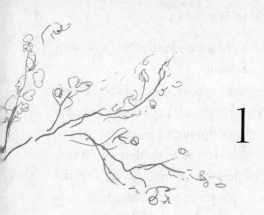

1

I sprinted up the steps at Venezia Santa Lucia station with minutes to spare before our train left without us, battling to keep up with Si, who was already several meters ahead and currently flinging himself through the glass doors of the station entrance.

"Come on, Hannah!" he yelled, disappearing out of sight.

I groaned under my breath, zigzagging through a group of about a hundred and fifty tourists who had decided that this was the perfect place to start fumbling about with maps.

"Sorry," I said, pushing past them, my breath ragged, my heart pounding in my chest. Missing the train was not an option; it would absolutely not be worth the fallout if we did.

I accelerated up the last few steps with beads of sweat trickling down my back, soaking through my flimsy cotton camisole and pooling at the waistband of my jeans, which I now bitterly regretted wearing given the thirty-degree heat. I'd thought I was being clever: it would be freezing on a train in the middle of the night, surely, and so I'd dressed accordingly, which wasn't ideal now, with the July sun beating down on my head.

I followed Si inside, struggling to keep pace, his blond hair bobbing in and out of view. My suitcase, clearly not designed for high-speed maneuvers, kept either tipping over onto its side or slamming painfully into my ankle. It was as though everything lovely about Venice had disappeared the second I ran through the doors of the station. I couldn't hear water taxis honking to each other anymore or take photos of the reflection of the sun setting over the Grand Canal. Instead there was incessant chattering and too-loud announcements in frenzied Italian and the wails of hot, tired children. It was disappointing that my lasting impression of beautiful Venice might now be tainted by this chaotic, fluorescent-lit concrete block of a station.

"You're slowing down!" shouted Si over his shoulder.

He waited for me to catch up and then grabbed my hand, pulling me after him. I must have looked ridiculous, my cardigan flying out behind me like a superhero's cape while my boyfriend propelled me unceremoniously across the concourse. My feet had never moved so fast as we weaved through the crowds, swerving the scarily long queues for the ticket machines because Si had had the good sense to print ours out before we'd left London.

"Right. Which platform?" he said breathlessly, dropping his bag and stopping so suddenly that I tripped over the back of his shoe and almost went flying past him. Really, part of me felt like calling the whole thing off and admitting defeat. We could spend another night in Venice, have a lazy dinner, a late-night stroll through the romantic backstreets of Cannaregio, the one area we hadn't properly had time to explore. If Si's sister, Catherine, hadn't been getting married in Amsterdam the following afternoon, that was. She'd never forgive us if we turned up late or—worse—not at all.

I wedged my hands on my hips, panting, watching Si's face as he concentrated on scanning the departures board, mumbling under his breath: "Roma Termini, Milano Centrale, Verona Porta Nuova." I was surprised by his excellent pronunciation of Italian place names, a talent I'd had no idea he possessed.

"Amsterdam, Platform 5," he said, flashing me a look and taking my hand. "Come on, Hannah. I think we can make it."

We started to run, racing past a place called Relax and Caffè, the name of which must surely have been ironic. Following Si's lead, I swung through the crowds, swerving to avoid the dangerously stealthy wheels of the mini-suitcases that kept creeping up on us at every turn.

"We're almost there," he yelled, pointing at something up ahead.

Our train, decorated patriotically in the three colors of the Italian flag, hovered on its rails, sleek and still, its doors open, as if to taunt us: you *could* make it, but will you? Si reached across me, yanked the handle of my suitcase out of my clenched fist and sprinted ahead with both bags held aloft. Gasping for air, and despite now having an excruciating stitch, I leaned forward like a sprinter about to cross the finish line.

A whistle blew.

"Fuck," shouted Si. "Wait!" he yelled to a guard.

We charged toward the nearest carriage. Si threw our bags inside, shoving me up the steps after them. I swung round to check he was behind me, wincing as the doors slammed into him and then bounced open again as he forced his way through before they shut for good. Almost immediately the train began to move, juddering at first, then accelerating smoothly, slipping out of the shadows of the station.

"You okay?" asked Si, wiping sweat off his forehead with the palm of his hand.

"Think so," I said breathlessly, rubbing at my right side.

I pulled off my cardigan, tying it around my waist and then leaning back, too exhausted to care that the nozzle of a fire extinguisher was pressing into my spine. When I held my arms out in front of me I noticed, in the golden light sifting through the windows, how tanned they were after a few days in the Venetian sun. How my usually dark brown hairs looked as though they'd been brushed with blond. We were flanked by the lagoon on both sides now; private water taxis were going full-throttle out on the water, back and forth from the airport, probably. They cost a fortune, those things, and so, needless to say, I'd spent the entire trip observing them enviously from the heaving queue for the water-bus.

Si bent down, unzipped his bag and plunged his arm inside, producing our tickets with a flourish. "At least one of us is organized," he said, chuckling to himself. "Seriously, Hannah. What would you do without me, eh?"

"Pretty sure I'd manage," I mumbled under my breath. I wasn't in the mood for his jokey comments about how useless I was.

He heard me and cocked his head, looking skeptical. "Not if the last hour is anything to go by."

Anyone would think I'd meant to leave my purse on the counter of the cute little gift shop near our hotel. I hadn't realized I'd lost it until I'd gone to pay for the water-bus tickets and then, of course, we'd had to run back for it, darting through the crowds, avoiding the throngs of tourists meandering at a snail's pace along the cobbled passages. The pretty, dark-haired local girl had retrieved it from under the counter, presenting it to me with a beaming smile. By the time we'd legged it back to the bus stop, the queue had quadrupled in size. I'd suggested we pool our last few euros and jump in a private taxi, but Si had point-blank refused, citing outrageous prices. Considering the amount of money he must have spent on the trip already, it had seemed like an odd place to draw the line.

He stood up and ruffled my hair. "We made it, that's the main thing," he said.

I nodded, picking up my suitcase, struggling to elongate the handle and then catching my finger on it in the process. I winced, sucking it to dull the pain. Si, who hadn't noticed, slammed the heel of his hand against a button, opening the doors through to the next carriage. I followed him like a lemming, stepping on someone's toes every other second and subsequently apologizing profusely.

"Here we go," Si said chirpily, stopping outside the first-class couchette he'd booked us as a treat.

I waited while he slid open the door.

"Oh," he said.

I peeped over his shoulder. A family was already inside, a couple and a young boy, their stuff spread out everywhere, a pile of colorful plastic toys in disarray on the floor.

"Excuse me, but this is actually our couchette," said Si, showing the man our tickets and dropping his bag territorially onto the floor. "See? Couchette 4, Coach H. Perhaps yours is farther down?"

The man turned to say something in French to the woman, who was sitting on the top bunk with her legs swinging off the edge. She had one of those sleek, shiny, perfectly symmetrical bobs that stopped just above her chin and I instinctively touched my own curls, which had gone wild and frizzy in the heat. We waited, both of us standing awkwardly to attention. I felt bad about the little boy, who was now hiding shyly behind his dad's legs, but it wasn't like they'd be without a cabin altogether, they were just in the wrong one.

After much shuffling of documents and hissed exchanges too fast for me to understand, the man showed Si a piece of paper. The two of us peered at it: their ticket looked identical to ours, the 19:20 Venice to Amsterdam, Coach H, Cabin 4.

"For God's sake," hissed Si.

There had obviously been a double booking. And they had a kid, so of course they should stay where they were. I had begun to suspect, though, that Si hated to lose at anything. A year together wasn't that long in the scheme of things and there was still lots to discover about each other, especially now we shared a flat.

"We'll find the train manager, then, shall we?" said Si, standing his ground.

"As you wish," said the Frenchman, shrugging dismissively.

I backed down the corridor. "Come on, Si. Let's leave it."

Eventually Si gave up and followed me, making a beeline for the first staff member we saw. He wanted to make an official complaint, he told her. She explained (much to his annoyance) that nothing could be done on board, that we'd have to go to the ticket office once we arrived in Amsterdam. Despite him having another rant at a steward with a drinks trolley along the way, we ended up in a cramped, rock-hard pair of seats a couple of carriages farther up in standard class. Si was fuming but pretending not to be.

"We'll be fine out here," he said, attempting to ram his bag into the overhead luggage rack and then kicking it under our seats when it finally dawned on him that it wasn't going to fit. I moved my knees to let him past. I'd given him the window seat because I'd been on a train journey with him once before and remembered that he'd moaned continually about people knocking into his shoulder "all the time." Also, I knew that once he got settled he'd be out like a light; it would be nicer for him to lean up against the glass. The only thing was, I was now stuck on this thing for the next fifteen hours and couldn't even daydream out the window, or pass the time by taking fuzzy photos of the view. I slid my fingers up and down the strap of the camera that had been almost permanently slung around my neck for the last few days, wondering whether I'd have time to shoot half a roll in Amsterdam before the wedding.

"Sorry about this, Han," said Si, looking sheepish. "What a fuck-up." He took my hand, stroking the skin between my thumb and forefinger. "This was supposed to be a special treat. You only turn thirty once, don't you?"

I swiveled my knees in his direction, holding his face in my hands. "It's fine, Si. Honestly. I'm having a lovely time."

"But I had our schedule all mapped out," he went on. "Tripadvisor raved about the first-class couchettes, called them cozy and romantic. I'd have booked us a flight, otherwise."

"It is romantic," I insisted. "And going without a bed for the night just adds to the adventure."

"Adventure wasn't exactly what I had in mind," he said, propping his elbow on the window ledge and pinching the top of his nose with his thumb and finger. I could tell it was killing him that things hadn't gone exactly to plan. *Welcome to my world*, I thought.

"Try to relax," I said to him, fanning myself with my hand, already too hot.

"There's no air-conditioning on this thing, I see?" said Si, wiping his upper lip on the shoulder of his T-shirt.

"There wouldn't have been in the couchette, either, then, probably," I reasoned, getting out my book and deciding it was best to leave him to stew for a bit.

I was halfway through *Gone Girl*, which my friend Ellie had lent to me because allegedly I was the only person she knew who hadn't read it. The female protagonist's psychotic tendencies notwithstanding, I thought there was something very appealing about the idea of dropping out of your current life and reinventing yourself as somebody else altogether. I supposed that, in a much smaller way, I'd changed myself, too, when I'd met Si. Had become a more contained, more settled version of myself. The sort of girlfriend I thought he deserved and that I'd always suspected I had the potential to be, when I met the right person. And after what I'd found in Venice, it looked as though it was working. I bit my lip, unable to stop myself from smiling as I tried to get comfortable, resting my head on Si's shoulder.

"I need the loo," he whispered into my ear after a while, stroking my thigh. "Sorry, sweetheart."

I sat up, stifling a yawn. "What time is it?"

Si looked at his watch. "Ten past ten."

A little over twelve hours to go, then. A full workday and then another half. My neck ached and I desperately wanted to stretch out my entire body, to fall asleep on my back with my legs flung out like a starfish. When I stood to let him pass, I felt unsteady on my feet.

"Back in a sec," he said, setting off down the aisle. I watched him go, marveling at the fact that even under these circumstances, he managed to look all groomed and neat in his emerald-green polo shirt and straight-cut indigo jeans. His hair was the same natural honey-blond at thirty-three as it had been at five, apparently, which annoyingly meant he still looked very young. He'd been asked for ID in Marks & Spencer recently, for example, something that hadn't happened to me for over a decade. To make matters worse, the week before we'd come away, I'd been brushing my hair one morning, pinning my choppy fringe to the side, just for a change, and it had been right there: my first gray strand. How could it be, when I was literally only just out of my twenties? I'd immediately started having dark thoughts about my impending death (which seemed closer than ever now) and about how I hadn't achieved half the things I wanted to achieve. I couldn't even blame my genes: Mum was fifty-seven and I'd never seen any gray scattered through her fine, dark blond hair. And I had no idea whether my dad had gone gray or not. His hair was dark like mine and he was olive-skinned, too. He was also short and stocky, like I thought I was, so perhaps I'd blame him for the gray. Why not, since he wasn't around to prove me wrong?

I sat back down, looking for signs of life out the window, anything that might tell me where we were. As we'd rattled on, I'd lost track of which country we were in, as though the train could be taking me anywhere and I would just let it. Outside, only the occasional light appeared on the horizon, like splashes of yellow paint on a black canvas. I could see the chatty American boys across the aisle reflected in the glass; they were asleep now, slumped on a parent each, their eyes closed, but not completely, so that you could still see a glimmer of white between the lids. I wondered whether that would be Si and me in a few years' time: the two of us traveling across Europe with a couple of kids in tow. Breaking up fights over sweets and who'd had longer on the Nintendo console.

Si's phone buzzed. It wasn't like him to go anywhere without his prized possession, a copper-gold iPhone that was pretty much welded to his hand. After feeling around on the floor with my foot, I found it in the gap between our seats. A message preview sat at the top of the screen and I half glanced at it, assuming it was his sister, who had been messaging him constantly in the run-up to the wedding. I put it on his tray table.

When I looked up, Si was standing next to me.

"Got us some drinks," he said.

"Great," I said, smiling at him. That should liven things up.

He edged past my knees, hurling himself into his seat and picking up his phone.

"Oh," he said. "Thought I'd taken this with me."

He scanned the screen.

"You got a message," I said.

"Yeah?"

He pressed a key, tutting.

"Who was it?"

"Work," he said, pushing his phone into his pocket.

"Not Dave, surely?" I said, referring to his nightmare new line manager. He'd made Si's life a misery since he'd started a couple of months before and was always on his case about something. Either that or he was trying to pin the blame on Si for mistakes he'd made himself.

"No, thank God, and he's the last person I want to think about tonight," said Si, pulling down my table with more force than was strictly necessary. "Here. I got you a wine."

I unscrewed the bottle with zeal, pouring fragrant, ruby-red liquid into a flimsy plastic cup. Oh, the glamour of train travel. Si did the same with his sparkling water. I was proud of him for sticking to his self-imposed no-alcohol rule, but given the stresses of the day, I thought he'd have been much better off with a brandy. It felt strange that he didn't drink anymore, and I was relieved to note that it wasn't just me who thought so—Ellie and her boyfriend, John, had been baffled by it when they'd come round for my birthday dinner last month, expecting the night to descend into the usual drunken revelry.

"That's exactly the kind of sound I like to enter a room to," Ellie had said, appearing in the doorway at the precise moment I popped the cork on a bottle of Prosecco. She'd edged round the table to pull me in for a hug. "Happy Birthday, Han."

I'd hugged her back, squeezing her tightly. "Thank you both for coming."

"Here, put this in the fridge," she'd said with a knowing wink, thrusting a bottle of wine into my hands.

Si and John had followed her into the kitchen, already deep in conversation about soccer. Apparently, Arsenal were doing well, which seemed to please them both. I'd branded Si a fair-weather soccer fan, as he only showed interest in his team when they were winning. Also, I thought he pretended to like soccer more than he actually did, depending on who he was with. I supposed I couldn't blame him for that; didn't we all do it, show relative enthusiasm for something based on how much we wanted to be one of the gang?

"Right. Drinks," I said, handing them round. "Oops, sorry, Si," I said, doubling back, grabbing the orange juice from the fridge and pouring him a flute of it. "Almost forgot you."

Ellie looked confused. "Not drinking, Si?"

Si scooted past me and I smiled up at him instinctively as he pressed his hands into my hips.

"I've given up, actually," he said casually.

"What, permanently?" asked John, already downing Prosecco like it was going out of fashion.

"Think so," said Si, putting on his apron. "On a bit of a health kick."

Ellie gave me a look; I shrugged. I hadn't mentioned it to her because I knew she'd make a fuss and, also, I wasn't quite sure how to explain it myself, because it seemed to have come out of nowhere. When we'd first moved in together, I'd loved how we'd chat about our day over a glass of wine in the evenings, one of us setting the table while the other one cooked. It had been something to look forward to when I'd been chained to my desk at work, struggling to stay focused in the afternoons. A chance for us to relax together, for me to shake off the frustrations of the day. Now things felt the tiniest bit more distant. He went straight from work to the gym most nights, and so by the time he'd come home and we'd had dinner, I'd be knackered and ready for bed. On the bright side, though, I was drinking less, too—it wasn't as much fun on your own, something that became glaringly obvious in Venice. One balmy late afternoon we'd been sitting in the most beautiful cobbled square, and I'd been trying to enjoy an ice-cold glass of peachy white wine while Si spent the entire time tutting over the extortionate price of sparkling water.

• • •

After an agonizingly slow-moving hour during which the train seemed to have practically come to a halt, I was desperately bored and not remotely tired. It was careering along nicely again now, rocking us rhythmically from side to side. The wine had helped so much that I'd gone to get another.

"Let's have some fun," I said, trailing my fingers across Si's knee.

He took one of his earphones out and leaned into me so that the tips of our noses were touching. "And how, exactly, do you propose we do that?"

We settled on people-watching, with Si providing a brilliant David Attenborough–style commentary about the imagined life story of whichever passenger we had decided to observe.

"He's going to visit a Dutch girl he met on holiday in Bali, and although he looks all cocky about it, he's secretly racked with nerves that she's going to reject him, like all his exes before her," said Si.

"You think?" I asked, dubious about his appraisal of the guy with the swagger and the hipster beard. "He looks very sure of himself."

"It's all a front," he said convincingly, reaching out to tuck my long hair behind my ears. "And she," he said, nodding at a nervous-looking woman returning from the buffet car with a mini-bottle of white wine and a plastic cup, "is going to visit the long-lost half sister she connected with on Facebook. She's terrified in case they hate each other. That's why she's drinking. She'll have another before the end of the night, you'll see."

I laughed. "I'll take your word for it."

Si's phone rang and he fumbled around in his pocket for it. "Hello?"

It would be Catherine, I bet.

He mouthed: *My sister.*

I knew it. My ears immediately tuned in to her shrill voice reeling off details of the latest minor setback she'd decided to turn into a catastrophe. After years of dating the good-looking but dull friends of friends from Durham University (that was how she'd billed it to me, anyway), she'd met her fiancé, Jasper, on a work trip to Amsterdam. He was ten years older than her, an art curator—a job title I still did not fully understand—and from a wealthy Dutch family who apparently owned properties all over the globe. Perhaps, for the first time in her life, Catherine now felt as insecure as the rest of us. She'd been preparing for her new role with great dexterity, however, and together with her mum, Pauline, had pretty much morphed into Berkhamsted's equivalent of Pippa and Carole Middleton. They'd thrown themselves into wedding preparations with a frightening intensity, sourcing bespoke invitations from somewhere on Mount Street and ordering personalized marshmallows for the wedding favors, because that's what Pippa had had, apparently. As for the dress . . . well, I had not been trusted with the details of the dress. I knew it was from some über-expensive New Bond Street boutique, but the actual design of it was shrouded in secrecy and whenever I asked, purely out of politeness, which fabric she'd chosen, or which shade of white, or whether she was wearing a veil, she made a zipping motion across her lips and I was put firmly in my place.

"Can't Dad do that?" asked Si wearily, rolling his eyes at me in an attempt at good humor.

I smiled encouragingly at him, opening my book to distract myself from the sound of Catherine's voice, which was increasing in volume as the conversation went on and she got herself in more and more of a state. Seriously, was this what planning a wedding did to you? Magnified every single neurotic trait you'd ever had?

"No, I'm sure Hannah won't mind putting the napkin rings onto the napkins," said Si.

I widened my eyes at him, hoping to convey the message that enough was enough, that he had to put his foot down. I'd already been allocated several tasks to ensure the wedding of the year went off perfectly the next day, including compiling the two-hundred-plus place cards (Catherine claimed I was the only person she knew with neat enough handwriting) and tying magenta chiffon around the stems of each bespoke bridesmaid's bouquet. It would have been much easier all round if she hadn't fired the hotel's in-house wedding planner, but when she'd dared to suggest that Catherine's color scheme would clash with the dining-room décor, there'd been no coming back. Pauline wasn't exactly the voice of reason, either. Honestly, the way she and Catherine had been banging on, you'd think the ceremony was going to be televised worldwide.

"Look, Cath," said Si, massaging the space between his eyebrows, "I'm going to have to go in a minute, all right? We're on a train here. And, oh look, we're slowing down and there's a station coming up. I might have to move some bags around or something."

I frowned playfully at him, kicking his ankle gently. We weren't stopping; the train was picking up speed if anything. I tipped my head out into the aisle, eyeing up what everyone else was doing (sleeping, mainly) and only half listening to Si placating his sister, telling her that everything would go smoothly, that she would look beautiful, that Jasper would be proud of her and that he, Si, was proud of her whatever happened. Even the two guys in front seemed amused; I saw them swiveling their heads to snicker at us through the slit between their seats, baffled, no doubt, by the weird gravelly tone Si reserved exclusively for his sister and which was about an octave lower than his usual speaking voice. When I'd first met Catherine, in the December after Si and I got together,

I'd immediately assumed we'd have nothing in common. She was one of those privately educated girls who was pretty and smart and popular and had never really struggled with anything as far as I could tell and therefore had the sort of extreme confidence I could only dream of. But when she wasn't talking about weddings, it turned out we weren't as different as I'd thought. We'd bonded over a love of wine and reality TV, and I'd thought we might actually have the beginnings of a proper friendship.

"I really am going to have to go now, Cath. Okay? See you tomorrow, yeah?" said Si.

He hung up and looked at me in disbelief. "Is it bad I'm going to be relieved when all this is over?"

I chose my words carefully. "She *has* turned into a tiny bit of a control freak."

"Turned into? She's always been one. It's been heightened by the wedding, that's all," he said, throwing himself back in his seat with a frustrated groan.

"Come on, let's have a look through your Venice pics," I said as the train rattled on and someone with an unnecessarily loud voice decided to make a phone call, despite it now being one o'clock in the morning. "That'll cheer us up."

I was too exhausted to read my book and too wired to sleep, stuck instead in some terrible, restless limbo. He handed me his phone.

"They're not great, though, Han. Yours will be much better."

"They won't," I assured him, although I thought they probably would be. I appeared to have finally found something I was quite good at, and rarely left the house without my beloved secondhand Canon AE-1 these days. It had been a Christmas present from Si and was the most thoughtful gift I'd received from anyone, ever.

I flicked through Si's camera roll, starting from the shot he'd taken of me when we'd first arrived in Venice. We'd been at the airport, waiting in the queue for the water-bus. For once, I didn't mind how I looked: relaxed in cut-off denim shorts, flip-flops and a black T-shirt, my hair curlier than usual because of the humidity, a guidebook open in my hand, a huge smile on my face because I was ecstatic to be there, in this place that I'd dreamed of visiting since I was a little girl, when Mum used to show me pictures of all the sights and make up stories about them. Then there was the selfie he'd snapped of us standing outside the Basilica di San Marco, which wasn't the most well-framed shot because at six feet two Si was ten inches taller than me, so it was practically impossible not to cut off either the top of his head or everything below my nose.

While I was sending Mum a WhatsApp montage of the photos Si had taken at the Doge's Palace, his phone vibrated and another message began to slide into view.

"Let's see?" he said, whipping it out of my hand and looking at the screen. "Fuck's sake," he said, tutting theatrically. "Work again."

"At this hour? What could they possibly want now?" I asked.

Not that it would make much sense if he told me, anyway. I still wasn't 100 percent sure what he did on a day-to-day basis. I knew it was something to do with selling pharmaceuticals and that he had to travel a lot and stay in Premier Inns and that he did presentations and that he didn't find public speaking the worst thing in the world.

"I'm not reading it on principle," said Si. "I'm on holiday, aren't I? And it's the middle of the bloody night."

I looked at him, hesitating. "Is everything all right?"

"'Course it is," he said, laughing hollowly. "You'd finished with the photos, right?"

"Not really."

"You shouldn't be on the phone—I read about it somewhere. The blue light messes with your sleep pattern," he said.

"It's too noisy to sleep anyway, so what difference would it make?"

"Why don't you put your earplugs in?"

"Left them in Venice," I said, picturing them on the bedside table at the hotel, my fluorescent-green saviors. I'd have to pick up some more when we got to Amsterdam.

"Well, I intend to get some rest even if you don't," said Si, sliding his phone into his pocket. "Otherwise I'll be of no use to anyone tomorrow."

He angled his body away from me, scrunching up against the window and closing his eyes, each breath becoming deeper and longer. Si was always short with me when he was tired, he admitted it himself. He'd be fine after a few hours' sleep. I, on the other hand, would most likely have to navigate the wedding with a severe case of sleep deprivation. I imagined getting drunk too quickly at the reception and telling inappropriate jokes before having a wine-fueled argument with somebody. My anxiety took over and doubled the twisting feelings of inadequacy in the pit of my stomach. Pauline would make snippy comments behind my back, I could picture it now: *This isn't her world, Simon. She doesn't know how to behave at an exclusive event like this.* Because Pauline consistently referred to the wedding as "an event," which I secretly found unbelievably annoying.

Massaging my jaw with my fingertips, I tried to put myself in the sort of blissful state conducive to sleep, which wasn't easy when the couple in the seats behind were whispering so loudly that they may as well have used their normal speaking voices, and somebody farther back was frenziedly eating a packet of crisps.

Si's phone buzzed again. Seriously, what was going on? It could only be Catherine. I inched my fingers toward Si's pocket, sliding the phone out as carefully as I could. I was going to put it on silent. He'd only just got to sleep, the last thing he needed was her sending him a slew of frantic messages. There was no point both of us being knackered at the wedding.

The phone vibrated for a second time as I tapped in his password, which he'd told me ages ago was 1956, the year his mum was born. A message sat at the top of the screen, from an unknown number.

Are you awake? It's me, Al.

I frowned. Presumably it was someone from his work, although he'd never mentioned an Al, and the only Al I knew of was Alison, one of Catherine's bridesmaids. She'd organized the hen do, a stupidly expensive weekend in Marbella that I'd tried to get out of because I couldn't afford it and because I didn't know anyone other than Catherine. I *had* gone, of course, mainly because I hadn't been able to think of a good enough excuse not to. Alison, I remembered, had seemed nice enough until she'd got drunk, argued with a Spanish guy she'd been getting off with all night and threw up in the swimming pool. If it was her, it was possible there was some sort of last-minute crisis. Catherine was probably doing her head in, too.

I scrolled up. There were other messages from the same number.

It's me, can you talk?

And before that:

I'm at the wedding. When are you getting here?
Urgently need to speak to you.

It was definitely bridesmaid Alison, then. I put his phone on silent anyway; whatever wedding disasters were occurring, there wasn't much he could do about it tonight. I tried to slide the phone back into his pocket without disturbing him, but it slipped out of my hand and clattered onto the carpet. I winced, praying I hadn't broken it. He'd go mad if I had. He stirred, and I looked tentatively across at him. His eyes were half open and he clasped his hands together, stretching them up above his head.

"Your phone fell out," I whispered, touching him lightly on the arm.

He patted his pocket, then ran his hand between our seats.

"It's on the floor," I stage-whispered.

Somewhere between sleep and wakefulness, he bent down and scooped it up. I noticed he put the phone into his far pocket before turning to lay his head back against the window. It was odd that he hadn't mentioned the other texts from Alison, but I was sure there was a simple explanation. He knew I was fed up with Catherine's constant demands, that was all, and probably thought I wouldn't want to hear it. I'd ask him about it in the morning.

I closed my eyes, squeezing them shut. Si began to snore softly. The doors kept hissing open and shut every few minutes and I could hear a group of lads shrieking with laughter in the next carriage along. Surely there must be a quieter spot somewhere on this train? I could go and sit somewhere else, just for a little while. The change of scenery might do me good. I pulled my straw shoulder bag onto my lap, careful not to disturb Si. Then I stood up, chucking my cardigan on the seat because it was still boiling and I didn't think I'd need it. My suitcase was in the rack by the door; it would be fine there, I'd be back to pick it up in the morning. I hesitated for a second or two, fingering my camera strap, thinking I should write a note. I'd only be an hour or two anyway, he probably wouldn't even notice I'd gone. With one last look at Si, I stumbled toward the front of the train.

2

I finally found a pair of empty seats in carriage A and threw myself into them, scooting across so that I could rest against the window. I hadn't intended to come this far up, but aside from the trio of wasted blokes making a massive racket in the carriage one up from ours, the one after that had smelled like mold, as though someone had left their clothes festering in the washing machine for days on end. Ridiculous of me to be so fussy, really; we were on a night train across Europe, what had I expected? In any case, I was here now and carriage A was seemingly the least offensive option, even if I would have to endure the tinny sound of crap dance music blasting out of some guy's headphones a few seats back. Was he playing the same song on loop? I looked over my shoulder at him, intending to give him a dirty look, but he was slumped on top of his bag with his eyes firmly closed. What kind of person fell asleep with their music on that loud?

In desperation I raked through my bag again, deciding I might as well put my own music on as an antidote to his. I almost cheered out loud when I pulled out my earplugs instead, which hadn't been left in Venice after all but had been tucked inside a leaflet advertising guided tours of the Gallerie dell'Accademia. I pressed them in, slipped off my shoes and tried to get some sleep.

• • •

Early-morning light was streaming through the carriage when I next opened my eyes. Disoriented, I reached for Si, forgetting that he wasn't next to me, that he was somewhere farther back, oblivious—hopefully—to the fact I'd moved seats at all. I took out my earplugs and rotated my head to the left and then the right, rubbing my aching neck, annoyed with myself for not having had the forethought to bring my cardigan so that at least I could have used it as a pillow.

I looked out the window, wondering where we were, watching the world slide silently by, the details all fuzzy and diffused, like one of those old-fashioned home movies shot on cine camera. The sun was almost entirely hidden by tumbling clouds, elephant-gray on the inside, then edged with a brilliant silvery white. I pressed my nose against the glass as we rocketed through a pretty village made up of fifteen or twenty houses with whitewashed walls and terra-cotta roofs. Its tiny, deserted station reminded me of a piece from a toy I used to have: the train set Dad had bought me for my seventh birthday. I could still recall that day, sitting cross-legged on the brown corduroy sofa in our living room, waiting for him to come home from work so that we could tuck into the hedge-hog cake Mum had made. I remembered he'd come in after a day on the building site, all dusty and tired, brandishing a huge box wrapped in shiny red paper. He'd left us a few weeks later, which must have been why the memory was so entrenched in my mind. Birthdays had never been the same after that.

I rotated my ankles to get some life back into them and scraped my hair up into a bun using the frayed elastic band that had carved an angry pink circle around my wrist overnight. Looking for the nude ballet pumps I'd flung off in the early hours of the morning, I jabbed around under the seat in front, eventually finding them and hooking them onto my feet. Then, yawning, I levered myself to standing, had a stretch and looked up and down the carriage. Most people seemed to be awake, flicking through guidebooks and magazines, stuffing sweaty, microwaved toasties into their mouths. The smell was making my stomach rumble. When I got back, I'd nip to the buffet car, grab Si and myself some breakfast. Croissants with jam and butter were his favorite; I'd get him two, and a nice strong coffee.

I picked up my bag and set off down the aisle, retracing my steps from the night before. The train kept lurching forward and I had to concentrate quite hard on not stacking it to the side, failing dismally at least once as my hip slammed into someone's shoulder. The train was getting livelier the farther toward the middle of it I went, with each carriage more populated than the last. I carried on, digging my fingernails into the felt fabric of the seats, nosing over people's shoulders to see what they were eating, until suddenly I couldn't go any farther. There was a door blocking my way with no window and no buttons to press and no way of getting through to the next carriage.

I stared at it, confused. Perhaps lack of sleep had made me delirious. I needed to think. I must have gone wrong somewhere, walked past my actual seat and the rack with my suitcase in it, which contained the change of underwear I was desperate for, and my wash bag so that I could nip to the loos and scrub my face and clean my teeth. I tried turning the handle, but it didn't budge. I'd only walked through four carriages and I knew, *knew* the train had been longer than this.

I turned round and headed back the way I'd come, clutching at seat backs as the train tipped and undulated, my head twisting from one side to the other, searching for Si's face, his shock of blond hair, the black cardigan I'd left on my seat. I was cold in my thin summer camisole now that we were farther north, in France, maybe, or in Holland already. The air-conditioning had finally kicked in, and I had nowhere near enough layers on. I passed the seat I'd slept in, arriving at yet another gray door, which, given that it said *No Entry* in three different languages, I could only assume was the driver's cabin. I leaned my back against it, looking down the aisle at a sea of heads and sticking-out feet.

I took a deep breath. My mind must be playing tricks on me. Obviously I'd missed something. Si must have been in the loo before, it would be as simple as that. I'd do the length of the train again and I'd find him. I checked the time on my phone: 6:14 a.m. We weren't due into Amsterdam until 10-something, so I had plenty of time.

I set out again, this time searching for any face I recognized: the American family, the Dutch couple who'd been sitting behind us, but I couldn't see any of them. A pulse throbbed in my throat. I reached the back end of the train again, turned and headed for the front, searching for clues.

After another futile round trip I sat back down in the seat I'd slept in with my hands clasped together in my lap, my palms now slick with sweat. I looked out the window again, trying to make sense of the landscape, seeing if I could work out where we might be stopping next. I searched for something recognizable: a building, a road sign. There were station names, but we were screeching past so fast that I couldn't make them out. I had the stirrings of a distant memory, a snapshot of something that flickered into my mind and then out again.

There was nothing for it, I would have to wake Si and ask him where he was. I got out my phone, prodding at the screen with clumsy fingers, dialing his number, waiting for him to answer. He wasn't going to be happy when he found out what I'd done. It rang and rang, eventually going to voice mail. I didn't bother leaving a message, he was obviously still asleep. The best thing would be to sort all this out before he realized anything was wrong.

I dipped my head out into the aisle, wondering whether I could ask someone, and what I could say:

Excuse me, but do you know where the rest of this train has gone?

Or perhaps *Hello, I seem to have lost my boyfriend.*

And then I heard someone barking Italian into a crackling radio and I perched on the edge of my seat, ready to pounce.

"*Mi scusi,*" I trilled as a guard sailed past, head held high, doing his best to avoid making eye contact with anyone.

"Madam?" he said, elongating the *m* sound at each end of the word and flashing a toothy smile. Resplendent in a navy-blue uniform and gold-trimmed hat, he clutched a ticket machine between his hands. He was an officious type, I could tell.

"*Un problema,*" I said to him, thinking he might appreciate an attempt to speak his native language. I tried to recall the few words I'd picked up at our school's Italian club, which I'd only joined because Ellie had persuaded me that we'd then be fully equipped to go Interrailing around Italy for the summer, where we could have flirty conversations with Italian boys, which of course we'd never had the money to actually do. "I cannot find my seat. It was back there, I think. Carriage F?" I waved my arm toward the other end of the train.

"What is your destination, madam?"

"Amsterdam."

He sucked air through his teeth. "Nooooo," he said, shaking his head slowly, as if to make sure I'd noticed. "No, madam, you are not on the right train. We are in Paris now. Look."

"What?" I said, my eyes darting toward the window. The wide boulevards lined with trees were just visible between the huge, brutalist apartment blocks and offices that sat alongside the tracks and blocked out almost all of the light. Paris. Of course. I recognized it now. I turned back to him, swallowing hard.

"But I was on the Amsterdam train!" I said.

"Madam, the train separated in Geneva at 3:38 this morning. There were many announcements. You did not hear them?"

"No," I said, covering my mouth with my hands. "I didn't hear anything."

My earplugs, I thought.

"The eight coaches at the back go to Amsterdam Centraal and this section here," he said, making a circular motion with a stubby finger, "will arrive in Paris Gare de Lyon in approximately seven minutes. This happens often with international travel in Europe, madam. And we always ensure that our passengers are sitting on the correct segment of the train."

"Well, I'm sorry, but you definitely did not do that this time."

I bit my lip so hard I could feel it tingle. This was crazy. It didn't seem possible that despite getting on the same train and sitting next to each other for several hours, I was now in one country and Si would soon be arriving in another. What about the wedding? And all my stuff? And Si's schedule, which was now well and truly in tatters? I already knew he was not going to take it well.

I looked around wildly, hoping for others who had made the same mistake, a group of us who could stick together, stage a protest, although what good that would do I didn't know; they were hardly going to turn the train round, were they? Was I really the only one who'd done this? Could I be the only person on this whole train who had no idea it was going to split quietly into two in the dead of the night? I noticed the guy with the giant headphones and the bad taste in music was poking his head above the seats. When he spotted the ticket inspector he stood up and staggered over to us, looking half asleep.

"Did you say this train is going to Paris, monsieur?" he said to the guard, running his hands through his dark hair, which was sticking out at all angles. He looked as confused as I felt. He was French, then, judging by his accent. I gave him a dirty look. If it wasn't for him, I would have heard the announcements in the first place.

"Sir, as I have already explained to this young lady, the train separated in Geneva at 3:38 this morning," said the guard wearily.

"We are not going to Amsterdam?" said the French guy, clutching his chest dramatically.

At least I wasn't the only one. "No, we're not," I snapped, catching his eye. "We're in Paris. See for yourself," I said, jabbing my finger on the windowpane.

He looked at me as though he'd only just noticed I was there.

"And by the way, if you hadn't disturbed everyone," I said,

swiveling in my seat so that I could look directly at him, "then maybe both of us would have heard the announcements in the first place."

He looked at me, screwing up his face with apparent confusion. "You are blaming me?"

"Yes, I am," I said. I thought I might be being a little unreasonable, but I was on a roll now. "I had to put my earplugs in to drown out all the noise you were making."

"What noise?" he said, seemingly incredulous.

"Your music?" I said, tutting. "It was far too loud. You probably kept half the carriage awake."

He shook his head at me as though I wasn't worth bothering with, turning his attention back to the guard, who was looking at his watch with barely disguised irritation.

"Monsieur," he said to the guard, "this is not acceptable. Not at all. I have a very important meeting in Amsterdam which I *absolument* must get to."

"Excuse me, but I was talking to the inspector first. We all have important things to do in Amsterdam," I snapped at him.

"There were many announcements, sir," said the inspector, "and madam," he added, smiling tightly, obviously unsure which one of us he should be addressing.

"Well, they were not loud enough!" said the French guy, looking as though he was about to start kicking things.

"There must be something you can do," I said to the guard, deciding I'd try to appeal to his more reasonable side. He must have one. "What's the best way to sort all this out?"

"If you wish to reach Amsterdam by train, you will need to travel across Paris to Gare du Nord, madam."

I closed my eyes for a second or two, trying to muster up a less defeatist attitude. "And how soon might there be a train from there?" I asked, doing my best to hold it together. All I could think about was Si, and what he was going to say when he finally worked out where I was. He already treated me like a child at times, and when I did stuff like this, it gave him the ammunition he needed to carry on doing it.

"You must inquire at the ticket office at Gare du Nord," said the guard. "There is nothing more I can do for you here, I am sorry."

"Sorry does not help us," said the French guy, who was now thumbing frantically through his phone.

"I presume you both have tickets for your journey?" asked the guard.

"Of course we have tickets," said the French guy, looking up. "Do you think we are idiots?"

I, on the other hand, began scrabbling around inside my bag knowing, almost instantly, that Si had our tickets, and our passports, for that matter, both of them, in the back pocket of his jeans. I closed it again.

"My boyfriend has mine," I said.

Si was much better at looking after things than I was; it had made sense for him to hold on to everything. Out of the corner of my eye, I was sure I saw the French guy roll his eyes. I was about to have a go at him for being so rude, but thought better of it. I had to stay focused on what was important: getting to Amsterdam in time to see Catherine get married. That was all that mattered.

"I wish you both good luck," said the guard, patting his machine. He was taking great pleasure in this, I was sure, and would regale his colleagues later with his tale of the stupid British girl who woke up on the wrong train in the wrong city. The French guy shook his head at both of us and stomped off back to his seat, muttering under his breath. At least when I explained all this to Si later, I could tell him that two of us had ended up on the wrong train. It might soften the blow.

I turned back to the window, resting my cheek against the pane to cool my skin, which felt all tingly and hot, the way it tended to when I started to panic about something. I tried to even out my breathing, counting eight tracks to my right and a never-ending tangle of wires above our heads. Graffiti was everywhere, sprayed onto the walls lining the tracks, most of it nothing more than fat white words that I didn't understand. I wondered how long it had been there; whether there was a chance I would have seen it last time I'd been here, almost ten years ago now. When other people talked of romantic weekends strolling along the banks of the Seine, my stomach actually turned, because I hadn't been on some cutesy mini-break. I'd been completely alone and looking for someone who didn't want to be found. It still hurt, and the memories of it seemed to seep into every inch of this city, and I'd rather be anywhere else in the world than here.

A crackly announcement in French, then Italian and then English, let us know that we would shortly be arriving at Paris Gare de Lyon and that the local time was 6:31 a.m. A blue double-decker train slinked past in the opposite direction and I wondered where it was going; how difficult it was going to be to find my way to Amsterdam from here. People were getting up out of their seats, shaking out their limbs, tidying their rubbish, gathering their things together. I got my phone out again, dialing Si's number, nibbling on my thumbnail while it rang. Voice mail *again*. Why wasn't he answering his phone? I knew it wasn't out of battery because he always, without fail, charged it overnight. Plus I'd seen him crawling around on the floor of our hotel room the morning before, un-plugging the charger, packing it neatly into his bag. Given that he wouldn't be arriving in Amsterdam for more than three hours, he was probably still asleep, that would be it. Then I remembered: I'd put the damn thing on silent.

I left a self-conscious message, paranoid that half the carriage was listening in.

"Si, it's me. You won't believe this but I'm pulling into Paris. The train separated in Geneva, apparently. I had no idea, did you? Shall I try and get a train from Paris to Amsterdam, do you think? Apparently, I've got to trek right across the city to a different station. I'm so sorry, Si. Call me, okay? As soon as you can. I really need to speak to you."

I put my phone in my lap, staring at the screen and willing it to ring. Si would know what to do, he was excellent in a crisis. Metal ground on metal as the train came to a stop, its brakes letting out a hiss of relief. The platform outside my window was laced with luggage trolleys waiting to be loaded up or, as in my case, not. I raked through my straw bag to see exactly what I had in there and what, if anything, might be of use. I had my credit card, at least, although I was pretty sure it was maxed out. Stupidly, in hindsight, I'd left my purse in Si's bag because he'd shoved it in there when we'd retrieved it from the gift shop in Venice and Si had paid for everything since then. I only had a few euros with me now—thirty at most—plus my book, three pens, a crushed biscuit and a ton of receipts. And still around my neck: my camera. If Si didn't get back to me soon, I'd head over to Gare du Nord, see what I could find out about the trains while I waited to hear from him. I made my way to the door noticing that, of course, the obnoxious French guy was at the front of the queue, first to step out onto the platform.

3

Light filtered through the glass roof of Gare de Lyon in misty strips of silver. I put my camera to my right eye and took a sequence of photos. I wasn't really in the mood and I couldn't remember a thing I'd learned from my beginners' photography book about composition, about framing, but it was too lovely not to try. It was the first beautiful thing I'd ever noticed about Paris; it felt right to capture it.

I followed the other passengers along the platform. The air was spiked with fumes, the way it always was in these gigantic stations, and a cool breeze made the hairs on the back of my neck stand on end. I folded my arms around myself, my shoulder bag bobbing up and down under my arm. It was easy to spot who was French and who was not, I thought. The local women looked chic and unruffled, even after the long and uncomfortable journey we'd had. They wore light jackets over expensive-looking fine knits, and had filmy scarves wrapped nonchalantly around their shoulders. I, on the other hand, was still clad in a wafer-thin camisole and skinny jeans that had gone all saggy at the knee.

Because I was lagging behind the rest of the crowd, it was eerily quiet, except for the turning over of a train's engine on a distant platform and the odd squeak of a suitcase wheel. I moved hesitantly toward the ticket barriers, knowing I was going to have to brazen this out. Hooking stray hairs behind my ears, I fixed on a smile and made a beeline for the less aggressive-looking of the two male ticket inspectors. I attempted to exude confidence by doing all the things I thought confident people probably did: I made eye contact, I relaxed my shoulders and, inexplicably, I casually hummed a *Hamilton* show tune under my breath.

He held out his hand as I approached.

"I haven't got my ticket, I'm afraid," I told him, keeping my expression apologetic yet assured, hoping he'd believe me when I told him that I wasn't an actual fare dodger.

"*Quoi?*" he said, groaning when a woman ran her massive suitcase over his foot.

"I didn't realize the train separated in Geneva," I explained, my voice coming out all singsongy in my rush to make my excuses. "And the thing is, I've got a wedding to get to in Amsterdam. Today, in a few hours' time. Can you tell me what I need to do?"

He laughed, throwing back his head, his mouth open so wide that I could see his tonsils.

"Why do you not keep your ticket with you? It is yours, *non?*" he said.

"My boyfriend has it," I said, struggling to keep my cool. "And he's currently on his way to Amsterdam. Where I should be going."

Seriously, what was it with ticket inspectors and their attitudes? Everyone made mistakes. Some more than others, as Si would say.

He sighed, shaking his head in disbelief. "*Un moment, madame.*"

I watched him shuffle off to speak to another—presumably more senior—inspector.

It was raining, of course, just to add insult to injury; I could hear it clattering on the roof of the station in violent, tinny bursts. Typical Paris with its grim, depressing weather. I'd get soaked at this rate, just what I didn't need with another long train journey ahead. If I made it that far, that was. The worst-case scenario would be that they'd make me pay a massive fine for not having a ticket. And I'd have to try my credit card and it wouldn't go through because I was probably over my limit. And then what would they do with me? Send me back to London? Detain me? I'd never make the wedding then, which, given how the day was already panning out, was looking more and more likely.

Another train snaked through the tunnel toward the platform, its windscreen wiper flicking back and forth across the front window. I watched as it squealed to a stop and the doors opened and about a thousand people cascaded off. What were they all doing here? I could never understand the appeal of Paris; I could think of a million better places to go. In a moment of rebellion, I thought I might be able to lose myself in the crowd, barge through the barrier behind one of them, like people sometimes did on the Tube. There was a name for it, an actual word, but I couldn't remember what it was. It was on the tip of my tongue. Piggybacking? Anyway, the younger, more defiant me might have tried it, but, well . . . I wasn't brave enough to do stuff like that anymore.

The inspector came back. "We will let you through," he said, opening the barrier with a fob. "You are lucky we will allow it, you understand?"

I nodded obediently.

"You must go directly to Gare du Nord, where you can buy a ticket for the train to Amsterdam. *D'accord?*"

I nodded again, whisking through before he changed his mind, calling a thank-you over my shoulder.

The clock on the departures board said 6:37. I needed coffee, but there was no time or money for that. I'd had nowhere near enough sleep and felt as though I was either deeply jet-lagged or coming round from an anesthetic. I began to walk, heading over to a pod of garish orange-and-green ticket machines, figuring there must be a train or a Metro I could catch. I stood in front of one, staring at the screen for a few seconds, prodding at all the buttons before working out that I needed to twiddle a dial to move the cursor. Eventually I found Gare du Nord, but I couldn't figure out which ticket to get, or which route I'd need to take to get there.

I whirled round, looking for some sort of information desk, catching sight of the French guy from the train disappearing down the escalator into the Metro with his too-big bag on his shoulder. I bet he'd have absolutely no problem swanning across Paris like he owned the place. Just as I resigned myself to the fact I was going to have to actually approach somebody and ask, I saw a sign for taxis and thought how much easier that would be. I felt around in the bottom of my bag, pulling out the twenty-euro note I'd seen earlier. It was a risk using up most of my cash so early on, but surely the most important thing was that I caught the next train to Amsterdam, even if it meant spending every last penny I had. I could go without food for a few hours, it wouldn't be the end of the world; I could stuff my face at the wedding instead.

I ran outside into the rain, holding my open book above my head.

Miraculously, because it was too early for the tourists, I supposed, there was only a short queue at the taxi rank. I watched the cars pulling up, one after the other, each one sporty and black with a flashy green logo on the side. When my turn came, I opened the rear door and flung myself inside, sliding my bottom across the slippery leather seat.

"*Bonjour, monsieur*," I said, reaching back to slam the door behind me. "Do you speak English?"

"A little," he said, looking at me suspiciously in his rearview mirror. Was I going to be too much trouble for him, he might be wondering; was the fare worth the hassle?

"I need to get to the Gare du Nord, but I only have twenty euros. Will that be enough?"

He shrugged.

Well, that was helpful. Anyway, I was here now, I would have to risk it.

"If the meter gets up to twenty, I'll have to get out and walk the rest of the way. Okay?"

"*Oui, madame*," he said, screeching away from the curb, his elbow hanging out the window, a cheesy French pop tune on the radio.

The rain had eased up and I wound down my own window, hoping the fresh air would perk me up. I could hear a siren, a creepy wailing sound, like something you might hear on one of those gritty French crime dramas. An undercover police car careered round the corner toward us, an old beige Citroën with a blue light stuck on its roof. In the passenger seat was a woman who looked like an actress playing the role of a detective; she was effortlessly beautiful, with long dark hair and a cigarette between her fingers, which she draped casually out of the window, as though chasing criminals around Paris on a Thursday morning was nothing out of the ordinary.

I sat back in my seat, combing my fingers through my hair, easing out a knot and then winding it back up into a bun. We were pulling out onto the roundabout at Place de la Bastille; I recognized its column with the golden angel perched on top. I got out my phone and googled directions from there to the Gare du Nord, bringing up a map and feeling better and more in control instead of at the mercy of this driver, who had a soccer emblem tattooed onto his neck and kept accelerating and braking so sharply that I was beginning to feel carsick. I checked the meter: nearly ten euros already.

I texted Si, wondering if he'd listened to my voice mail yet. I'd been so caught up in getting to the station that I hadn't really considered what it would be like for him to wake up and discover I wasn't sitting next to him. What would he do when he worked out that the train had uncoupled in the night and that his girlfriend was not in fact in the loo or the buffet car, but was hundreds of miles away, in a country she had absolutely no desire to be in?

> Hey. I left you a voice mail earlier, which you
> probably haven't heard yet. I'm fine, so don't worry.
> I'm in a taxi on my way to Gare du Nord. Call you
> when I know what's happening with the trains xx

I knew he would worry no matter what I said, it was what he was programmed to do. Not only would he feel like a failure for not getting me safely from A to B, he'd assume that I would fall apart without him. And he had a point—it was what I'd always loved about him, the fact that he was so capable and together, and that from the very beginning he had made me feel more cared for and looked after than anyone I'd ever met. For the first time in my life I didn't have to try to work everything out for myself—he did it for me, and much more successfully than I'd ever managed. So I'd let him, happily taking a back seat when it came to anything vaguely organizational. According to Ellie, he was one of life's "fixers," which I'd suspected she hadn't meant as a compliment.

I checked the meter again: seventeen euros and ten cents.

"Um, are we nearly there?" I asked the driver, leaning forward, projecting my voice through the Perspex hatch.

"Two kilometers," he mumbled.

Seventeen euros and eighty cents. And the traffic was terrible.

"Remember I only have a twenty," I said, in what I hoped was an authoritative manner.

"I remember."

I looked out the window, drumming my fingers on my knee, begrudgingly noticing how pretty the buildings were with their wrought-iron balconies and their window boxes bursting with color and the French windows thrown open behind them. I tried to follow the journey on my phone, twisting it this way and that, wondering where we were in relation to the Seine. That was what I remembered most from the last time I was here: walking alongside the churning water, angry at every single one of the smug, camera-wielding tourists chugging past on their sightseeing boats, and internally railing against the unfairness of life in general. Killing time before my return train, although since I'd been too miserable to enjoy the city anyway, in hindsight I might as well have sat brooding on a bench in the Eurostar terminal.

We turned onto one of those busy boulevards you see on TV whenever there's some sort of transport strike, which even at the best of times appears to be permanently loaded with cars and funny-colored buses and crazy cyclists weaving their way through it all. It was so vast, Paris, and even more hectic than London, although perhaps it was me who felt all over the place in this city I didn't know and didn't particularly want to know. It was disconcerting to think that only one person in the world—in fact, perhaps not even him, yet—knew I was here at all.

"It is at twenty, *madame*," said the driver.

Fuck.

"Stop, *s'il vous plaît*."

He pulled over. I thrust my sweaty note at him and climbed out of the taxi, spinning around full circle, struggling to get my bearings. The taxi driver beeped his horn and waved at me, trying to help, pointing straight ahead. I gave him a relieved half wave back and began to run. Paris was at its rush-hour worst, with horns beeping relentlessly and bus fumes muddying the air. Because the road sloped uphill, I was out of breath within minutes and had to revert to power-walking, my ballet pumps slapping and sliding on the pavement. The sky was a dark ominous gray, with clouds so low it felt as though they were skimming the tops of the buildings. Sure enough, I felt a big splat of rain on my forehead, and then another and then of course it poured down. It would have to rain on me now, when I was completely exposed and didn't have time to stop and find shelter.

I broke into a jog, swearing loudly when I plunged straight into a puddle that was deeper than it looked, soaking my shoes. I squelched on, up the same never-ending road with its identikit restaurants and their drab scarlet awnings, until at last I saw a sign for the Gare du Nord. Keeping my head down to protect my face from the now near-horizontal rain, I swung off the main road into the station forecourt, darting between cars with their trunks flung open, sprinting through the nearest entrance.

4

The Gare du Nord was ridiculously busy, like Waterloo at its worst. It was a stunning building, I had to give it that, all peaked roofs and arched windows, but not quite beautiful enough to make up for the crowds and the noise and the slippery floors and the irate drivers outside in the taxi rank. And the fact that I was freezing cold, soaked through and wearing what I suspected was now a completely see-through camisole.

I joined a cluster of people huddled around a departures and arrivals screen, my lungs burning with the exertion of charging uphill, my eyes scanning through a list of places I'd never heard of. I needed there to be a very fast train to Amsterdam leaving pretty much immediately, which, given that I couldn't seem to catch a break today, was possibly asking a bit much. I spotted one, though, halfway down: the 07:20, calling first at Brussels, then at Antwerp, Rotterdam, Schiphol (which I thought was the airport) and finally Centraal. I had no idea how long all this was going to take, although Holland sounded far away, and I would have passed through two other countries to get there. It was 7:09. I had eleven minutes to buy a ticket and board the train, and then at least I would be on my way. There would be some good news to report to Si when he called me back.

I spotted a sign for *Billets* at the back of the building, although it was the most stylish ticket office I'd ever seen and looked more like the open-plan office of some sort of creative start-up, with wooden desks and computer screens and huge pewter lampshades numbered 1 to 13 hanging over the pods. I ran to join the back of the queue. People were grumbling to each other and looking at watches and nobody seemed to be moving and even when they did, they fussed and dithered about which desk to approach. There were two guys standing at the front dressed in black: I had no idea whether they were security guards there to control the crowds or ticket officers strategically placed to help. I stood on tiptoe, struggling to gauge what the situation actually was. There were at least fifteen people in front of me and although there were several kiosks open, each transaction seemed to be taking forever, with people taking out maps and pointing at things, then fumbling around in their backpacks. I was pretty sure that whatever it was they needed, they could have got it ready while they were waiting in the queue. I felt like shouting: *Just buy your ticket and fucking well go!*

From the depths of my bag I heard a ringing sound. It must be Si. *Finally.*

"Hello?" I said, pressing my finger to my ear.

"Hannah? It's me."

"Oh Si, thank God."

"What's happened? Are you seriously in Paris?"

"You got my messages, then," I said, cringing. I could just

imagine his face, the way his eyes turned from green to slate-gray when he was annoyed about something.

"Eventually," he said, "but only after I'd walked up and down the length of the train about five times wondering what the fuck was going on. I've been out of my mind with worry here, Han."

The queue moved forward by about an inch. If I'd had the guts I would have waltzed straight to the front, begged someone to take pity on me, charmed them into letting me cut the queue.

"I can imagine, Si, honestly, I can. I should never have moved seats. I couldn't sleep and I panicked."

"Since when do trains just split like that, anyway?" he said, sounding out of breath, like he'd just come back from one of his runs. "I'll be calling the train company the minute we get home. They absolutely did not make their instructions clear."

"I know," I said, relieved that it wasn't me he was blaming, at least not entirely.

He sighed. "Look, the main thing is that you're all right. You are, aren't you?"

"'Course," I reassured him.

"Jesus, Han. Are you even going to make it in time for the wedding?"

There was a sudden surge of activity and I moved about five places forward.

"There's a train in nine minutes," I told him, glancing back up at the screen. "I'm nearly at the front of the queue."

"Call me back, then, when you know what's happening."

"Where are you now?" I asked.

"Still on the train. We've got another couple of hours at least. God, I'm going to have to explain this to Mum and Catherine when I get there. Wish me luck."

A window came free and I scrambled over to the counter, telling the cashier what it was I wanted in a garbled mix of English and French.

"Si, I'll speak to you later."

"I've got your suitcase, okay, so don't worry about that. It'll be waiting for you at the hotel."

"And tell Catherine I'll be there, whatever it takes."

I then became one of those people I had literally just vilified, beginning a frantic search for my credit card, pulling things out of my bag, lobbing my phone and my book and a handful of coins on the counter. I felt all jittery, like when I'd drunk more than one espresso on the trot. Why wasn't it in the zipped section of the bag where I'd put it? After a bit more rummaging I found the card for the joint account, which Si had instructed me was to be used only for bills and household emergencies. It must have fallen out of my purse at some point in Venice, and since this was clearly a matter of urgency, I handed it to the cashier without hesitation. Si would understand. I watched her punch digits into the card machine, doing a double take when I realized it was going to cost me 180 euros.

"Is that the cheapest ticket?" I asked, gutted that a one-way train journey could cost that much.

"It is, *madame*," she said, looking down her nose at me. Admittedly, I doubted I was looking my best, all sweaty and grubby and dripping all over her counter.

"I'll take one," I said, having very little choice. If this was what it took to get everything back on track, then it would be worth every penny.

"Your card is declined, *madame*," said the cashier a few moments later, looking up from her screen.

I gripped the counter. "What? It can't be."

"It is," she said, apparently about to lose the minuscule amount of patience she'd had with me to begin with.

I didn't know whether to cry or laugh out loud at the ridiculous run of bad luck I'd had all morning. Nothing had gone right, literally nothing, and now this, at the final hurdle, when there'd been a chance I could have made it to the wedding and everything would have been all right again. With the cashier staring me down, I returned to searching the depths of my bag like a maniac. Just as I'd been about to tip the whole thing on the floor in a last-ditch attempt to find my credit card, I slid it out from under a travel-sized packet of wipes and handed it over. With shaking hands I tapped in my pin number, willing it to work. I had no idea what I was going to do if it didn't.

"*Voilà, madame*," said the cashier, looking ever so slightly put out, as though she'd wanted the small triumph of denying me a ticket.

I thanked her anyway, stuffed everything back into my bag, slung it over my shoulder and ran. Platform 19, she'd said, which was, of course, right down at the other end of the concourse. I wondered if there was something weird happening in the universe, some planet in retrograde that might explain why over the past twenty-four hours I'd done nothing but run frantically around stations and nearly miss trains. Upping my pace, I simultaneously raked around for my phone, wanting to check the time. As I ran, my hand swiped back and forth, checking every corner of my bag, up and down, under things, between pages, everywhere. I couldn't find it. I swallowed hard, slowing down; this couldn't be happening, not now, not after everything. I had an awful thought: Had I picked it up again, after I'd emptied everything out at the ticket office? I couldn't think, my brain had gone all fuzzy. Had I, in my panic to catch the train, left my phone on the counter?

I whirled round, looking for a clock, running over to the nearest departures board: 7:16. I had four minutes.

I sprinted back in the direction of the ticket office. If I didn't have my phone, then Si wouldn't be able to get hold of me and I didn't want him to worry or—more to the point—think me incapable of looking after myself. I charged past the queue, waltzing right to the front this time, explaining to the irate-looking security officers, one of whom had held out his hand to stop me, that I had left my phone on counter number 11 and that I wasn't pushing in, just checking. He reluctantly let me through and, ignoring the shouts of protest from somebody in the queue, I ran over to the desk I'd been at a few moments before. The cashier was serving someone else now, a middle-aged businessman who unsurprisingly gave me a weird look as I scanned the counter, then flung myself to the ground, crawling around next to his feet to see if it had fallen on the floor.

"Excuse me," I said to the cashier, jumping up, waving my arms around semaphore-style. "Excuse me, but did I leave my phone here a minute ago?"

She shook her head, the tiniest of smug smiles fluttering across her face. Great, I'd just proved to her that I was indeed the dimwit she'd thought I was. I put my hand over my mouth, telling myself to keep a clear head. If I wanted to catch the train, I had to forget about my phone and run. It was more important that I made it to Amsterdam, whatever the cost. Phones could be replaced, but Catherine would never have another wedding day. So I ran, out of the ticket office and back across the concourse, toward the platform, my breath ragged, my ticket clutched in my hot, damp hand. I was halfway to Platform 19 when out of nowhere and as if in slow motion, a huge black bag slid across the floor in front of me. I reacted pretty quickly, I had to say, flailing my arms around, trying to slow myself down, digging the balls of my feet into the ground, but it was no good, I couldn't stop or even swerve in time to avoid it. I flew forward, the floor of the station zooming toward me at such alarming speed that I reckoned I was going to knock myself out. I put out my hands to save myself and landed sprawled on my side, twisting my ankle in the process.

I lay there for a second or two, breathless and somewhat dazed, before everything came back into focus and I became aware of legs all around me, of painted toenails in sandals and the bottoms of jeans, of an announcement about a train to Lille and a searing pain in my ankle.

When I blinked and looked up, someone was standing over me, a man, wearing a black leather jacket. I couldn't believe it. Or actually, I could, because with the day I was having it just *had* to be the arsehole French guy from the train, didn't it? I might have guessed he'd be selfish enough to chuck his stuff about all over the place.

"*Je peux vous aider?*" he said, breathing heavily as he held out his hand, which I ignored.

"No, you can't," I said, knowing I had to get up, had to keep on running. I tried to stand, but more pain shot through my ankle, so I used my other leg to push myself up, grabbing at his bag for leverage.

"Can you walk on it?" asked the French guy, already backing off. He was catching the same train I was, presumably, and obviously had no intention of hanging around to check whether or not I was okay.

"Just go," I snapped at him, bending to gather up the contents of my bag, which had scattered all over the floor.

"I can call somebody to assist you," he said, looking wildly around, scooping up my book and a pack of tissues and shoving them at me.

"What I need is to catch this train," I said, snatching them out of his hands. The platform looked even farther away than before and I could hardly sprint at full speed now, could I? Running wasn't my forte at the best of times. "Go and get your train. Seriously," I told him. Why was he still standing there, staring, being of no use to anyone whatsoever?

"If you are sure?" he said, hauling his bag onto his shoulder.

"There's no point both of us missing it, is there?" I said, starting to hobble toward the platform.

He fell into step beside me, rubbing his hand over his mouth.

"Go!" I said, massively pissed off. I didn't want him blaming me if he didn't catch his precious train.

He went to walk off, looking back over his shoulder as though he was unsure what to do and then finally breaking into a run and accelerating so fast that he was out of sight within seconds.

I pushed on, attempting a painful half run because there was always a chance the train would be delayed. Someone might have pressed the emergency alarm, for example. There could be a minor signaling problem that would temporarily hold things up. Just as I neared the end of the concourse and veered left onto Platform 19, a whistle blew and the train—my train—began to move, slinking casually out of the station as though it hadn't just added yet another terrible layer to this hellhole of a day. I leaned on a luggage trolley for support, trying to regulate my breath, taking the weight off my ankle. And then I saw him, the French guy, striding toward me, his monstrosity of a bag thrown over his shoulder, the train snaking into the distance behind him.

"So," he said, slamming his bag on the floor.

I put my hands on my hips, squaring up to him. "How did you manage to miss it?"

"I was here," he said, throwing his arms about. "One minute before, at 7:19. But they had closed the doors early and that *imbécile*," he said, scowling over his shoulder at a guard, "would not open them again."

"Right," I said, too fed up to even pretend to care.

"I should have been on that train," he said. "Now I will be late for something very urgent, very important to me."

"Join the club," I said.

"Well, perhaps if you had been looking where you were going," he said, raking his annoying floppy fringe out of his eyes.

"I hope you're not suggesting that any of this is my fault?" I said.

He looked at me. "You must take some responsibility, *non*?"

I did a mock double take. "Please *do* explain."

He laughed.

"And don't laugh at me." I couldn't stand these arrogant Parisians. Who did he think he was?

"You feel guilty," he said, still chuckling to himself. "Admit it."

"I do not."

"You do."

"What have I got to feel guilty about?"

He looked up at the ceiling, pretending to think. "Hmm. Let me see . . . perhaps it is because you were running around like a crazy person in a busy train station. Falling over people's things. Holding them up."

My mouth actually hung open. He was unbelievable. "Well, I'm very sorry that I didn't notice your *massive* bag, which for some reason you decided to fling right across my path."

He made a huffing noise. "I put it down for one second only to search for my ticket. If you had opened your eyes, you would have noticed it right there in front of you."

"I could have been seriously injured."

"If it had not been my bag you'd fallen over, it would have been somebody else's."

I pressed my lips together. This was getting me nowhere. I should be finding out when the next train was, not standing around arguing with someone I would thankfully never have to see again.

"Right. Well, this was a delightful conversation, but I'm going to go now," I said, shaking my head in an exaggerated way so that I could be sure he'd noticed. I felt a bit dizzy afterward, actually.

"Maybe you can slow down this time," he said, bending to get something out of his bag.

"You know, you're very rude," I said to the top of his head. He didn't even look up. I went to say something else and then checked myself: I didn't need to get into it. Holding my head high, I turned and strode purposefully down the platform, which wasn't easy with a limp.

"And you are very clumsy!" he called after me.

I clamped my hands to my sides to stop myself from giving him the finger. I couldn't believe he was trying to shift the blame onto me; I could have broken my neck out there. When I reached the end of the platform, I glanced back to check he wasn't following me. I'd had enough of his appalling attitude for one day. I needn't have worried, he'd obviously forgotten about me already and was sitting on top of his bag scrolling manically through his phone. I tutted indignantly to myself and walked on, trying to stay positive. I still had ten hours to get to Amsterdam in time for the wedding—how hard could it be?

5

There was a pod of wooden benches underneath the escalator up to the Eurostar terminal and, lowering myself onto the last empty seat, I stuck my foot out and bent to examine it. I hoped it wasn't going to swell—I'd never get my wedding shoes on then.

I was busy prodding the flesh around my ankle bone when a huge black bag—*the* huge black bag—dropped out of nowhere, landing with a bang on the floor next to me.

I looked up in disbelief. "What are you doing here?"

He shrugged. "It is okay, your foot?"

"Not sure why you're pretending to care," I said, feeling petulant. For some bizarre reason I was suddenly acting like a sulky teenager.

He knelt down on the ground in front of me and gently slipped off my ballet pump.

"What are you doing?" I asked, swiping my foot away, embarrassed.

"I am checking over your ankle," he replied patiently, easing my foot back toward him and resting my heel on his thigh.

"Now who's feeling guilty?" I said.

"It has not become red, that is good," he said, peering down and ignoring my childish retort.

"What, are you a doctor or something?"

"No," he said, giving me a condescending look. "I am not a doctor. But I do know a broken ankle when I see it."

"Broken?" I said, shocked.

Surely it wasn't that. How was I supposed to get to work every day on crutches? I'd never get up and down the escalators on the Tube.

"Does this hurt?" he asked, twisting it to the left.

"Yes." I winced.

"And this?" He turned it the other way, more gently than I'd expected.

I took a deep breath in and then out. "A bit."

He smoothed his thumb across my instep, over the place where my toes ended and my foot began.

"Yeah, you can stop now," I said, finally succeeding in moving my foot away, aware that the teenage girl sitting next to me, who had previously been scrolling through her phone, suddenly looked very interested in what was going on.

"I think it is just a sprain," he said confidently.

"I'm pretty sure I could have worked that out for myself," I said. Trust him to make a big deal of stating the obvious.

I looked up at the nearest departures screen: 7:28. Our train had been erased from the schedule as though it had never existed. Now not only had I lost my phone, but it was touch and go as to whether I'd make it to the wedding at all. I imagined Catherine and her parents, waking up in their executive suites, cracking open the champagne. No expense had been spared on this wedding, that much I knew. When I'd first met Si's family, I'd had to hide my surprise when Si pulled up outside a sprawling detached house that was at least five times the size of the one I'd grown up in. I'd looked up at it in all its double-fronted glory, trying not to gasp out loud at the perfection of its double bay windows, its grand, brass-laced door and its brickwork covered with ivy. Their sweeping driveway, flanked by expansive, manicured lawns, was large enough to house about six cars. For when they hosted their posh dinner parties, probably, and the whole village came.

"Here we are," Si had said, chirpily. "Home sweet home."

"Well, this is lovely," I'd said, smiling inanely at him, trying to hide how annoyed I was that he hadn't warned me his family was loaded. I supposed this was so normal to him, this life, that it hadn't even crossed his mind that I might like to know. That I might have wanted to prepare myself. I immediately felt underdressed, in high-street jeans and a bobbly black turtleneck jumper, which I'd been convinced had looked chic and French when I'd flattened myself against the wall of my tiny room in my shitty house share in Manor House to check myself out in the mirror. I'd been kidding myself, obviously: it was hardly sophisticated enough for this spectacle of a house.

* * *

The Gare du Nord was getting busier by the second, which I wouldn't have thought possible. I watched people rushing in from outside, their summer clothes wet with rain, flicking water off their umbrellas, leaving tiny, shiny puddles on the floor. I didn't know how long I was going to be stuck in this station for, but I'd already had enough.

"Am I missing something here, or are there no Amsterdam trains on the board?" I said, pointing at the nearest screen.

French Guy stood up to see for himself, brushing dust off his knees.

"I cannot see anything, either," he said, looking at me over his shoulder and ruffling his hair with confusion.

When I spotted a guard striding past, I seized my opportunity, waving my arms about to flag him down.

"*Excusez-moi, monsieur!*" I shouted. "When is the next Amsterdam train, please?"

He pulled a timetable out of his jacket pocket and flicked through it for a few agonizing seconds, shaking his head. This didn't seem like a particularly good sign.

"This afternoon, *madame*," he said. "The 13:40, arriving in Amsterdam Centraal at 16:57."

I put my head in my hands, trying to think. The wedding was at 5:30. Would that give me enough time? If there were no delays, would half an hour be long enough to get to the hotel? When I looked up, French Guy was strutting around gesticulating madly as the guard explained that there were engineering works on the line, that two trains had been canceled and that there was nothing that could be done. I looked away because I was trying to keep calm and he wasn't helping. It was possible, if everything went smoothly and the train left when it was supposed to, that I might just make it. I needed to hold on to the tiniest bit of hope.

"Okay?" asked the French guy after a while, standing in front of me with his arms crossed, completely blocking my view of the concourse.

"Yes," I lied.

"What is it you must do in Amsterdam?" he asked.

"I'm supposed to be at a wedding."

He shrugged. "Not such a disaster, then."

I squinted up at him. "You don't think missing someone's wedding, the day they've spent months planning, that you're supposed to be helping set up, whose family are expecting you, is a disaster?"

"I do not," he insisted, doing an annoying pouty thing with his mouth.

"And what world-changing event are you required at this afternoon?" I asked.

"Work," he said, putting his hands on his hips and expelling air through pursed lips. "A meeting that can change everything for me."

"You're right, that does sound *much* more important," I said, rolling my eyes.

"And I do not care what that guard on the train said, the announcements were not loud enough. How are we supposed to listen when we are all asleep? It was the middle of the night," he grumbled.

"I know," I said, reluctantly agreeing with him. "I didn't hear a thing, either."

"I wish, now, that I had stayed where I was," he said. "I moved because there were some guys laughing and shouting in my carriage and I could hear them all the time, even with my music on at maximum volume."

"That's why you had your music on that loud, then, was it?"

He sighed and flicked his eyes to mine. "You still try to blame me?"

"It's as clear as day: if your terrible dance music hadn't been booming out of your headphones, I wouldn't have had to put my earplugs in."

He raised his eyebrows. "Terrible music?"

"In my opinion."

"And now we find ourselves here," he said, looking enigmatically around the concourse.

"But you're French, right?"

He nodded. "I live here, in Paris."

I tutted. "Hardly a disaster for you, then, either, is it?"

He bent down to retrieve his bag.

"You always think you have things much worse than everybody else?" he asked.

"Only when I actually do," I said, although his comment stung. It was something Mum used to say, that I was always feeling sorry for myself.

"So," he said, hoisting his bag onto his shoulder. "I go."

"Bye, then."

He hesitated. "You need anything?"

"Can you conjure up a train?" And then a thought occurred to me. "Actually, if you're serious, could I borrow your phone?"

I didn't particularly want to give him the satisfaction of helping me, but while he was standing there, with his phone in his hand, it seemed foolish not to ask. Besides, I very much wanted to avoid having to use one of the Gare du Nord's disgusting, rancid pay phones.

"Here," I said, delving into my bag, "I've got some change somewhere. I can give you some money for the call."

I tried to pass him a handful of coins, which he waved away.

"Why do you not have a phone?" he asked.

"I lost it. Left it on the counter at the ticket office."

He looked doubtful. "I do not think that is what happened."

"It must be."

He shook his head. "*Non*. The Gare du Nord has a problem with pickpockets. Very bad. They snatch things from you so quickly that you do not even notice."

"I reckon I just lost it. I'm always losing stuff."

"Why would somebody not hand it in, if you left it on the counter, with the cashiers right there?"

"I don't know," I said, irritated now, suspecting he was one of those guys who always had to be right.

Admittedly, the idea that I might have been pickpocketed hadn't even occurred to me, but then I was a bit slow on the up-take with things like that. It was the same with films: Si would guess the plotline before it had barely begun, and I'd constantly need clarification about what was going on. Problem-solving was not something I was proficient at.

"Oh well. Either way, I've lost it. Doesn't really matter how, does it?"

He handed me his phone. "I think it does matter. Because one way it is your mistake, and the other way, it is not."

I shook my head. The sooner I could use his phone and give it back to him, the sooner he'd go. Annoyingly, when the teenage girl sloped off, her handset now clamped to her ear, he took a seat next to me, spreading out his legs at an acute angle, locking his hands behind his head as though he was watching TV on the sofa at home.

The call to Si went straight to voice mail again; I was planning to leave a message, but then I got stage fright with this nosy stranger sitting next to me, listening to every word I said. I noticed that the hems of his jeans had risen up, revealing black ribbed socks and well-worn white Converse trainers. Si would not have been seen dead in trainers that tatty.

I handed back the phone.

"There is no answer?"

I shook my head. "Nope."

Because he was now at eye level, it was the first time I'd noticed how good-looking he was, which probably explained the swagger and the attitude. He was slightly younger than me, I'd have said, late twenties perhaps. His tanned skin was sparkling and golden, as though he spent his summers frolicking naked on the beaches of the French Riviera (which he probably did). He clocked me staring and I pretended to look for something in my bag, emerging with my trusty lip balm. I slicked some on, pressing my lips together, attempting to give him the impression I was completely fascinated by a poster advertising day trips to Versailles. Out of the corner of my eye I saw him smirk to himself. He probably thought I fancied him or something. Frenchmen thought they were God's gift to women, didn't they?

"Your ankle is still sore?" he asked.

I tentatively twiddled it around. "Not really."

He looked at me as though he didn't believe me. "You need to get an X-ray."

"I don't want an X-ray."

"I can direct you to the nearest hospital."

"No, thank you."

"Why do you not want to check?" he asked, swiveling in his seat.

Seriously, what was it with this guy and his probing questions?

"Because I already told you, it's not that bad. And because I'd rather wait here. I need to make sure I don't miss the next train as well."

"So you will sit in one place and be miserable?" he asked.

"Precisely," I said, picking at the chipped red nail polish on my thumbnail, wondering if I'd have time to repaint it at the hotel. Catherine was bound to have something to say about me turning up in such a state as it was.

The other reason I didn't want to go to the hospital was because I didn't have any travel insurance and there was no way I could afford an expensive doctor's bill. I hadn't given insurance a thought until we were already on the plane to Venice, and strangely, neither had Si, who was usually very on the ball about such things. Even he had reassured me that nothing could go wrong in the space of a few days. That was a laugh. If my ankle had been broken, I would have been in real trouble.

"There is a long time to wait," said French Guy.

"Thank you for pointing that out."

He squinted at me, as though he couldn't quite decide what I was about. Because he looked the way he did, he was probably used to women fawning all over him. Hanging on his every word. Well, not me, absolutely not.

"You do not have a suitcase!" he announced, having only just noticed. He leaped up to do a sort of mock scan of the area around my feet.

"I travel light," I snapped back, hoping he'd get the hint and go.

"I do not, as you can see," he said, nudging his bag with his foot as he sat back down and turned to me.

"Clearly."

He almost smiled. "Too much?"

"What have you got in there? You could do some serious damage with that thing."

"I suppose you are blaming my bag, now, for your injured ankle."

"Pretty much."

"Nothing to do with you running too fast?"

"Nothing at all," I said. I had my story and I was sticking to it. "So are you going to tell me what you've got in there, or not? I'm going to start suspecting it's something illegal otherwise. A dead body, perhaps?"

"Nothing so sinister. It is vinyl. Records. I buy them wherever I go."

"And lug them around everywhere?"

"I suppose. Do you like music?"

"'Course I do," I said, immediately on the defensive. My knowledge was very, very limited.

"What kind of music do you like?"

"All sorts," I said.

I looked up. The rain had got heavier and was now hammering on the roof. Perfect. Now I couldn't even go outside for some fresh air.

"You like dance music?" he prompted me. "Wait, I know you do not like it, since you referred to it as 'terrible.'"

"To each their own."

"Rock, then? *Classique?*"

"Anything, really," I said, being deliberately vague.

My musical tastes were dodgy, even I admitted that. I owned an Olly Murs album, for example, although in my defense it had been a Christmas present from Mum and my stepdad, Tony. Also,

Ellie and I had gone to the Take That reunion concert at the O2, which I wasn't totally ashamed to admit, but there was no way I was going to mention it to this guy. Because whatever edgy, alternative bands he was into, I could pretty much guarantee I wouldn't have heard of any them. He was probably only asking me so that he could make a pretentious comment about it afterward to make himself look good and boost his already massive ego.

He pulled a pack of cigarettes out of his pocket. "Six hours to wait, eh? Not good."

He offered me the packet, but I shook my head, even though I badly, badly wanted one. I hadn't smoked for nearly a month. Si had nagged me about giving up from the moment we'd met. Obviously I'd tried to stop before, for years, but the timing had never been right; I'd enjoyed it too much and I had terrible willpower. But once Si and I had moved in together and I was spending most of my time with him, I began to cut down, eventually managing to go without altogether. I didn't even really crave them anymore. Except at times like this. Then I missed it.

He took a cigarette out of the packet for himself and slipped it behind his ear.

"Do you know anybody in Paris?" he asked.

His voice was low and scratchy, as if he had a sore throat, or he'd had too many late nights. Probably the latter.

"No. No one."

I shivered, longing for something warm to slip over my shoulders. Stupid of me to leave my cardigan on my seat. Ridiculous of me to waltz around moving carriages in the middle of the night in the first place. What had I been thinking? I suppose I hadn't been, that was the problem.

"Here," he said, throwing his bag to the ground and combing

through the insides of it. He pulled out a red hoodie. "I suppose you could have this."

I held my hand out to stop him, horrified. "No. No way."

"Take it," he said. "I have many clothes in here. And it is raining. You cannot walk around Paris in your camisole."

He threw it at me, not quite meeting my eye, and I caught it clumsily, suddenly self-conscious about the lack of clothes I was wearing.

"Thank you," I said, pulling it on, wrapping it around myself like a dressing gown. I wouldn't usually wear clothes belonging to someone I'd only set eyes on an hour ago; in fact, I'd likely be grossed out by the thought of it. But nobody would be happy if I turned up at the wedding with hypothermia. I noticed his top smelled like he did, of tobacco and leather and vinyl.

"You are a photographer?" he asked, pointing at my camera before zipping up his bag.

"Not really," I said, running my thumb and middle finger up and down the strap. "It's just a hobby."

He took the cigarette from behind his ear and hesitated, leaving it hovering a centimeter from his bottom lip.

"*Alors*, I am going to walk," he said. "All this time in the Gare du Nord? It is not possible."

I thought it sounded like a nightmare, too, but I couldn't risk leaving the station, just in case, by some miracle, an earlier train was announced.

"Good luck," I said.

Once he was gone and I was alone again, I'd be able to think more clearly. Make a proper plan.

"You can come if you want," he said gruffly, as though there was nothing he would like less.

I laughed. "I think I'll pass."

"Too risky for you?"

I fiddled with the sleeves of his hoodie. "It's called being sensible."

"Ah. You think I am a criminal. A murderer. That I will kidnap you and make you stay in Paris forever."

"Very funny."

As if I was going to go off God knows where with a man I barely knew. No, I was going to stay at the station and drink the cheapest coffee I could find and read my book and probably get very bored, but still. It was the mature thing to do.

"You will not see any of the city?" he asked, sounding disappointed. I had no idea why he cared whether I saw it or not. Was he an ambassador for the French tourist board or something?

"Well, there's the problem of my ankle," I pointed out.

He did up his jacket and slipped both hands into his pockets, his thumbs hanging over the edges.

"Ah, yes," he said, giving me a look that suggested he thought a slightly sprained ankle was a feeble excuse for not dashing out to sightsee around his precious hometown.

"My name is Léo, by the way. *Et vous?*" he asked, the cigarette now dangling from his lips.

"Hannah," I told him hesitantly.

He nodded, adjusted the strap of his bag for a second or two, and then he was off, merging seamlessly with the crowds, zigzagging across the concourse. He was tall and lean, like a long-distance runner or one of those insane Parisian guys who leap about from building to building. I shook my head at the way his bag sat on his back like a turtle's shell, so big it took up as much space as an actual other person. There was nothing spectacular about his clothes: a biker's jacket and black jeans slung so low I could see a flash of the white waistband of his boxers, but against the backdrop of the Gare du Nord, with hundreds of commuters blurring into insignificance around him, he managed to make the scene look like an editorial spread in a fashion magazine.

I watched until he almost disappeared. At the last second, he swiveled his head to look back at me, dragged his hair out of his eyes and raised his hand in a sort of dismissive wave. I resisted the urge to wave back, and then he was gone.

6

Standing up to test my foot, I limped over to the nearest café, thinking how the Gare du Nord was marginally less dingy than I remembered. This time I couldn't help but notice the warm, buttery lighting, and the delicious-looking pastries sparkling in glass cabinets. I joined the queue, looking longingly at the stacks of baguettes jam-packed with colorful fillings and the rainbow-hued display of macarons. Exercising great restraint, I bought a *pain au chocolat* and a small cappuccino instead, crossing my fingers that my credit card went through.

This was a familiar feeling. Ellie joked that I was old before my time, with the kind of lackluster social life you might expect from someone in their sixties, not their twenties. But that's how it was when you were broke. One day I was determined to be debt-free. To have a better job and a bit of disposable income. I'd go to the theater in the West End and out for nice dinners and for weekends away in the kind of trendy, boutique hotels I read about in *Stylist* magazine. And yet here I was, thirty and still stuck, living in one of the most exciting cities in the world, unable to fully appreciate it because I was permanently overdrawn.

I walked across to the *Office de Tourisme*, which was closed until *9 heures*, according to the timings etched on the door. I leaned back against the glass and stuffed sweet, comforting pastry into my mouth, gulped down the coffee, and felt warmed from the inside out. Then I headed to the main concourse, turning a full circle, looking for the sign for telephones. It was a strange sensation being phoneless and uncontactable. There was something liberating about it, but also, what if something terrible happened and nobody could get hold of me?

This was exactly the kind of irrational thought my mum would have, I realized. She had a habit of coming up with the worst, most unlikely scenario and convincing herself that it was guaranteed to happen to her/me/someone she knew. Another thought occurred to me: What if I missed out on an amazing job opportunity (I couldn't imagine what) because I'd not seen an e-mail in time? This, I told myself, was even more unlikely than the medical emergency I'd been worrying about a second ago.

I watched a train pull in; it was painted red, with a pointed front, like a rocket. They were very fast, these European trains; I'd read about them somewhere. In which case, surely there was still a chance I could make it to the wedding if there were no more delays. I wasn't giving up on the idea just yet. I watched a Eurostar come in on another platform, feeling a pang of longing for home. I was probably closer to London than I was to Amsterdam. I could be sitting on my sofa with my feet up in three hours' time.

Looking for a pay phone—didn't they exist anymore?—I walked carefully out the nearest exit, taking it easy on my ankle. The paved area outside the station was shiny and wet, with giant raindrops bouncing off it in vicious little splashes. I watched people run from the bus to the station entrance with jackets and newspapers held over their heads. Zipping Léo's hoodie up so tightly that I would only be visible from the nose up, I ventured out into the rain.

This was near where the taxi had dropped me off this morning, I remembered, and it seemed as though everyone had had the same idea because I counted at least fifteen cabs, their doors opening and shutting, luggage being dragged out of trunks, horns beeping, wheels sloshing through puddles the size of small ponds. I took a couple of grainy photos of the building opposite: five stories of traditional Parisian apartments stacked on top of a row of red-canopied restaurants. I was particularly drawn to an attic room where somebody was, very ineffectively given the weather, putting their washing out to dry, hanging wet towels out a window carved into the gray zinc roof. Then I people-watched for a bit and read road signs and billboards to test my French. I realized that, for the first time in ages, I was doing fine on my own. I couldn't get hold of Si and therefore there was no point in waiting around for him to save me, which was the dynamic we appeared to have fallen into. As though we were living out our own version of a fairy tale, with Si cast as the handsome prince galloping around on his trusty white steed. I loved having someone there to take care of things. Whatever I needed, Si would find a way to provide, I only had to ask. But we were living together now and contemplating spending the rest of our lives together and I couldn't help wondering whether Si had come along and rescued me before I'd had the chance to work out if I could do it for myself.

After watching at least a hundred more passengers file through the entrance to the terminal, I spotted a row of pay phones against the far wall. A twitchy-looking homeless man skulked around near the curb, rather worryingly holding a white rope tied into a noose. Keeping him in my peripheral vision, I put my coffee on the ground next to me and picked up the closest handset, polishing it with the last wipe from my travel pack. Pointless really, as it had zero germ-eradicating properties as far as I knew, but still . . . it made me feel marginally less squeamish.

I thought I'd try Mum first. This was a risky strategy; she was going to have a fit when I told her what had happened. But I needed someone to know where I was, that I was safe and well. And I knew what Si was like; he'd probably end up calling them anyway, particularly if he was in a panic. I'd rather they heard it from me and for it to be delivered in a calm and matter-of-fact manner, which I'd learned was the best way to break any kind of news— good or bad—to Mum. Anyway, she might surprise me: we'd been in touch more than usual over the past few days. I'd sent her tons of photos and she'd loved hearing what we'd been up to. She'd always wanted to come to Venice herself but had never been able to afford to, and I felt faintly guilty that I'd essentially taken her dream and lived it out for myself.

I dialed Mum's home number. It was 7:55 in Paris, so an hour earlier in Enfield. I imagined Mum, all rolled up under the duvet in the same bedroom she'd slept in for the past thirty-something years. I couldn't imagine her ever leaving Thirlmere Drive, a street which, to me, had always had a sort of bleak and hopeless quality about it. Every flat-fronted house was identical to the next, for a start, except for those whose inhabitants had splashed out on a porch or a loft extension. It was as though the street had a uniform. I wondered why nobody had broken free of the mold. Why somebody hadn't thought to paint their magnolia-colored house a different, brighter shade, or even to dispense with net curtains.

I was prepared for Mum to sound all groggy, and to quickly become near hysterical as her mind ran away with her, jumping ahead to whatever terrible fate she thought might have befallen her disaster-prone daughter now. You'd have thought that at my age I'd have stopped caring what she thought, but somehow, because she was the only parent I had, I supposed, it hurt that she always assumed the worst of me. That I had to work extra hard to prove her wrong. To show her that I wasn't the complete fuck-up she seemed to think I was. Although that wasn't easy when I had— as was the case on this occasion—actually fucked up.

It rang seven times before she picked up.

"Hello?"

Her voice was vague, as though she thought she might be dreaming.

"Mum, it's me."

Silence.

"Hannah?"

"Yes."

"What's happened?"

She breathed heavily into the mouthpiece.

"Nothing. I'm fine," I said in the most soothing voice I could muster.

"Thank God," said Mum. "You're not in any trouble, then?"

"'Course not," I said casually. "Nothing terrible, anyway. It's just that I've lost Si."

More silence. And then, "What do you mean, lost him?"

I knew she'd be fighting the urge to go all dramatic. I tried to explain.

"The train from Venice divided into two in the middle of the night and we didn't realize and now I've ended up in Paris and Si's on his way to Amsterdam."

"Oh God, Hannah!"

"And he's got all my stuff. My suitcase. My purse, although luckily I've got a couple of cards with me," I said in a rush. "Oh yeah, and my phone's been stolen."

Might as well get it all out there.

"What about Catherine's wedding?" she screeched. "You'll miss it, Hannah! Honestly, trust you. Why do things like this always happen to you?"

Mum was going to be mad about this turn of events because she'd been much more invested in Catherine's wedding than I'd ever been. She'd made me relay every little detail of the day and was particularly obsessed with Pauline's outfit, which I'd avoided telling her probably cost more than Mum's entire wardrobe put together.

"I don't know, Mum, why do they?" I replied, exhaustion creeping up on me.

Our relationship had always been more on the volatile end of the spectrum. There had been bickering, door-slamming and ignoring each other for days on end when I was a teenager. Even now, she had the ability to wind me up within seconds, as though she knew exactly what my insecurities were and made a conscious (or, perhaps, to give her the benefit of the doubt, unconscious) effort to go ahead and play on them anyway.

"Tony!" I heard her shriek. "Wake up. It's Hannah, she's got herself in a right mess."

I closed my eyes for a second or two. I would have called Ellie if I'd known her number by heart.

"Mum, don't panic. I'll sort it out. I've got a ticket for the next train to Amsterdam. If it runs on time, I should just about make it in time for the ceremony. It's not until 5:30."

"And Paris. Is it even safe? You've never even been to France before, Hannah!"

"Hmm."

This was hardly the time to tell her about that one ill-fated trip.

Tony groaned in the background—he could sleep through anything, Tony—and I heard Mum telling him in a high-pitched, garbled voice what had happened. She made it sound much worse than it was.

"Tony said give us the number of the phone you're using and we'll ring you back. You need to save your money, Hannah. Have you had anything to eat? Are you warm enough?"

There she went, going off on one as usual, talking to me as though I had the common sense of a four-year-old. I gave her the number, replaced the receiver and waited. It rang a minute or so later.

"Hannah?"

"*Non, pardon*, you must 'ave the wrong number," I said, putting on a French accent in an attempt to lighten the mood and also because I knew it would piss her off.

"Who is this, please? I'm looking for my daughter, Hannah."

I laughed lightly. "It's me, Mum. I'm joking."

"For God's sake. I'm worried sick now and so is Tony."

"He hasn't gone back to sleep, then?"

A pause. "Well, yes, but that doesn't mean—"

"Never mind."

I imagined Tony with his rapidly receding hairline, the beige Bermuda shorts he insisted on wearing no matter the weather hanging neatly over the back of the chair next to his bed. He told me it was because he was a postman and he'd built up an immunity to the cold over the years. As stepfathers went, he was actually pretty cool. He liked the Rolling Stones and soccer and watching documentaries about real-life crime. And he'd never taken sides, even in the early days, when he and Mum had first met. I'd been fifteen then and had fallen out with a group of friends at school and hated Mum (and everyone else) and he'd been very patient with me, very gentle, and had let our relationship develop slowly, over time. He'd never been a replacement for Dad, I think we both knew that, but I suspected that if I ever needed him, he would be there in a heartbeat. Not that I'd ever really tested the theory, but still. It was nice to know.

"Look, I'm guessing Si hasn't been in touch yet, but if he calls, tell him I'm fine and that I'll be there as soon as I can," I said to Mum.

I heard a sigh and a rustle of sheets. She'd be getting back into bed. Eight o'clock was when she got up and not a moment before.

"Poor Si, he'll be going up the wall," she said.

Of course Si would be the one she felt sorry for. He was like the son she'd never had. Lately, when she called the house phone, I'd noticed she sounded disappointed when it was me who answered and not him.

"He's *lovely*, Hannah," she'd said with a rare burst of excitement when I'd taken him home for the first time. We'd been out in the kitchen making tea for everyone.

"Don't sound so surprised," I'd said, reaching into the cupboard to get out four mugs.

"He's very good-looking," she whispered conspiratorially.

I laughed softly. "He is, isn't he?"

Mum arranged four paper napkins in the shape of a fan on the tray. "I hate to say it, but I'd almost given up on you finding someone."

I concentrated on rearranging the mugs, spacing them out evenly.

"Really? Didn't realize you'd written me off so quickly."

Mum cleared her throat. "It's not that. It's just, well . . . when you think about the other boyfriends you've brought home."

She was right, of course, they'd all been awful, but it wasn't for her to say.

"That's what being in your twenties is all about, though, isn't it?" I said flippantly, wanting to keep things light. "Trying things out. Having relationships that don't work. Making mistakes."

Mum got the milk out of the fridge and poured it into her best white china jug, which she put on the tray alongside a plate of chocolate digestives.

"We've all made our fair share of those," she said.

I filled the teapot with water from the kettle, adding it to the tray.

"Are you talking about Dad?" I asked quietly.

We rarely mentioned his name, hadn't done so for years. I'd learned not to. I'd been seven when he'd left and hadn't had a clue what was going on, except that he wasn't there anymore and I missed him. Whenever I'd asked Mum about it, she'd disappear upstairs and come down ten minutes or so later with red-rimmed eyes and then I'd feel bad. As though I'd been solely responsible for upsetting her.

"Don't waste your time wondering about him, Hannah. Because I can guarantee that wherever he is in the world, he won't be thinking about you."

"You don't know that," I said, defensive, even after all this time.

She sighed. "If that's what you want to believe, Hannah. If it's easier for you that way."

I put the tea bags away in the cupboard, shutting it carefully.

"Come on, let's take these in, shall we?" said Mum, picking up the tray and giving me a tight smile. I knew what that look meant. It was her way of letting me know that the conversation was over, that now wasn't the time. It wasn't, of course, with Si sitting next door, but the thing was, it was never the time.

*   *   *

I hung up on Mum, resting my forehead against the keypad and promptly vaulting off it again, remembering how many fingers touched those buttons on a daily basis, not all of them clean. I shoved in a few more coins and dialed Si's number. I supposed I'd better tell him about the missed train. Reassure him that I was still doing my best to get there. It felt strange for us to be so out of touch, because I could usually get hold of him instantly, whenever I needed him. He was very dependable like that, not like other guys I'd dated. On the odd occasion he went out with friends—he preferred to stay at home with me these days, he said—he always, *always* gave me a blow-by-blow account of where he was and what he was drinking and what time he'd be back, and so I'd end up feeling part of it, almost as though I was there with him.

After a few rings it went straight to voice mail again. I pushed the heel of my hand into my eye socket and left another message. Surely he'd worked out it was on silent by now. I didn't want to be the one to mention it because then I'd have to explain how I knew that in the first place. It would be much better if he assumed he'd mistakenly changed the settings himself.

"*Hey, Si. It's me. There's a delay my end, I'm afraid. Engineering works, apparently. Don't reckon I'll get to Amsterdam until gone five now, so it'll be very tight, but I'll make it. Tell Catherine I'm sorry. Oh, and my phone's been stolen. Gare du Nord is notoriously bad for that, apparently. Nothing's going right for me today, is it? Anyway. Not sure how you'll get hold of me from now on. I guess I'll have to call you. Bye, then.*"

I stood still for a bit, letting my heartbeat return to its normal, resting rate, filling my lungs with cool, damp air. I didn't know why I hadn't told him the truth, about missing the train. Or about Léo's bag and my ankle. It was funny how relationships changed over time. How some of the things you loved about each other to begin with now irritated you beyond belief. And vice versa. Of course vice versa. And because Si and I were very different, in terms of the things we liked and disliked, in the childhoods we'd had, there was lots to get used to about each other.

In a way, it was a miracle we'd met in the first place. I remembered that day vividly: the scent of honeysuckle and beer in the air, how it had been one of those balmy summer London evenings. I'd been on my way to Ellie's, coming up the escalator at Highgate Tube, rooting for my sunglasses in my bag, which I'd found, put on and then promptly pulled back off my face because I really didn't need shades underground. I'd turned to check out a poster for a new theater production starring someone I was sure I'd seen in a Channel 4 drama about a missing girl and then, distracted, I went to put my hair up into a bun, knocking off my sunglasses in the process, wincing as I heard them land on the step below.

"Shit," I said, turning to look. I'd paid twenty-five pounds in Zara for those and now they were probably smashed to pieces.

The person behind me bent down to pick them up.

"These yours?" he'd said, stretching his arm out to reach me.

"Yes. Thanks." I held out my hand, taking them from him, my fingers knocking clumsily against his. I met his eyes and smiled, caught off guard by how attractive he was. He was blond, looked like he worked out and was very tall and slightly tanned. His face was completely symmetrical, with everything from his nose to his jawline perfectly aligned. He reminded me of an Irish boy-band member, or a kids' TV presenter. I was so caught up with examining his bone structure that I didn't realize the top of the escalator was behind me until my heels banged against the metal teeth and I stumbled onto the concourse. Flustered, I attempted to regain my composure by whipping my Oyster card out of my bag in a brusque and businesslike manner, as though I was in a terrible hurry.

"Do you live around here, then?" he called from behind as I bustled through the ticket barriers.

I looked over my shoulder at him, shaking my head. "No. My friend does, though. She's just round the corner, off the Archway Road."

"Oh, me too," he said.

I wondered whether he had a girlfriend. A wife, even. Probably. He wasn't my type, mind you. I much preferred guys who were flawed and a bit messed up like me, to whom I wouldn't feel eternally inferior.

"Well, it was nice to meet you. Briefly," he said, buzzing through behind me.

He had a big, wide smile that was perfectly symmetrical, just like the rest of him. And he must have had highlights; nobody's hair was that color. I made a mental note of his features so that I could describe him to Ellie later.

"You too," I said. I liked the way he had his suit jacket slung casually over his arm, the way he'd undone the top two buttons of his shirt.

I turned and walked away, toward the exit for Archway Road. Just before I started up the steps I heard footsteps behind me.

"Excuse me?"

It was him again, one hand in his pocket, a shimmer of sweat on his top lip.

"Hi," I said, moving to the side so that people could get past.

"Um, I know this is weird and feel free to say no," he said, "but would you fancy going for a drink sometime?"

I remembered trying to play it cool, to look as though getting asked out on the Tube was a regular occurrence. Not only did he look as though he'd walked off a movie set, but he was creating a scene straight out of a Richard Curtis rom-com. Perhaps the sequel to *Notting Hill. Highgate Village* had a nice ring to it. When I'd described it to Ellie later, she'd said it sounded like something that would happen to Jennifer Aniston, which I'd thought summed it up perfectly. I'd presumed I'd never see him again, anyway, because I could count on one hand the number of times a guy had taken my number and had actually called. I'd worked out over the years that it was something they (men) did to avoid awkwardness; a cowardly get-out clause when they decided that they didn't fancy you enough to bother after all.

7

It was now 8:10, according to the huge clock on the front of the station. God, it was like time was standing still. Even from out here the continuous announcements about trains arriving and trains departing and whistles blowing felt as though they were drilling into my brain. The rain had slowed, at least, and had morphed into the sort of fine, misty drizzle that made Paris look all foggy and romantic. Would I have felt differently about being here again, I wondered, if the circumstances had been different? If Si had been with me? If we'd come to see the sights together, had got the lift to the top of the Eiffel Tower to take photos of the view? I wondered whether I would have been able to forget about the past and let myself appreciate it for what it was. Because I couldn't find much to like about Paris. It had a darkness about it, although I suspected that might come from inside me as well as from the city itself. Although I had actual evidence now that bad things happened to me here: there had already been the missed train, the twisted ankle and the stolen phone. I could only imagine what terrible event fate might throw at me next. The sooner I could get out of this place, the better.

After killing a few minutes by wandering aimlessly around outside the station entrance probably looking highly suspicious, I noticed a blond-haired woman wearing a peacock-blue cardigan running across the forecourt. Something about her reminded me of Alison the bridesmaid. Not that I could recall her in much detail. She was very pretty; I remembered thinking that at the hen weekend. Even shorter than me, maybe five feet one or five two. Northern accent; I thought she'd said she was from Manchester originally, and had moved to Berkhamsted after her parents divorced and her mum got remarried to some local business owner. She was an old friend of Si's family, and after getting a first at Cambridge, she was now in corporate law (or something).

I felt a stab of envy about how sorted she sounded and then instantly berated myself for comparing myself to other women. It was nobody's fault but my own that I was stuck in a job I hated. The thing was, though, loads of people were in the same boat. They had bills to pay and kids to feed and had long ago given up on any dreams they might have had. If I wasn't careful, I knew I'd end up being one of them. I wondered how things were going with the wedding preparations, whether whatever drama she'd been texting Si about in the middle of the night had been resolved. I thought about them all getting ready in Catherine's room without me, sipping champagne as they struggled to keep her calm. I would have been flitting in and out, getting drinks and passing on messages and reassuring an increasingly irate Catherine that I'd done everything she'd asked me to. Si and I would have been smiling at each other over some ridiculous demand she'd made.

"Hannah!"

I turned my head, imagining I'd heard somebody calling my name. It couldn't have been, though, since as far as I was aware, not a single person I knew was in Paris.

"Hannah! Over here!"

And then I spotted Léo, standing next to a motorbike, a helmet in his hand, his hip resting against the bike's frame.

I gave him a half-hearted wave, wondering where he'd magicked the bike up from so quickly. I supposed he must live nearby. Unsure what to do next, I went to walk away, back inside the station. When I glanced over my shoulder, I saw that he was jogging across to me, stepping straight out in front of a taxi.

"*Va te faire foutre!*" shouted the driver, braking sharply. He beeped his horn but Léo waved him off, seemingly not bothered that he'd narrowly escaped death.

"*Un moment*, Hannah!" he called to me.

I stopped. What did he want now?

"Hi," he said, coming to a stop in front of me, catching his breath.

"Hello."

"What have you been doing?" he asked conversationally, the motorbike helmet lodged under his arm.

"In the thirty minutes since I saw you last? Not much, funnily enough," I countered. What did he think I'd been doing?

The air was still hazy with rain, but when I held out my hand to catch some, it was so fine I could barely feel it. The air felt warmer, too, as though there was a chance the sun might break through.

"Oh, right," I said as it dawned on me what he wanted. "You came back for this," I said, unzipping the hoodie.

He put his hand out to stop me. "Of course not. It is yours to keep."

I looked at him quizzically. "Are you sure?"

"Yes," he said with a slow smile.

"Do you always give your stuff away to complete strangers, then?" I asked, tucking my hair behind my ear.

"Not usually."

It wouldn't surprise me if there was a plethora of other women wandering around Paris wearing items of his clothing.

"I have been thinking," he said. "You must report your lost phone to the police. If you have insurance? Otherwise you will have to buy another. They are expensive, *non*, these phones?"

I hadn't thought of that, of course, what with being eternally disorganized. I presumed I did have some sort of insurance, though, because my monthly repayments cost a fortune and I was always complaining about them, particularly because my direct debit came out right at the end of the month. I sighed; he was right. I'd at least need some sort of crime reference number, or whatever the French equivalent was, if I was going to submit a claim. I couldn't really afford not to.

"Would I need to go to an actual police station, do you think?"

"Yes," he said. "Of course."

"Isn't there one inside the station?"

"There was once, but it is closed now. There is the central police station in Rue Louis Blanc, not far from here." He gestured vaguely in the direction of the city.

"Couldn't I just ask a police officer? There must be loads of them inside," I suggested. I had the creeping fear that I was going to leave the station, get stuck filling in form after form and miss the next train, even if it wasn't leaving for several hours.

"No," he said, seemingly irritated by my incessant questions.

"You cannot. Because you will need to complete a document. Which is only available at a police station."

I tutted. "Typical."

"Come, I will take you."

"Take me?" I asked, frowning in confusion.

"I have borrowed my friend's bike," he said, wafting his arm toward the road. "There is a spare helmet, I think. Let us see."

I laughed, incredulous. "You're not seriously expecting me to get on that thing?"

He flashed me a look of utter confusion. "Why not?"

I shook my head in wonderment. "Because I don't even know you."

"And?"

"And I don't have a death wish."

He cocked his head to one side. "You worry a lot, Hannah," he said after a long pause.

"That's just not true."

"It is. I can see it. You are always thinking."

It was frustrating that it was that obvious, even to someone I'd had only a handful of conversations with.

"You must go to a police station, yes? And you cannot walk properly, *non*? And the next train is more than five hours away. So, this is the solution. It will take half an hour, no more. And then you can sit on your bench and wait for your train."

I looked around, wondering what other people in my position would do. Would Ellie go with him? Not that it mattered, she wasn't here. It was me who needed to make the decision, something I was notoriously bad at.

"I'll tell you what," I said, coming up with a compromise. "I'll go to the police station myself. You can point me in the right direction."

He crossed his arms, looking at me pensively.

"Let me take you. Otherwise I will feel bad," he said.

I shook my head. "Really? So this is about you, then, is it?"

He shifted his weight from one foot to the other. "You are right, it is a little about me. But it is mostly about you."

"You're still feeling guilty for tripping me up," I said triumphantly. "Aren't you?"

He held up his thumb and forefinger, indicating that he was, just a tiny bit.

I looked into his eyes. Could I trust him? What would happen, I wondered, if I took a chance and agreed to go with him? I did need to report my missing phone, otherwise I'd have to pay for a new one when I got home and there was no way I had the money to do that. And it probably would be quicker to go with him now rather than trying to walk to the police station on my own when I had no idea where I was going.

"I am a very safe driver," he said enticingly.

"Why don't I believe you?"

He grinned. "Are you afraid of Paris, Hannah? Is that what it is?"

"That's a ridiculous thing to say," I protested. Did he really think I was that pathetic?

"Then a motorbike is the best way to get around the city," he said, as if I'd already agreed. It was infuriating.

"Is it, though?"

If only I could see the world like I used to, again. Transport myself back to a time when I would take risks and do things just for fun and assume that people were inherently good until proven otherwise. I'd lost some of that spark, I knew I had. I'd become more cautious and paranoid as I'd got older. As though I was turning into my mum, which was the absolute last thing I wanted.

I bit my lip. "You'd have to drive slowly."

"Certainly."

"And I can't be gone long."

"Fine with me."

I followed him hesitantly over to the bike, a huge, shiny black monstrosity that looked as though it had a life of its own. There was still time to change my mind. Right up until the last second if need be, I told myself.

"Where's your bag, by the way?" I asked, thinking that if he was planning to have that huge thing slung over his shoulder, it would probably tip us both over.

"You are concerned about the dead body inside?"

I gave him a sarcastic smile.

"It is at my friend's apartment. I will collect it later," he said, shaking his head to himself.

While I waited for Léo to find a second helmet, I checked my ankle, slipping off my ballet pump and wiggling my foot around. It was still uncomfortable, but the pain was definitely easing off. I put my shoe back on and grimaced. They were soaked through and had started to leak; there was even brown sludge in the grooves between my toes. I crouched down to smear it off with my thumb.

"Ah! Here," he said, after opening a compartment under the seat.

I stood up, taking my hair out of its bun and then putting it up into a neater, tighter one. I'd never even been on one of those little mopeds you zoomed about on in Greek holiday resorts because I'd always assumed that if I did, I'd be the girl involved in a fatal crash on the main road out of Kavos. As soon as I'd turned fourteen and had become more independent, going into London on my own and so on, Mum had kicked off her campaign to let me know that the world was a terrible, unsafe place full of evil people who were out to get me. She went on and on about all the bad things that could happen, telling me—in unnecessarily minute detail—about the awful stories she'd heard over the years, usually gleaned from either the local paper or the "real life" articles in *Take a Break* magazine. I brushed them off at first, doing all the things she'd warned me about anyway, like getting off my face for seven nights straight in Tenerife when I went with Ellie and her parents, and accepting lifts from older boys who'd only just passed their tests. But after a while I began to see how much it was affecting Mum; she'd even cried one night when I'd told her I'd be back from Ellie's at ten and hadn't got in until nearly midnight. She'd wanted to keep me safe like any mother would, I got that. But in hindsight, I wondered whether there'd also been a part of her that didn't want me to be out having fun. She was stuck at home, scrabbling around to pay the bills, while I still had my whole life ahead of me. I could travel the world and have a rewarding career and fall in love with anyone I liked. Before she'd met Tony, Mum had always felt hard done by, and even now some of that sadness had stayed with her. She just never seemed happy. It was as though she'd wanted more from life and was angry with herself for not getting it.

"I'm really not sure about this," I said, my heart beginning to hammer harder in my chest.

"What is it you are afraid of?" asked Léo.

I looked around at the other motorbikes lined up next to us.

"What if we have an accident?"

"We will not."

I nibbled on my thumbnail. "Nobody gets on a bike expecting to crash, though, do they?"

"You think about death a lot, Hannah."

"I don't," I said, although I knew I did.

He handed me the helmet. "If we imagined the most terrible things that could happen every time we step out of our apartment, we would never do anything, *non*?"

"I suppose."

I took it from him, swinging it about like a kettlebell. He did say it was the most efficient way to get around Paris. And the odds of surviving the journey were statistically in my favor.

"Okay," I said, taking a deep breath. "Let's do it."

I put the helmet on before I changed my mind. He fastened and tightened it for me, his fingers tickling the underside of my chin as he grappled with the clasp.

"There. Ready." He shrugged off his leather jacket. "You must wear this," he said.

"What for?" I asked, noticing how everything sounded muffled now, as though I was underwater.

"It can be windy on the back."

I thought it was more likely to be in case I fell off—the leather would offer my skin some protection, wouldn't it? I took it from him, anyway, slipping my arms into it. I could still feel the heat of his body on the quilted lining.

"You promise you know how to drive this thing?" I shouted.

He laughed and vaulted onto the bike. He was Parisian, they probably all knew. I thought briefly about what Mum would say if she could see me now; what Si would think. And then I climbed on anyway.

"Ready?" Léo called over his shoulder.

"Not really," I shouted back.

The helmet was heavy on my head and the strap felt too tight under my chin, but I didn't want to make a fuss. He turned on the engine and I felt the power of it shuddering through my body, making my bones vibrate. I wasn't sure what to do with my hands, so I placed them tentatively on his hips.

"Hold tighter," he shouted back to me.

This was more embarrassing than I'd realized. Did we really need to sit this close together? Cringing, I slid my bottom toward his, wrapping my arms around his waist, clasping my fingers together on the other side. I tried not to notice his stomach muscles as my thumbs brushed over them. Then Léo twisted his head to the left, checked behind him and pulled off into the road.

I closed my eyes at first, not daring to look, not wanting to know how close we were to other cars, whether we might be boxed in between two buses and an articulated lorry. And then, as the minutes passed and we were still upright, I opened them just a slit, and then a little more, until they were fully open and my chin was almost resting on Léo's back, and when I peeped over his shoulder I could see we were on a manic main road lined with grocers selling exotic vegetables, and Chinese restaurants from which I could already smell the aroma of steamed dumplings as we passed. There were shops with trays and trays of gold jewelry on display, and another with beautiful Indian fabrics rolled up in the window. The road was slicked with rain and because there were so many cars and buses and taxis, we were constantly stopping and starting and not gaining much speed, which suited me perfectly. But then we turned off to the right, down a quieter side street, and he began to accelerate.

"Everything cool?" he yelled.

"No! Slow down!"

He ignored me, of course.

We flew past abandoned shops with their shutters clamped down, and tatty-looking burger bars, and hairdressers with garish pink signs advertising *Coiffure*. When we finally pulled over to the curb and he cut the engine, I could still feel the throb of it under my skin. I slid off the bike, stumbling as I put too much weight on my bad foot.

Léo steadied me with his hand. "*Ça va?*"

I nodded, unclipping my helmet and yanking it off. My legs were stiff from being pried apart at an unnaturally wide angle and I kicked them out, rotating my good ankle to get the blood flowing again.

"See? I did not kill you," said Léo, taking the helmet from me.

"It was touch and go at times," I said, patting down my hair.

The truth was, I wasn't sure how I felt. I knew that my heart rate was off the scale and that I'd had a proper adrenaline rush for the first time in ages and that I'd thought I was going to die at least once. Whether that was a good feeling or not, I couldn't quite tell.

Léo directed me up the steps of the police station, an intimidating, black office-like building on the opposite side of the road. Inside was a large room, dimly lit and sparsely decorated, except for three rows of gray plastic chairs laid out on a shiny lino floor and a wooden desk with a police officer sitting behind it, his face hidden behind a computer screen. I hesitated for a second until Léo nudged me forward, then hung back while I approached the desk.

I coughed self-consciously.

"*Bonjour, monsieur,*" I said to the police officer. "*Pourriez-vous m'aider, s'il vous plaît?*"

He was tapping away on his keypad and took ages to look up.

"*Oui, madame?*"

I didn't appear to be able to recall any French whatsoever, with odd words popping into my mind and then disappearing before I could do anything with them. The French words for "lost" and "stolen," for example, seemed to have permanently evaded me. Perhaps I felt too on display to grapple for the phrases I hadn't used for years, what with Léo watching me and the officer giving me a stereotypically steely gaze. I resorted to "*Parlez-vous Anglais?*"

"A little," he said, looking at me blankly.

I glanced nervously at Léo, who was busy tapping away on his phone.

"Um, I was in the ticket office at Gare du Nord and I put my phone on the counter while I tried to find something. And then when I looked for it about five minutes later, it wasn't in my bag. I thought I'd left it behind on the counter at first, so I—"

"Stolen?" said the officer. "Pickpocket?"

"Maybe. Yes. I think so."

"Fill this out, please."

The officer slid a document across the counter and I went to take a seat next to Léo, who was already sprawled out, taking up two of the chairs on the back row.

I started filling out the form, managing to complete all the basics: name, address, telephone number. When I got to the bit where I had to describe the nature of the crime that had been committed, I was stuck.

"What's the word for ticket office, again?" I asked Léo, who was rubbing his face and stifling a yawn.

"*Guichet,*" he said, stretching.

"*Guichet?*"

"Yes. *Guichet.*"

I was pretty sure that wasn't the word I'd learned when I was revising for my high school French, but I could hardly argue about it. He was probably using the colloquial form or something, but it would have to do. I wrote it down.

"How do you say 'stolen'?" I asked him about a minute later.

"*Volé.*"

Honestly, none of these words were looking the slightest bit familiar. Plus I kept getting distracted by the comings and goings at the station. At one point, a police officer strode through the room with a machine gun in his belt, which made me wonder exactly how volatile and unsafe Paris might be, and about how going off on a bike with someone I barely knew was a bad idea. What if something happened? How would I ever explain it to Si? A few minutes later a drunk guy was manhandled through the doors, swaying and shouting as someone tried to determine his name. *Quel est votre nom? Votre nom!* I rushed through the rest of the form, handed it in, had some sort of receipt shoved back at me and then we left. It was all over with very quickly and yet was the sort of thing that I would usually have procrastinated about for days while I went back and forth over the pros and cons of reporting my phone stolen, struggling to make a decision.

I was relieved to get outside and tipped my face toward the clouds, squinting into the light, which was dazzling after the dinginess of the police station.

"It's drying up, at least," I said.

The rain had finally stopped, and there was the tiniest smattering of blue poking through the gray sky.

"Perhaps the sun will come out," said Léo, going over to the bike and wiping rain off the wing mirrors with a cloth he found in the box on the back.

I watched him for a bit, not sure what to do with myself.

"I suppose I should get back to the station, then," I said.

Because what if, by some miracle, the engineering works had finished early and a train was announced that would get me to Amsterdam sooner?

"Sure. One moment," he said, polishing the handlebars intently.

"Here," I said, taking off his jacket. "I seem to have taken all your clothes, you must be cold."

"No, please. I am good," he said, although when I looked at his arms, I could see his dark hairs standing on end, sharp and spiky, as though it might hurt to run my hand across them.

I put the jacket back on. The sleeves were too long for me so that only the tips of my fingers poked out of the bottoms.

He pulled a packet of cigarettes from his pocket. "You do not smoke, right?"

"No," I said, taking one anyway.

He looked surprised and I shrugged. I thought it wouldn't do any harm; I'd make sure it was just the one. He lit mine for me, then his own. I almost gasped in ecstasy when the first drag filled my mouth and nicotine swept into my bloodstream. Oh, how I'd missed it.

Léo looked across at me. "Good?"

I nodded, holding the cigarette at arm's length, relishing how familiar it felt in my hand. "I'm supposed to have given up."

I watched a policeman inside the building; he was standing by the window, barking instructions into a handset.

"Good for you," said Léo. "One day, I will do the same."

"Why does everything fun have to be so bad for you?" I wondered out loud.

He shrugged. "Perhaps it is the thrill of it you enjoy, rather than the thing itself? The idea that you are doing something you shouldn't be."

Thrills were few and far between these days, it seemed. I could count on one hand the number of times Si and I had been for a proper night out since we'd moved in together. I wasn't complaining: I loved sharing a place with him, having him to come home to each night. Trying out recipes I'd found online, chatting about his day while we ate. And on the plus side, I was also managing to avoid the earth-shattering lows that used to spring themselves on me in between all the highs. I much preferred things as they were, a steady stream of normality, of feeling looked-after and settled and loved. I didn't think I'd change that for anything.

"What were your plans in Amsterdam, then?" I asked.

We perched on the edge of the curb. I watched him send rings of smoke silently up into the ether. Si would go mad if he could see me now. He'd been ecstatic when I'd managed to stop completely and was now on a one-man crusade to get me to join a gym.

"A meeting," he said. "To discuss a project I have been working on."

"What do you do?"

His phone rang and he looked at it, shaking his head and rejecting the call.

"I write music," he said.

"You're a composer?" I said. Creating music required a certain sensitivity that I wouldn't have thought he possessed.

"A composer," he said, mulling it over. "It sounds very grand when you say it like this."

I wrapped my arms around my knees. "Do you play an instrument, then?"

"Piano," he said. "And guitar."

I widened my eyes, I couldn't help it.

"This is not what you were expecting," he said, smiling.

I looked down at the ground, rubbing at the stained satin of my shoe. "Not really."

"And you?" he asked. "You play something?"

I shook my head. "I always wanted to try the piano, but we couldn't afford lessons."

He looked at me, frowning. "So why do you not learn now?"

I considered his question. "It feels too late, I suppose."

He shook his head, as though I'd said the wrong thing again. "So your life is already over, at the age of—what—twenty-six? Twenty-seven?"

"I'm thirty, actually."

"So your life is over at thirty."

"Feels like it, sometimes. Why, how old are you?"

"Twenty-eight."

"A baby."

He stood up, doing a side stretch, one way and then the other. "You look younger than thirty, anyway."

I tutted. "Yeah, right."

"You do not believe me?"

"Nope."

"You have a complex about it, your age?" he asked, flicking his cigarette onto the road.

"No. I do not."

I did, though. A little bit.

"You are always this negative?" he asked, grinding the butt into the ground with the toe of his trainer.

"Not always, no," I said snappily, fed up with his persistent nitpicking. He didn't like me; he was only here because he felt guilty about making me miss my train. I got it.

"It is only an observation," he said, holding up his hands in surrender. "For example, I give you a compliment about your age and you assume I am lying. That is negative, *non?*"

I shrugged. "Whatever." If I'd wanted a character assassination, I could have given my mum another call.

He sat down next to me again, leaning back on his elbows. A group of women walked past, giggling together over something one of them had said.

"I have upset you," he said.

"I'm feeling sorry for myself, that's all."

"You have not had a good day. A lot of bad luck."

"I'm honestly not usually this miserable."

He raised his eyebrows. "You are not?"

There was no fooling him. "Well. Not *this* miserable."

It was hardly surprising, was it, with everything that had happened? The shock of finding out I was on the wrong end of the train. The stressful transaction in the ticket office, cards being declined, falling over and hurting my ankle; the pain that still spiked through it when I walked. I swallowed hard, suddenly feeling very tearful. Which was weird, because I hardly ever cried. And on the odd occasion when I couldn't stop myself, I made sure I did it in secret, completely alone, ashamed that I'd got to that point at all. I stood up so quickly that I felt dizzy. I brushed dirt off my jeans and tidied my hair and desperately tried to stop my eyes from sprouting tears, because now I'd started, I couldn't seem to stop.

"Are you all right, Hannah?" asked Léo, coming to stand beside me. A crying girl he barely knew was probably his worst nightmare.

I looked away, frantically brushing away the tear that was very inconveniently sliding down my cheek at the worst possible moment.

"I'm fine," I said, clearing my throat. What was wrong with me? It wasn't like he'd said anything that bad.

"It is my fault?" he asked, chewing on his lip.

I shook my head. "Not really."

"But it was—how do you say?—*insensitive* of me. To say that you are negative. I do not know you, do I? You could be a very positive person usually. Super happy. All of the time."

Another tear appeared, in the other eye this time. For God's sake, what was it about this guy? On one hand he was the most annoying person I'd ever met, and on the other I'd been more emotional around him within an hour of knowing him than I was around anybody else I knew.

"I feel very bad," said Léo.

"That seems to happen a lot, doesn't it?"

He put his hand over his mouth again, like I'd seen him do at the station.

"Anyway, it's not about you," I said. "Which I know must be *very* difficult for you to understand."

He smiled. "Even if it is not about me, there must be something I can do, *non*?"

"Unless you can turn back time and make it so I don't switch seats on the train, I don't think there is," I said, scrabbling in my bag for a tissue, finding one eventually among all the paraphernalia.

"Let me show you Paris," he said with over-the-top exuberance. "You want to see the Eiffel Tower? The Champs-Élysées? The Arc de Triomphe?"

I blew my nose. "I saw most of that last time I came."

"You have been here before, Hannah? Why did you not say?"

What did I mention that for?

"It was ages ago now," I said dismissively, hoping he'd drop it.

"How long did you spend here?" he asked.

"A day."

"A day? Then of course you did not see everything. Did you get a boat along the Seine? Did you have coffee in Montmartre? Walk through the Jardin des Tuileries?"

I shook my head. "It wasn't that kind of trip."

We both looked up as a commotion broke out on the steps of the police station, watching as a man was dragged up the steps in handcuffs.

"What kind of trip was it?" he asked.

I took my hair out of its band, twisting it over my shoulder.

"It's a long story. But let's just say I'm not the biggest fan of Paris."

Léo was quiet for a moment or two and then he reached out and put his hands on my shoulders. "I would like to show you around my city, Hannah. And prove to you that it is as beautiful as everyone says."

I shook my head. "I need to get back to the station."

He took his hands away and I immediately wanted him to put them back again. It was because I was exhausted, I told myself, and I felt like a mess and my head was all over the place. Anyone could have reached out to me and I would have felt the same way.

He looked at his watch. "It is only 8:40. We have plenty of time."

I felt myself starting to waver. Once I'd got used to the sensations of it, I'd felt so free on the back of the bike. When was I going to get the chance to do something like that again? What harm could come of taking a little detour on the way back to the station?

"You will come?" said Léo. "A small ride around Paris?"

I pulled the zip of his jacket up and down a few times, noting where it snagged, where the run was smooth.

"We'd have to be quick."

"No problem. I also have things to do. There is something I must give to a friend."

I raised my eyebrows at him, twisting my hair up again.

"Nothing illegal," he said, winking at me. He had a dimple in his left cheek that I'd only just noticed.

"Shall we go?" he said, holding out the helmet.

I narrowed my eyes at him. "Okay."

"This must be scary for you, *non?*" he said, waiting while I put on the helmet and then fastening the clasp for me again.

"What must be?"

"You are out of your comfort zone, Hannah. You are not used to it, I can see."

I would have disagreed with him if I'd had the energy. He couldn't read me as well as he thought he could. I'd taken risks all the time, once. Maybe not these days, but once. I slid onto the bike behind him, already regretting agreeing to go.

"Hold tight," he shouted over his shoulder, starting the engine.

8

We'd been driving for fifteen minutes or so when Léo pulled over. My adrenaline was pumping from the journey, a fast-paced set of twists and turns along narrow backstreets and across grand cobbled squares, the bike tipping so violently as we navigated some of the sharper bends that I'd imagined us crashing to the ground at any second, skidding across the tarmac like bowling pins. I'd had to hold on to him more tightly than ever, my face pressed into the back of his neck in a sort of blind panic.

"Here," he said, thrusting his helmet at me and sliding off the bike, his knee missing my face by about a centimeter. "Wait here one minute."

I gave him the universal sign for okay, because I couldn't be bothered to project my voice out of the depths of the helmet. I liked how it made me feel cut off from the world. It was nearly silent inside there; a place where nobody could see me and I could barely hear them, which most of the time was how I preferred it.

I watched Léo run into a place a couple of doors down. There was a queue out onto the street, which he seemed to have by-passed completely, disappearing inside. I hung his helmet on the handlebars and then unclipped my own. I ought to find a way to call Si. But then, how would I explain where I was?

I looked up at the beautiful, pristinely preserved creamy colon-nade above my head, with its old-fashioned lanterns hanging from each arch. We'd parked right in front of Le Meurice, a luxury ho-tel, by the looks of it. It was one of those places with uniformed doormen outside and black executive cars sliding in and out of the loading bay, dropping people off, Louis Vuitton luggage being pulled discreetly out of trunks.

. . .

"Hey."

Léo was back in what seemed like a nanosecond clutching two dusky pink paper cups.

"The best *chocolat chaud* in Paris," he said, handing one over, looking to me for a reaction.

"Great," I said, underwhelmed. I liked hot chocolate, but how good could it be? Of course he would think it was the best; accord-ing to him, the best of everything originated in Paris.

"What is that place?" I asked, more impressed by how estheti-cally pleasing a disposable cup could look. The color reminded me of Catherine's wedding invitations: she'd gone for cream, with this exact shade of pink running around the edges.

"It is called Angelina," he told me, ripping off his lid and drink-ing hungrily. "The café has been here on the Rue de Rivoli for over one hundred years."

I could smell molten chocolate before I'd even taken a sip, its scent curling through a tiny hole in the white lid. I looked over at the café, which had a grand black awning bearing its name in gold lettering hanging over the door.

"Coco Chanel used to have tea there," said Léo. "And Proust. It was the place to come if you wanted to be noticed in the early 1900s."

I gingerly took off the lid and blew on the surface before taking my first mouthful. It was like nothing I'd ever tasted: thick and smooth and rich and sweet all in one, like a melted chocolate pudding. I resisted the urge to groan out loud, not wanting to give him the satisfaction of admitting how sensational it was.

"It's nice," I said, pretending to be nonchalant.

Léo leaned on the front of the bike, watching me suspiciously. "Just nice?"

"Hmm," I said. "Lovely."

"Unbelievable, *non?*" he said, gulping his down.

I nodded. "Not bad at all."

I sipped mini-mouthfuls of delicious froth, wanting to prolong the experience as long as I could. It felt properly Parisian in this area, upmarket and chic. Even a workman walking past in a yellow hard hat with paint-splattered jeans had impressively chiseled cheekbones.

I tipped the last dregs of hot chocolate into my mouth, already craving more. Léo took the cup from me.

"I can get you another if you want?" he said, as though he could read my mind.

"Better not," I said, making a mental note to google *Angelina* when I got home. I wondered if they had an online shop. I could just imagine having a version of it at home, especially in the winter, Si and I all curled up with a hot drink each in front of the TV.

Léo went to throw the cups away and then jogged back. I

noticed he had a tattoo on his right arm, a barbed-wire design that curled itself around his biceps. I'd recently decided to get a tattoo of my own, although everyone I'd told had launched themselves at me with ferocity, informing me what a terrible idea it would be. Mum had warned me about the perils of navigating a job interview with "a body covered in tattoos," as though I was planning to be riddled with them from the neck down. Si branded them trashy on women, which I'd told him was both insulting and misogynistic, and Ellie reckoned I'd regret it when I reached old age and my skin sagged, distorting the image beyond recognition. I fully intended to do it anyway. I wanted to find a really beautiful quote. Something about hope and moving forward and not looking back. I'd have it etched on my wrist so that I could look at it every day.

"Next: the Champs-Élysées," announced Léo.

I ran my fingers along the handlebars of the bike. I should say no. I should think about Si and I should say no, that he must take me back to the station, right this second.

"Do we have time?" I asked.

"It is 9:20. The train does not leave for more than four hours," he said. "You can relax a little, Hannah."

I got back on, still not sure if I was doing the right thing. Before I could decide if I was or if I wasn't, he pulled off, pointing out the Jardin des Tuileries on our left, which I thought might lead up to the Louvre. I held on tightly as we carved our way through gridlocked, beeping traffic on the biggest, most chaotic roundabout I'd ever seen in my life. It was like a Wild West of cars and bikes and mopeds coming from all directions, as far as the eye could see. There were no road markings, either, so how you were supposed to know which lane to be in, or how to cut across to come off at your turning, I had no idea.

"Where are we?" I shouted.

"Place de la Concorde," he called back. "Marie Antoinette was beheaded right here, in this square."

"Seriously?" I yelled, turning my head as if to catch a glimpse of some relic from the past.

"So you can think about death again," he said, laughing to himself.

Somehow we fought our way through to the other side, passing the Hôtel de Crillon on our right. Wasn't that where they held those ridiculously old-fashioned debutante balls? A film crew was gathered outside, their camera equipment by their feet, some sort of location truck parked in the bay out front.

"A beautiful hotel," said Léo when we stopped to let a stream of cars out in front of us. "But even the simplest room costs over one thousand euros per night."

And then we turned onto a very long, straight road. The Champs-Élysées, I thought, spotting the Arc de Triomphe standing majestically in the distance. Red brake lights snaked in front of us like ticker tape, hundreds of them, four lanes deep.

"What's that?" I asked him when we stopped at a junction, daring to hold on with one hand while I pointed to a building with glass domes and bronze chariots sprouting out of its roof.

"The Grand Palais," Léo replied over his shoulder. "A very nice exhibition space and art gallery. In the winter, you can skate on the biggest ice rink in the world."

Another thing that was "the biggest in the world." I was beginning to think his—admittedly quite interesting—facts about Paris were ever so slightly biased.

We pulled off the Champs-Élysées and Léo accelerated now that there was less stopping and starting, whizzing past trendy hotels with smoked-glass windows, chic *patisseries* and boutiques advertising haute couture. I spotted Alaïa; Christian Dior Atelier. It was like a different world, this street; I could picture the wealthy women who shopped here sliding in and out of chauffeur-driven cars, stopping for long lunches that probably cost as much as my weekly salary.

"Hold tighter," he shouted as we drove up onto a bridge and whipped across the Seine. The wind was blowing through my hair, which had long ago escaped its bun; the sun warmed the back of my neck and I could see the Eiffel Tower shooting into the sky right in front of us. I'd always dismissed it as tacky, branding it nothing more than a tourist trap, but now that I could see it properly, or perhaps because of the angle I was seeing it from, it took my breath away.

On the other side of the bridge, we turned onto a side street where Léo pulled over and turned off the engine.

"Come. There is something I want to show you," he said, leaping off.

"What is it?" I asked him, a buzz of excitement rippling through me. I hadn't felt like this in ages. He beckoned for me to follow him.

"You will see," said Léo mysteriously, stepping out onto a zebra crossing despite my worrying that the oncoming bus wasn't actually going to stop.

I hesitated.

"What are you doing, Hannah?" he asked, throwing his arms in the air.

"Do cars have the right of way or people?" I called to him.

He waved me after him. "People, of course. You show the traffic you intend to cross, and then you cross."

"But what if they don't see you?"

He shook his head and marched off. I followed him nervously, not sure which way to look first, and of course the traffic simply stopped to let me pass, as I should have guessed it would. What had I imagined? Honking cars full of angry Parisians shaking their fists at me? A pileup, with me stranded in the middle of the street surrounded by twisted metal? I watched Léo striding off, so carefree and sure of himself, and I wished that I could just do things, too, without driving myself mad with all the reasons why I shouldn't.

A small crowd had gathered on the corner and Léo had already joined them by the time I caught him up. I wondered what all the fuss was about, but when I looked up and saw what they could see, my mouth actually dropped open. Sandwiched between two cream-colored balconied apartment buildings was the most perfect view of the Eiffel Tower, right there in front of us. With the cobbled street, the sky with a hint of blue behind the clouds, the pop of green from the trees growing under its arch, I could see why it was every Instagrammer's dream shot. I immediately put my camera to my eye, trying to capture it in a way that did it justice. I wanted to feel the essence of it and its size, which was much more imposing than I remembered from before, although of course I'd been farther away from it then.

"As you can see, we are not the only ones who know about this place," said Léo, watching, amused, as a girl in a beret and a striped Breton top took pictures of herself using a selfie stick. A Japanese guy was photographing his friend, who was looking enigmatically up at the top of the tower with his hands in his pockets.

"It's such a lovely view," I said, framing an abstract shot of just the very top of the tower.

"You enjoy taking photographs?" asked Léo as I crouched down to look at the scene from a different perspective.

I nodded, standing up, suddenly unable to contain my enthusiasm. "I've loved it since I was a little girl," I told him. "Every year I'd ask for one of those disposable cameras for Christmas—do you remember them?—and I'd spend ages deciding how best to use those twenty-seven frames or whatever it was. I'd take covert photos of people doing something that summed up who they were as a person: my mum ironing, for example. The boys from across the road whizzing past on their BMXs, standing up on the pedals. Or I'd go to the park and take what I thought was a very arty shot of a rusty old set of monkey bars."

"Sounds fascinating," said Léo, smiling to himself.

"Well, I thought so."

"You were happy with how they turned out?" he asked.

I shrugged. "I can't remember. I never showed them to anybody, so it was difficult to be objective."

After a few more minutes of snapping away and a change of film, we walked closer to the tower, dodging the crowds of influencers taking their best *I'm in Paris!* photo. We passed a restaurant with tables spilling out onto the terrace. Léo stopped, reversed and peered through the window.

"*Un moment,*" he said, holding a finger up to me and opening the door to go inside.

What was he doing now? While I waited, I watched a glamorous woman wearing a red dress and heels leaping through the air as a professional-looking photographer tried to capture her with both feet off the ground.

"*Voilà!*" said Léo, reappearing with a bottle of red wine and two plastic glasses. "You cannot appreciate the full glory of Paris without a glass of French wine in your hand," he said. "Come, let us sit."

He ushered me over to a bench, handing me one of the cups. I took it reluctantly.

"Isn't it a bit early for this?" I said, covering the top of the glass with my hand. "I don't want to turn up to the wedding drunk, do I? Plus, you're driving."

"I promise you I will be careful," he said. I watched him pour a small amount of wine into his own cup. "Relax, Hannah. You will not be in Amsterdam for hours, have some fun."

I moved my hand so that he could fill my glass. "You're very tuned in to everyone else's flaws, aren't you?" I said, bristling at the fact he'd branded me uptight already, without giving me the chance to prove him wrong.

"It is no problem," he said, clinking his cup against mine. "We all have them."

I took a few sips in quick succession, swilling the bold, spicy wine around my mouth to get the full taste sensation. "It's good," I admitted reluctantly. My gaze rose to his lips as he took a sip of his own drink, his Adam's apple bobbing up and down when he swallowed.

"How tall is this thing, then?" I asked, looking up at the tower. From here I was close enough to watch the lift slide up and down through the center and to make out the shapes of tourists milling about on the lowest platform, clamoring to get near the window, cameras flashing.

He frowned. "I cannot remember the exact measurement. Around three hundred meters, perhaps."

"It's huge. Much bigger than I'd thought."

"When it was built in 1889, it was supposed to be a temporary

structure only," he explained. "It was part of an exposition to cel-
ebrate the French Revolution."

"Seems like a lot of work only to have it ripped straight down
again," I said.

"Exactly. The architect—Gustave Eiffel—had to prove that
not only did it attract many visitors, but it had other attributes, too.
It was used as a radio tower in the First World War, for example."

I took off the leather jacket and put it on the bench between us.

"You are warm now?" he asked.

I nodded, putting my camera to my eye to snap a few more
shots of the tower, and the velvety-smooth grass nearby that was
scattered with people relaxing in the sun, lying on peeled-off jump-
ers, their heads propped up on bags while they pored over guidebooks or flicked through their phones. I couldn't remember the
last time I'd done something like that, had an unplanned picnic in
the park, or sat out in the sun all afternoon with friends. Perhaps
that was what happened in your thirties. People moved away,
bought houses out of town; every meet-up took a bit more planning. Being here, on this bench with Léo, felt like the most spon-
taneous thing I'd done in months.

"So tell me, what is this wedding in Amsterdam you are so
desperate to get to?" asked Léo, who had stuck his long legs out
in front of him, crossing them at the ankle.

"My boyfriend's sister is getting married at 5:30 in some swanky
hotel."

"Shame you will miss it," he said, glancing at me out of the
corner of his eye.

I tutted. "Talk about me being negative. If the train gets in
just before five, I don't see why I can't jump in a cab and get to the
ceremony on time. Amsterdam is tiny compared to Paris, isn't it?"

"I suppose," he said.

I swirled wine around in my glass. "You don't think I'll make it, do you?"

He stretched. "Maybe." I noticed how his white T-shirt rode up to reveal a tiny strip of flat, tanned stomach and I drew my eyes away, putting my camera to my eye and playing about with the focus dial.

"Let's go," I said after a while, standing up. "I need to get back."

I'd call Si again from Gare du Nord.

Léo peeled himself off the bench, checking his watch.

"It is 9:55," he said, handing me the wine and his cup to put in my bag. "Better rush, *non?*" he said, walking off and laughing at me over his shoulder.

9

I ran my fingers along the metal frame of the bike. Because the engine had only just been switched off, it was still hot under the pads of my fingers.

"Everything okay?" I asked.

"It was making a strange sound," said Léo, his voice muffled as he bent down to check the front tire and then the back one, his brow furrowed with concentration, his long fingers prodding at the rubber.

The way my day was going, I wouldn't be surprised if the bike *had* broken down, leaving us stranded on the wrong side of Paris, miles from the train station. I rubbed the back of my neck, trying to remain calm. This was an adventure, I told myself; a glitch in my otherwise very ordinary life. And anyway, if I had to, I could walk back to Gare du Nord. We hadn't run out of time yet.

"It is fine, I think," he said, standing up, wiping his face with the hem of his T-shirt, revealing his perfect abs again. He probably had them out at every opportunity.

"Is it safe to drive?" I asked.

He patted my shoulder reassuringly. "Do not worry, Hannah, the bike is not going to explode on us."

I gave him a withering look.

"So. Come," he said with a typically Parisian shrug. "A look at the river. And then we must go."

"It's just a river," I said, grabbing his jacket and following him begrudgingly across the grassy promenade. I had no desire to see the miserable view of the Seine I still remembered. "We do have the Thames at home, you know."

The two of us leaned on a wall overlooking the water and directly across from the terminal for the Bateaux Mouches tourist boats on the opposite bank. They slid elegantly up and down, swinging in and out of the jetty, enthusiastic tourists sitting out on the decks, cameras poised. Surprisingly, I wasn't finding them anywhere near as irritating this time around.

"Impressive, *non*?" said Léo.

"If you say so," I said, putting my camera to my eye and zooming in on the glass roof of the Grand Palais glittering in the distance.

I caught him watching what I was doing.

"Do you like photography?" I asked.

I'd told him loads about myself and he was full of questions, but I realized I knew very little about him.

"I never tried," he said, peering at my camera with interest.

"You want to have a go?"

He nodded and I pulled the strap over my head and looped it over his. He brought the camera up to his left eye and swiveled from side to side, looking for a subject. Settling on a flat, sleek-looking boat called the *Catherine Deneuve*, which was moving slowly past us, he clicked the shutter.

"How do I focus?" he asked, his voice heavy with concentration, and I had to stop myself from smiling.

"Here."

I reached over, our cheeks almost touching, my wrist bone resting on his shoulder. I felt my neck begin to flush.

"Rotate this button gently, until the picture is crystal clear."

He took a few shots and then turned the camera on me.

I put my hand over the lens. "Don't you dare," I said, laughing.

"You are shy?" he said, grinning at me, and it struck me that we already felt comfortable enough to tease each other.

"Very," I said. "And I don't photograph well."

"I do not believe that," he said, handing the camera back to me, then ruffling his hair and looking out at the water. I glanced at him out of the corner of my eye.

"You did not say how it is that you are alone here," he said. "With no suitcase and no warm clothes."

He pulled a cigarette out of its packet, lighting it for me and handing it over. I shook my head, clamping my hands behind my back. If I had one more, I knew I'd be on a slippery slope. I wasn't the sort of person who could smoke now and again, when I was under stress, or when I was with a particular group of people. I didn't function that way: it had always been all or nothing with me. Things were either great or they were terrible; I either loved someone or I hated them.

"So, we were in Venice."

"Who is we?"

"Just me and Si."

He looked confused.

"My boyfriend. Simon."

It was breezier down here, and a few degrees cooler even though the bright sunshine now glistened over the river. I slipped his jacket over my shoulders.

"*Simon* . . . ," said Léo. The name sounded nicer in French. "Ah. That is who you called. When we were on the train."

I turned to face him, wedging my hands on my hips. "Were you listening in on my conversation or something?"

He smirked. "I could hardly help it. The entire carriage could hear."

"They could not."

"You were very loud."

I looked sulkily out at the Seine. A dredger passed by with a dog charging about on its decks, which didn't do anything for my nerves because I was convinced it was about to jump into the water and drown right in front of my eyes.

"It was because you were upset, *non*?" said Léo, still going on about it. "Your volume was up here," he said, reaching his hand up toward the sky to demonstrate just how much of an idiot I'd made of myself.

"You're exaggerating," I said.

I'd made a concerted effort to talk quietly.

Léo laughed. "Tell me, what did you do in Venice?"

"The usual. Sightseeing. Eating my body weight in pizza."

The whole time I'd been there I'd had this feeling of familiarity, I nearly told him, as though I'd been there before. Perhaps it was the photos I'd seen of it in the past, the brochures I'd leafed through, the pictures of George and Amal Clooney on their wedding day.

"He must *really* want to impress you if he takes you to Venice," he said.

I thought that maybe he had, but it had still been a massive shock when I'd found out where we were going, particularly since he'd never been one for grand gestures before. He'd told me at my birthday dinner, in front of Ellie and John. I wasn't quite sure why he'd done that and if I was honest, I'd have preferred it to have been just the two of us. I hated having multiple pairs of eyes on me and could never relax when I was the center of attention.

"As you guys know better than anyone, next Saturday, the very amazing Hannah and I will have been together for a year," Si had dramatically announced the second we'd finished dinner.

"Nice one, Si," said Ellie, winking at me.

Si cleared his throat. "It has, and I can say this without hesitation, been an amazing journey. When I walked up that escalator at Highgate Tube station, I had no idea my life was about to change. That I was about to meet the woman who would prove that love at first sight is an actual thing."

I put my head in my hands, embarrassed. What was he *doing*?

"What a sweet talker," said Ellie, nudging me jokily.

"And so," he went on, pausing only to take a mouthful of water, "I wanted to get you something extra special. A sort of thirtieth birthday cum anniversary present. To show you how much you mean to me."

"Okay," I said, warily, peeking through my fingers.

He produced a box from under the table. I swallowed, tearing off the wrapping paper, part intrigued, part mortified. I didn't think I'd done anything to deserve all of this. Inside the paper was a gray box with a Mulberry logo emblazoned on the front. I was confused. Money had always been a touchy subject between us, although I'd assumed it was because we were still working out the logistics of living together—opening joint accounts for the bills and setting up direct debits and all that other organizational stuff that I'd never been brilliant at. We had to save, he'd been drumming into me, for a deposit on a home of our own. To me, this seemed like a pointless exercise, because how were we ever supposed to save enough for a property in London? I'd rather have spent the money on having a good time now and worried about the pros and cons of mortgages later, although that was me all over. No wonder I was permanently overdrawn.

"Look inside the box," he said.

There was something flat and rectangular lying on the bottom of it. I pulled apart the tissue, revealing an oxblood leather passport holder.

"Si!" I said, my mouth literally dropping open.

"Open it," he said, crouching down next to me.

I looked at him quizzically, doing what he'd asked. My passport was already inside, along with a British Airways ticket. I shook my head in disbelief, scanning it for a destination, barely able to take it in: London Heathrow to Venice Marco Polo. Sunday, June 30, 2019.

"I'm taking you to Venice," he said, beaming. "I know you've always wanted to go."

"Blimey," said Ellie, looking flustered for once, as though she couldn't quite find the right thing to say.

"But we're already going to Amsterdam in July," I said, confused.

"For the wedding, you mean?" scoffed Ellie. "That's hardly a holiday."

"Exactly," said Si, taking it in good humor. "I know you've booked the whole week off work, so I thought we'd spend a few days down in Venice first."

I raked my fingers through my hair. I didn't understand.

"And then I've booked us on a night train from Venice up to Amsterdam on the Wednesday night. I thought it sounded more romantic than flying. We'll have our own little compartment with pullout beds. Brandy nightcaps as we whizz across the Pyrenees."

I thought I might actually be in shock. Si looked pleased with himself and excited, like a kid at Christmas.

"Say something, for God's sake," said Ellie.

Suddenly I shot up out of my seat, threw my arms around Si's neck and pulled him into me. "I love you," I whispered in his ear, my heart racing. "And I can't believe how lucky I am to have you."

• • •

The midmorning sun was glittering on the Seine and I took a series of photos, widening the shot to capture the buzz of the river.

"It is 10:20," said Léo, checking his watch for the hundredth time that day. "Shall I drive you back to the station?"

"Sure," I said, grabbing my bag off the ground, surprised to feel a swirl of disappointment.

"I would offer to show you some more of Paris. But since you hate it so much . . ."

"I never said I hated it," I protested.

He gave me a look.

"Okay, I do sort of hate it."

"You have seen all of this before? The river? The Eiffel Tower?"

"Sort of," I said, remembering how bleak everything had felt that day. How I'd berated myself for coming at all, for believing for a second that he wanted to see me. For opening myself up, being prepared to forget about everything that had gone before.

"I suppose you are too afraid to see the more authentic parts of the city," said Léo, walking off toward the bike.

I jogged to catch up. "What do you mean, afraid?"

"I am a complete stranger to you. You would not risk coming with me to my *arrondissement*, for example. It would be too risky, *non*?"

He handed me the helmet, which I managed to do up myself for the first time.

"Where is your *arrondissement*?"

"The 10th," he said, straddling the bike. "You know it?"

I shook my head.

"It is very beautiful," he said, adjusting the wing mirror. "It is a shame you will not see it, you could take some very good photographs."

"How far is it from here?" I asked, sliding on behind him and lifting my voice as he turned the key.

"It is north of the Gare du Nord. Fifteen minutes, perhaps?"

He revved the engine.

"Okay," I said nonchalantly before I changed my mind. I could always use his phone and call Si from there.

Léo swiveled to look at me over his shoulder, his eyes challenging. "Okay, what?"

"Okay, I'll come and see your *arrondissement*."

"You will?"

"But I can't stay long."

Another half an hour or so wouldn't hurt, I told myself as I wrapped my arms around his waist.

He pulled off into the road and when we stopped at a set of lights, he turned to look at me again.

"You surprise me, Hannah," he shouted. "Perhaps you are not as scared of everything as I thought."

10

There was so much to see on the drive to the 10th *arrondisse-ment*, it was like discovering a whole different side to Paris, one that hadn't been photographed a hundred times over. I noticed little details along the way, like the woman polishing the counter in an empty *boulangerie* and the colorful wooden toys in the window of a quirky little toy shop. I loved the feeling of darting round the city, being able to zip down the narrow streets that cars would struggle to navigate. I was almost disappointed when we pulled up next to a cobbled quayside.

"This is where I spend much of my time," said Léo, pointing downstream. "In these cafés along here. There is a juice bar selling very delicious smoothies, can you see? And over there is an exhibition space and gallery. They have some very cool new artists showing there."

The area was already bustling with locals sitting outside restaurants and coffee shops on those quintessentially French woven chairs. Waiters in white aprons whipped in and out of doorways carrying plates of eggs and toast and coffee. It was obviously a popular running spot, too, because I counted at least twenty people jogging past in the space of a minute. Across the other side of the canal, a group of young guys were cheering and laughing, enjoying an early-morning basketball game.

"What did you say this place is called?" I asked him.

"Canal Saint-Martin," he said. "The canal was built by Napoleon in the early 1800s to bring fresh drinking water in to Paris."

I picked up my camera and took some pictures of the smooth, dark green water that was so still it looked like glass.

"How far does it go?" I asked.

"Until it reaches the Seine. But a little farther along, at Place de la République, it goes underground for two kilometers, into these dark, eerie tunnels. You can take a boat there."

I took a photo of a sightseeing boat against a backdrop of some very cool graffiti, and then I turned to look upstream and captured a boxy block of flats framed by a canopy of plane trees.

"You know the song 'Les Mômes de la Cloche'?" said Léo, resting his back on the railings next to me.

I took a nice shot of three buildings in the distance, just on the bend of the canal: they were painted in mint green, rose pink and sunshine yellow, one after the other, like a trio of gelato.

"Never heard of it."

"Edith Piaf sang a version of it. It is about the Canal Saint-Martin and the children who lived on the streets here. There is this one line that says: *When death takes us, it is the most beautiful day of our lives.*"

"Jesus," I said, putting my hand on my chest.

He smiled. "You do not like sad songs?"

"No," I said. "Is that what you write?"

He shook his head dismissively. "Not really. You are hungry?"

I narrowed my eyes at him. "Are you changing the subject?"

"Absolutely not," he said innocently. "Now let us get back to you. You need to eat, *non*?"

"I'm fine," I said, looking at him suspiciously. He was definitely avoiding something.

"It was not your stomach I heard growling?" he said.

"Can't have been," I lied. "Anyway, I can eat at the wedding."

He looked at me as though I was mad. "That is hours away, Hannah."

I riffled around in my bag, finding a pack of old chewing gum in the bottom. That would stave off hunger for now. "You like your food, then, I see," I said, offering him the pack.

"Of course. You do not?" he said, taking one and throwing it into the air, catching it in his open mouth.

"Sure. But I don't think about it every second of the day."

I didn't know why I couldn't admit how hungry I was. It was a pride thing, I thought: I didn't want him feeling sorry for me, or feeling obligated to buy me something.

"Come," said Léo, motioning for me to follow him.

I stayed where I was. "Where are you going?"

"To eat cake," he said.

"I said I wasn't hungry," I called after him.

He pretended not to hear and had already crossed the road, stopping outside a burgundy shop front with *La Patisserie* painted in gold on the window. When he realized I hadn't followed him—which blatantly he'd expected me to, as though I was incapable of making my own decisions—he turned to look at me with his hands on his hips.

"Come on, Hannah!"

Outside the bakery, groups of young, trendy Parisians were clustered around shiny zinc-topped tables stuffing flaky pastry into their mouths. I'd have to get the cheapest thing and pray my card went through. My stomach rumbled again and I walked over to join him, purposely taking my time.

"Why did you take so long?" he asked, seemingly genuinely baffled.

"This is embarrassing to admit, but I don't actually have any money," I said, deciding honesty was the best policy.

He looked confused. "None at all?"

"Not really. I used the last of my cash to get a cab to Gare du Nord. And I've got a credit card, but you know . . . there's not much actual credit on it."

He looked surprised.

"I left my purse in my boyfriend's bag," I said. "I've got money in there, obviously." I didn't want him thinking I was a charity case.

"You should have told me before," he said, looking annoyed. "I will give you some euros, Hannah. You cannot go for so many hours without money, that is crazy."

"I don't want your money," I said firmly.

He waved a hand in front of his face. "It is no problem."

"Well, it's a problem for me. I can manage for a few hours more. Being a bit hungry is hardly the end of the world, is it?" I said.

"Ah, so you *are* hungry." The grin split his face and irritation rose up inside me. I hated him knowing he'd been right.

We moved forward in the queue, stepping inside the shop, but I couldn't quite see past the people already at the counter.

"Are you going to be too proud to let me buy you something?" asked Léo.

"You don't need to do that," I said quickly, although the offer was seriously tempting.

"I know I do not need to."

We were here now and it did seem a shame to be in Paris and not try at least one local delicacy.

I caved in. "Well, only if you're sure," I said, ignoring his far too cocky smile.

The queue moved forward and finally I was able to see the display in its full glory. Behind the slanted glass were rows and rows of the most perfectly presented, colorful, ornately decorated cakes I'd ever seen.

"Better than your English bakeries, *non?*" he said.

"What are they all?" I asked, wondering how I was ever going to choose.

"So these are *baba au rhum*," he said, crouching down so that he could see through the glass, pointing to a line of squidgy, treacly-looking sponge cakes topped with a crest of cream. "And these here are *Paris-Brest*, a soft pastry with praline inside of it. Then we have many different types of *éclair*, *tarte Tatin*, *clafoutis*, *puits d'amour* and at the end, *Mont Blanc*, a kind of puréed chestnut meringue."

I shook my head, overwhelmed. "I can't decide," I said.

"What have you never had before?" he asked. "You must try something new."

"I've definitely never had a *Mont Blanc*."

"Good choice." He nodded and took his turn at the counter. "*Bonjour, madame, comment allez-vous? Alors . . . deux Monts Blancs, s'il vous plaît.*"

The shop assistant took a white paper bag with the *patisserie's* logo on it in one hand and with the other she slid two mountain-shaped cakes inside.

"Ready?" he asked, once he'd paid.

"Sure," I said casually, trying to play it cool when really I was salivating at the thought of the mouthfuls of sugary sponge cake to come.

We perched on a nearby bicycle rack overlooking the water. I was careful to put as much space between us as I could, which wasn't easy on a thin piece of steel. Léo took his cake and handed me the bag.

"How on earth do I eat this?" I asked, peeking inside.

It felt fragile in my hand, as though it was going to disintegrate the second I took a bite. I peered at it, marveling at the crispy pastry base and the spaghetti-like chestnut cream piped all over it, roughly forming the shape of a mountain. Presumably Mont Blanc, which I thought might be in the Alps.

"Hang on," I said suddenly, "hold this for a second, will you? I want to take a photo of it."

"Be quick," warned Léo, who had been uncharacteristically quiet while demolishing most of his own, his *Mont Blanc* already just a pile of crumbs. "Otherwise it will collapse and you will lose it."

I focused on the cake cupped in the palm of his hand, taking the shot.

"Perfect," I said.

He passed it back to me.

"What do you like to take photos of now, then?" asked Léo, wiping his hands on a napkin. "You have moved on from rusty climbing frames?"

Nobody had ever asked me that before. Not even Si, who I

suspected considered my passion for photography nothing more than a fun little hobby. An incentive for me to pootle about taking pretty photographs of Portobello Road on a Sunday afternoon, or whatever. But for me it had never been just that. It symbolized the part of me that wanted more. I thought my dad might have felt that way about it, too.

"I like beautiful buildings," I said slowly. "Old ones and new. And the way light falls on objects: on a staircase, or rooftops, or a tree. And reflections. How water distorts everything, gives something solid and inflexible a sort of otherworldly quality."

"What else?" he pressed, crossing one leg over the other and turning toward me so that his knee was practically touching my thigh.

"I love the feeling I get when the composition is just right," I said, getting carried away. "When I've captured the mood of something. Or when I've caught a moment on film that will never, ever happen again, at least not in that exact way."

I tried to concentrate on not dropping my *Mont Blanc* all over the front of Léo's hoodie. Photography was the one subject I could go off on a tangent about, but I thought it was a bit much for most people.

"But you say you are not a photographer?" asked Léo, his voice gentle.

I shook my head to indicate that, no, it was not my job. I couldn't actually answer him because my mouth was full of the silkiest, nuttiest cream I'd ever tasted in my life.

"Mmm," I said, giving him a thumbs-up.

"What is your job, then?"

"I'm a human resources administrator. For a small law firm in the city," I told him in between mouthfuls.

"Do you like it?"

"Quite the opposite," I said, laughing lightly. "I can't stand it."

I pulled off a chunk of crispy pastry and popped it into my mouth.

"Actually, it's not the job, not really. It's me," I said, chewing. "I've been thinking about leaving for the last three years and have done nothing about it. They keep trying to send me on these management training courses but I make excuses not to go. Last time, I said I couldn't make it because I had food poisoning and then I had to take an extra day off sick to make it look realistic. And the worst thing was that the following day it was somebody's birthday and there was cake in the office and I had to pretend that I felt too queasy to risk it, even though—as you now know—cake is my favorite thing on earth."

He laughed. "You are funny, Hannah."

"And you ask too many questions."

"And here is another one. Why do you stay in that job if you hate it so much?" he asked, looking sideways at me.

I dabbed at the side of my mouth with my fingertips, licking a smidgen of cream off my thumb. I'd wondered the same thing myself, hundreds of times. Fear of the unknown, I supposed. The idea that if I stayed where I was, I wouldn't have to deal with the inevitable disappointment of trying something I actually cared about and being shit at it. And so I continued to get up, go to work, sit on the Tube alongside millions of other Londoners, and I accepted my lot, assuming that I couldn't have it all.

"It's reality, isn't it?" I told him. "I can't afford to take risks. I've got bills to pay. Commitments. Things I have to save up for."

"Like what?"

A tourist boat beeped its horn as it passed, its decks filled with tourists enjoying the sun, their cameras glinting and flashing against a backdrop of bright blue sky, which was now feathered with just the wispiest of white clouds.

"I don't know. Property?"

He looked surprised. "You want to buy a house?"

"I mean eventually. Yeah."

"And in the meantime you remain bored and fed up in this job that you do not like?"

"Well, yeah. That's the sacrifice, isn't it, as you get older? Most of your hopes and dreams have to go out of the window."

"Do they?"

"Yes."

"Do they have to?"

I looked down at my ankle, turning it over to check it wasn't swollen.

"Actually," I said, wondering whether I should tell him. "There's this photography course I'm thinking of doing."

He took the empty paper bag from me and lobbed it into a bin about a meter away; it was a clean shot.

"Like at a university?" he asked.

I lifted my camera and took a quick shot of a pretty mint-green arched bridge downstream.

"It's a pre-degree course at Central Saint Martins."

When I'd mentioned it to Si, I'd felt like he'd tried to put me off. He'd said it sounded like a good way to spend money I didn't have. That he didn't know why I'd want to give up every Saturday for six months when we could be spending that time together. We'd never be able to go away for the weekend, he'd pointed out, and I'd said: When do we ever go away for the weekend? I hadn't mentioned it since.

"It's an art school. In London," I added.

"I know Central Saint Martins, Hannah."

His know-it-all tone made me want to stop talking.

"Sorry," he said, softening. "Carry on."

I struggled to find the right words now that I'd lost my flow. How had I got started on this particular topic of conversation, anyway?

"The course has got some complicated name," I said tentatively, wondering what scathing observation he was going to make about it all. "Something about professional practice and a portfolio. It's only part-time, but there's loads of work outside of class."

He pulled his phone out of his pocket, tapped out a short text and then put it away, focusing his attention on me again. "This is possible for you?"

I nodded. "I think so."

"And you have made an application?"

I twisted my lens cap back and forth. "Not yet. The closing date is next Wednesday."

He got up and went to crouch on the edge of the bank, gazing at something in the water.

"You must do it, *oui*?" he said, looking at me over his shoulder.

"I don't know," I said, wishing I hadn't said anything. "I'd have to upload a portfolio of fifteen or twenty shots."

"You have those?"

"Yes," I said quietly. "Probably."

To him—to most people, in fact—it was probably a no-brainer. It was only a short course; it wasn't like I was committing to years of study. And I could just about afford it. I'd have to give up all the little extras like my morning Starbucks and my glossy-magazine fix. I'd take my own lunches in to work, that sort of thing. It was just that the idea of taking photography seriously, of thinking about it in terms of an actual career, felt like something that wasn't meant for someone like me. And in some small way, chipping away at the back of my mind, I felt bad doing the one thing I knew Dad would have loved to do, if he'd only had the chance.

Léo stood up and I lifted the viewfinder to my eye.

"Stay there," I instructed.

He did what I'd told him to, putting one hand over his eye, pretending to be shy about having his photo taken.

"Relax," I said, adjusting the focus, taking five or six shots. "You look all stiff. Oh, and wipe your nose, there's cream all over it."

He laughed, swiping his hand across his nose, and I caught him in a moment, looking relaxed and natural before he started posing and it looked wrong again.

"Do I make a good subject?"

"I don't know until I get them developed, do I?" I replied.

"You like using film?" he asked.

I nodded. "I prefer it. I like the romanticism of not knowing what you're going to find. Sometimes I leave it months before I get a film developed so that I completely forget what's on there. Then I can look at the images with fresh eyes."

I still got excited about collecting the old-school sealed envelope, its contents smelling of warm ink. The opening of it, the flicking through glossy print by glossy print, making a pile of my favorites.

"It is the same with my music," he said.

"In what way?"

He hesitated, searching for something in his jacket pocket.

"Actually, it doesn't matter. Tell me more about this course."

"Oh no," I said, realizing what was happening. "You're not getting out of it that easily. I've just told you a whole load of stuff I've never told anybody. Now it's your turn. What about your music?"

He tipped his head to the side. "You are good at reading people, aren't you, Hannah?"

"Yes I am. Now, tell me."

Raking a hand through his hair, he turned toward the canal and then back to me again. It was the most uncomfortable I'd ever seen him look.

"When I am working on a song . . . ," he said, rubbing his hand over his mouth.

"Yes?"

"I need to distance myself from it. For some time, if it is possible. When I have put it to the side for some weeks, a month or more, there is a chance I can hear what is not right with it. What is working and what is not."

"Okay." I nodded encouragingly. "Go on."

"But this, of course, cannot be done if I have a deadline. If I have to follow somebody else's timeline. Produce a finished product when somebody else says so."

I tapped my fingernails on the bicycle rack.

"Have you got a deadline at the moment?"

"Kind of."

"It's got something to do with Amsterdam, hasn't it?"

I waited. Then I widened my eyes at him, as if to say: *Has it?*

"Yes," he said, looking as though even admitting that had been too much for him.

"Why is it so difficult for you to talk about?" I asked.

"I am used to being the one who asks all the questions," he said.

"You don't like talking about yourself?"

He shook his head. "I do not," he said. "And do not even think about asking me why, which I know is going to be your next question."

"Okay, okay," I said, holding my hands up in surrender. "God, I thought *I* was closed off."

I lifted my face up to the sky and breathed deeply. This part of Paris smelled different from where we'd been before. Sweeter, woodier. Less like car fumes.

"Come," he said, standing up, shielding his eyes from the sun. "Follow me. Five minutes' drive from here is the Parc des Buttes-Chaumont. The views are crazy, you will make some very cool photographs for your portfolio."

I bit my lip. "I shouldn't, you know."

I'd already been much longer than I'd meant to be. I couldn't risk it.

"Think of your project, Hannah." He bent down to tie his shoe-laces. "And it is not too much of a detour," he reassured me, look-ing up.

"Just for a minute or two, then," I said, running my hand along the railing as though it was a musical instrument, listening to the different notes it made.

"It is 10:52, before you ask," he said, waving his wrist in my face and making a big show of checking his watch. "We still have lots of time."

11

We set off on the bike, crossing over the canals and driving uphill through an area that felt more suburban and lived-in than the other places we'd been to. Less of the apartment blocks with balconies and shutters I'd seen near the station and more of the sort of architecture I was used to in London, a mishmash of old and new, some seventies-style buildings, a hospital, a school, some sort of sports center. After navigating a mad roundabout where stopping at a zebra crossing with somebody on it didn't appear to be a legal requirement, Léo pulled over and cut the engine.

"Through here," he said, pointing to a set of green iron gates. And then he stopped. "Your ankle," he said with quiet concern. "It is a short walk, but it is uphill. It is too much?"

I shook my head. "It's much better," I said. "I'll be fine."

We walked through the entrance to a shady park with a sort of rocky, mossy feel; a different atmosphere again from the canals and the more central parts of Paris we'd already explored. I looked up, breathing in the scent of pine, noticing the way the treetops popped against the sky. I couldn't quite believe I was here again, in this city I'd despised for so long.

"I have another interesting fact about death for you," announced Léo.

"I don't know why you keep harping on about it," I replied, irritated. "I'm no more obsessive about it than anyone else."

"You want to hear the fact or not?"

"Not."

"You are sure? It is a good one, about what was once below our feet, here in this park. *Très macabre.*"

"In that case, definitely not."

I noticed how long his stride was compared to mine, how I was doing nearly two steps to every one of his. There was something oddly comforting about the twinge of pain I felt every time I put pressure on my twisted ankle.

"Where are these amazing views you've been bigging up, then?" I asked.

"This way." He steered me across to a wide pathway that curved off uphill. "You will see, it will be worth the climb."

"It better be," I said, my thighs already burning. I took off the hoodie, tying it around my waist, glad I'd left his jacket with the bike.

"So tell me," he said, his breath catching in his throat as we hit a particularly steep section. "How is it you are so good at reading people?"

I swung my arms back and forth to try to build some momentum.

"I'm not always," I said. "Not with everyone."

He stopped to hook a tiny pebble out of his shoe and I was grateful for the chance to rest.

"But sometimes you understand what is inside someone's head?" he asked, setting off again.

I'd noticed that when he asked a question, he actually seemed interested in the answer, and not in that fake, faux-polite way that people sometimes were, because I was very tuned in to things like that. I noticed when people asked me something and then glazed over before I'd had a chance to answer, causing me to falter to a halt, deciding that my story wasn't worth telling after all.

"Not exactly. It's more that I get a sense of what they're thinking. Specifically, what they're thinking about me."

He stopped walking for a second or two, looked across at me and then carried on.

"I think I would rather not know what people think of me," he said.

I fiddled with my camera strap, loosening it a little so it wasn't so tight across the shoulder. "That sounds like a healthier approach."

"*Oui*, I think so."

"For example, I have this thing where I'm constantly trying to work out whether people like me or not. I have a compulsion to know. I pick out all the little things that most people are probably oblivious to—their body language, the tone of their voice, whether their eyes flicker away from mine, whether they're looking over their shoulder for someone more interesting to talk to and so on. And if I don't get the validation I need, I instantly assume the worst: that I'm an awful person and therefore they must hate me."

There was a burst of something sweet in the air as we walked past an explosion of tiny purple flowers pushing between the cracks of a rock face to our right. I stopped to take a photo.

"You think people are thinking bad things about you all of the time?" he asked me.

I thought about it. "Not all the time, no. But I can tell when they are."

He shook his head. "It is your own paranoia, surely."

I ran the tip of my middle finger back and forth across my thumbnail, considering his reply.

"I don't think it is. Not entirely, anyway."

"Perhaps people like you very much, but they back off because you are so defensive that you give the impression that *you* do not like *them*."

"So you think I imagine it all?" I asked, skeptical.

"The mind can play tricks on you. People can be nicer than you think, Hannah."

"Ever the optimist."

"I dare not suggest that you are anything other than positive," he said, giving me a sideways look, the trace of a smile on his lips.

I pulled a leaf off a passing tree and shredded it into pieces, leaving a trail of green fibers behind me.

"What, worried I might cry again?"

"Look," said Léo, sweeping his arm out in front of him. "This is what I wanted you to see."

I couldn't even hide my surprise this time. The park had opened up into a beautiful Japanese-style garden complete with a suspension bridge leading to a fairy tale–like island made up of craggy cliff faces. The soft green fronds of weeping willows draped onto the surface of the lake below. When I turned full circle, I realized we were surrounded on all sides by cream-colored buildings with zinc roofs and balconies, like a sort of Parisian Central Park.

"Do you see the temple on top?" asked Léo, raising a hand to point.

I nodded, thinking how much I loved this place.

"It is a copy of the Temple de Vesta in Tivoli, Italy," he said. "If you go inside it, you can see for many miles, all the way to Montmartre."

I immediately lifted my camera and leaned against a post, snapping away, trying to capture the haunting quality of the temple. Then I zoomed in on a couple standing a few meters away. I liked the way they were leaning over the side, pointing at something in the water, whispering softly to each other. I became lost in the world I could see through my camera lens, losing track of the number of photos I'd taken. By the time I looked up again, Léo was already halfway across the wooden bridge, which shifted slightly as I stepped onto it, as though it wasn't quite as stable as it looked. I held the railing for support.

"Scared of falling, Hannah?" he called to me.

"Well, given how *clumsy* I am . . ."

He laughed, waving for me to catch up. The higher we climbed, the busier it became. Everywhere I looked someone was exercising, out for a run or doing press-ups on a bench or even yoga under the shade of a tree. It appeared to be a city of dog lovers, too, as I noticed most of their pampered animals were on ridiculously long leads, as though Parisian pets could not possibly be restrained.

"You are tired? Enough walking?" asked Léo as I came up slowly behind him, the fact I'd only snatched a couple of hours' sleep on the train finally catching up with me.

"I'm fine," I said, reluctant to admit I could do with a break. "Can we stop for a sec, though?" I asked. "I should try Si again."

Léo handed me his phone. "You need to check in?"

"No, but he'll be wondering where I am," I said, wondering why I felt the need to explain myself. "That's what couples do for each other," I added. I pitied Léo's poor girlfriend, if he had one. He hadn't mentioned anybody.

"You will tell him where you are?" asked Léo.

"Of course. Why wouldn't I?"

I moved off the pathway, perching on the arm of a bench that had someone's name carved into it, a dedication to somebody who had died. Those inscriptions always depressed me. I calculated their age in my head: sixty-eight. Too young. Nowhere near enough time to do everything you wanted to do. I glanced over at Léo, knowing he'd have something sarcastic to say if he knew I was thinking about death again. He'd crouched down, his back pressed against the trunk of a tree. I positioned myself so that I couldn't see his face and dialed Si's number. It rang three times before he answered and my heart began to race because I wasn't sure what kind of mood he'd be in if, by some miracle, he did pick up. He was a sucker for a schedule, and for everyone sticking to it, and I'd have disappointed him with my inability to follow instructions and to be in the right place at the right time. It was past eleven now, so he'd have checked into the hotel. Catherine probably had him ironing tablecloths already.

"Han?" he said breathlessly.

"Yes, Si, it's me."

"Are you all right?"

There was music in the background, the clink of glasses.

"I'm fine."

"I've been so worried about you, sweetheart. Where are you now?" he asked.

It was good to hear his voice. I imagined him perched on a stool in the hotel bar, could picture the frown lines he got between his eyes when he was worried about something. The way he pulled absentmindedly at strands of his hair when he was on the phone.

"Paris, still," I said.

From somewhere in the park I could hear children shrieking, the sound carried on the wind, most likely, from the playground we'd passed earlier.

"Jesus. This is a nightmare, Han. I'm having to reallocate all the jobs you were supposed to do, when everyone's already snowed under."

I brushed imaginary dirt off my jeans. "How did Catherine take it?"

"How do you think?" he said, with the exasperation of someone who'd had his highly strung sister in his ear for the last half hour and was at the end of his tether.

I glanced at Léo, who was pulling up strands of grass and rolling them between his fingers.

"If we'd been in the couchette like we were supposed to be, none of this would have happened," said Si. "So it's partly my fault, isn't it, for not being organized enough? I should have insisted they find us another first-class cabin."

"Oh well," I said, not wanting him to get wound up. "There's nothing we can do about it now."

There were lots of different voices in the background, and the clatter of glasses knocking together. Tables being set, perhaps. Things being polished and laid out. Every detail had been carefully considered, that was how Si's family rolled. They didn't do anything by halves, which I'd always been the tiniest bit intimidated by. When Si described his childhood, it sounded like the kind of idyllic life I'd only ever seen in American films, where the characters had wealthy, doting parents who had homemade cookies in the oven when you arrived home from school. And your friends had endless parties at which everyone would want to talk to you/get off with you and somebody would get too drunk and then everyone would jump in the pool.

"What are you up to?" I asked.

"Down in the restaurant," he said. "Helping Mum with the table plans."

I imagined him there, delegating jobs, organizing everyone, bossing them about with such easy authority that you couldn't help but nod and agree.

"What's the hotel like?"

"Amazing. Super modern. There are these huge, dramatic light installations hanging from the ceiling. You'll love it."

The hotel was called the Lux and was the sort of pretentious place I usually went to great lengths to avoid. I'd seen pictures of it on the website, which had pretty much been a permanent fixture on Catherine's laptop since I'd met her. It was a different world, all of this, which had only served to fuel my suspicion that Si's family must think he could do better. That an administrator from a council estate in Enfield wasn't exactly what they'd had in mind for their beloved son/brother. He, of course, was oblivious to the differences between us and had even suggested that we invite my mum and Tony over for lunch in Berkhamsted one Sunday, so that all the parents could meet. I hadn't been able to imagine anything worse than an afternoon spent pretending we were all getting along and very likely culminating in my mum saying something inappropriate about Brexit. And so I'd shut down that bright idea of his *very* quickly, convincing him that it was too soon for all of that but that we'd definitely arrange something at some point in the future (i.e., never).

"How's your sister bearing up?" I asked.

I sneaked another look at Léo, who was now trying to skim stones through the trees and into the water.

"She's, um, naturally a bit tense," said Si.

"Yeah. I reckon most brides would be."

I heard a woman's voice in the background. I couldn't hear what she was saying, not exactly, but there was an accent. Something about a ring, the end of the word pronounced with a hard *g*, like they did in Manchester. It was Alison, I knew it was. Si started talking, but his voice was muffled, as though he'd purposely held the phone away from his mouth.

"Sorry, Han," he said eventually, coming back on the line.

"Who was that?"

He hesitated. "One of the bridesmaids. The makeup artist hasn't turned up, apparently."

"Oh, right. Which bridesmaid's that, then?"

"Um, one of Cath's old friends. Alison, her name is. You might have met her at the hen do."

I dug my thumbnail into the arm of the bench, leaving an impression of my nail in the soft wood, like a new moon. Why hadn't he told me about her messages on the train? And it made me think that if he'd kept that from me, what else was there? A couple of months ago I'd accidentally bashed the hoover into a box of handwritten letters stashed under his side of the bed. When I'd got down on all fours to make sure I hadn't damaged them, I'd peered at them for ages, wondering how old they were, who it was he used to write to. And why he'd kept them. But in the six months since we'd moved in together he hadn't mentioned them once and for some reason I hadn't dared to ask.

"I'd better go, actually," said Si. "Mum's waving me over."

"Okay."

"When can you get here?" he asked.

"Should be just after five."

"Jump in a taxi and get to the hotel as soon as you can, all right? You've got the address and everything?"

"Sure," I said. Except all the info was on my phone, which I now didn't have. "What's the name of the street again?"

He sighed. "It's near the Anne Frank House, Hannah. The taxi driver will know it."

"All right," I said, feeling small.

"Whose phone are you using, by the way?" he asked.

This was obviously the point at which I should mention Léo. It wasn't as though I had anything to hide, and so what if Si didn't approve? I was a grown woman, it was fine to disappoint people. Inevitable, in fact. And then I bottled it and lied.

"Someone lent me their phone," I said, pushing the palm of my hand into my eye socket.

"So you're still at Gare du Nord?"

"Yeah," I said quietly, glancing over at Léo. Fucking hell, what would he think of me if he could hear me lying through my teeth? And, more to the point, why was I doing it at all?

"It's very quiet," said Si.

"I'm outside. Round the back, getting some fresh air."

"Right. Well, don't go wandering off, just stay where there are phones and people to help if you need it. Don't be tempted to go off looking around Paris or anything, will you?"

"'Course not," I said, wondering whether he'd always treated me like a child and I just hadn't noticed.

"Bye, Han."

I hesitated for a second. "I love you."

"Love you, too," he said.

He ended the call and I stayed where I was for a minute or two, watching a sparrow pecking at something on the grass near my feet. I thought about why I hadn't told him the truth about where I was and whom I was with. Probably to avoid the inevitable lecture about going off with strangers. Stranger danger—wasn't that something you taught five-year-olds? And it was pretty obvious that he was keeping things from me, too, otherwise why wouldn't he have mentioned Alison's texts? If we couldn't be truthful with each other now, whatever the cost, what would we be like in a few years' time, if we did get married, once the honeymoon period had worn off?

Realizing I couldn't sit there brooding without drawing attention to myself, I walked across to join Léo.

"Everything is okay with your boyfriend?" he asked.

I nodded.

"He has not sent out a search party?"

"Very funny."

"I think it is going to rain again," said Léo, pointing upward at the band of dark cloud above our head. "Come, let us try to find some shelter. There is a café at the top of the hill, perhaps we can make it there."

I'd noticed the cooling air when I was on the phone, but now the wind picked up out of nowhere and huge raindrops launched themselves out of the sky.

I groaned. "Not again."

We raced across to a giant pine tree a few meters away. I fumbled about with the hoodie because I'd tied the knot too tightly.

"Let me do it," said Léo, moving my hands lightly aside.

He undid it for me, shaking it out, slipping the fabric over my arms, one at a time, pulling up the hood and slowly doing up the zip. The entire time he didn't once look me in the eye. He had droplets of water on his eyelashes and for some reason I thought about wiping them away with my thumb. The rain was pounding all around us, smashing noisily through the needles of the tree so that it was like standing under the crest of a waterfall. Over Léo's shoulder I watched a family charging past, braving it, the woman's umbrella blowing inside out.

"You are cold," he said when the rain began to ease. I wiped my face with a sleeve.

"A bit," I admitted, wondering about the tension that had suddenly sprung up between us.

"You must get warm," he said firmly.

I nodded in agreement. "Is there anywhere to get food around here?" I asked, shivering. "I feel like a hot drink might help."

"You would like to go to a café with me, is that what you are saying, Hannah?"

I felt myself turning red again, lowering my head so that he wouldn't notice. "I thought you might be hungry again, that's all. Since food is so important to you," I said, trying to find that easy balance again.

He crossed his arms, smirking at me. He knew he was making me uncomfortable and was relishing every second of it.

"But you are out of money, *non*?"

"I can try my card," I said, wishing I'd never suggested it.

He laughed, glancing at his watch. "I am teasing you. I will buy you an early lunch."

"You don't have to."

"I want to."

"I'll pay you back."

"Just say yes, Hannah!" he said, exasperated.

He set off, out from under the tree, without waiting for my reply. Then holding out his palms and looking up, he flicked his head for me to follow him. "It has stopped. Let us go. I know a good place."

I lagged behind for a couple of seconds before running to catch up.

12

The handful of wooden tables outside the restaurant were taken, so we pressed our foreheads against the window, checking if there were any seats free inside. The smell of lemon juice and salty fries hung in the air and I could hear the tinkle of cutlery knocking against china.

"It is very popular, this place, as you can see," he told me.

The words *Café et Chocolat* were etched on the window in white, both of which sounded unbelievably appealing right about now. There was a menu written on a blackboard propped in the window; I scanned it, not understanding a single word. If I'd wanted the authentic Parisian experience, I'd got it.

"*Oui!*" exclaimed Léo. "Come. There is a table free."

Léo greeted the waiter like an old friend and we were shown to a banquette pressed up against the back wall. I chucked my bag under the table and half fell onto the red velvet seat, from where I had a near-perfect view of the entire café and the impressive zinc-topped bar in the center of it. Léo took a seat opposite me, immediately calling the waiter back.

"What would you like, Hannah?" he asked.

"Coffee, please," I said, amazed I'd made such a quick decision instead of the usual procrastination about whether I wanted wine or water; whether I fancied coffee or tea. Ellie teased me about it every single time we went to a bar—according to her, by the time I'd decided what to have first, everyone else was on their second round.

Léo rattled something off and the waiter nodded and disappeared behind the bar, scribbling on a minuscule white pad as he went. I looked around, making a mental note to take some photos before we left. It was the quintessential Parisian neighborhood bistro with mirrors covering almost every inch of the wall and a floor made up of hundreds of higgledy-piggledy fragments of tile stuck together to make a kaleidoscopic pattern beneath our feet. Delicious smells emanated from the kitchen, and soothing, ambient dance music played softly in the background. I immediately felt myself starting to relax.

"Tell me something I do not know about you, Hannah," said Léo.

The waiter brought our drinks and I picked up my coffee, letting the heat of it warm my hands. I was fascinated by the tower of wineglasses in the middle of the bar.

"I've told you tons of stuff already," I said. "More than I've ever revealed to someone I've known for half a day, let me tell you."

He leaned back in his seat, putting his hands behind his head. "It is because we are strangers. We can say anything to each other and it will not matter."

I peeled off the wet hoodie, wishing I could do the same with my jeans, which were stuck to me like a second skin.

"Because after today, we will never see each other again," I said.

"Exactly," he said, looking at the menu for about two seconds and then flinging it onto the table. "So . . . you live in London?"

I nodded, following suit and picking up the menu, scanning through it. "In the northwest of the city, in an area called Kensal Rise," I said, trying to decide if I fancied an *omelette et frites* or a pretentious take on a *croque monsieur*: a *croque focaccia*. "It's busy, but I love it. I like being where there are crowds and lights and traffic and color."

For some reason I felt safer among the chaos of London than I did almost anywhere else. It hadn't been like that where I grew up; you could go for a walk around the block and not see a single other person, which I'd always found disproportionately depressing.

"It is you and your boyfriend only?" asked Léo, watching me intently.

I nodded, clearing my throat. "We've only been there a little while."

I missed our flat. I was still reveling in my newfound maturity, in the idea of cohabiting and living in a place that didn't resemble a student dorm room. It had come fully furnished, but I'd added my own little touches and had spent hours flicking through lifestyle magazines and creating a collage of photos of brownstone walk-ups in Brooklyn, which our purpose-built seventies-style flat above a pet shop bore absolutely no resemblance to.

"How long were you together before that?" asked Léo. "Before you decided to live in this apartment?"

"Six months or so."

Sometimes—although I'd never admit it to Si—it felt as though our relationship was moving at double the speed of everybody else's. We'd only properly been together for a few months when he'd suggested moving in together. And he'd chosen the least romantic place to ask me: the upstairs landing of Mum and Tony's house. I'd gone up to help him find a spare dining chair when we'd gone round for dinner one night. He'd taken my hands on the landing, clutching them earnestly.

"There's something I've been meaning to ask you," he'd said softly, his eyes glittering.

I'd laughed brightly at how nervous he seemed. "Go on."

He coughed, taking a deep breath. "I wanted to ask you if you'd move in with me."

I swallowed hard. "What do you mean?"

"The lease is coming up for renewal on my place," he said, keeping his voice low. "And I thought to myself: we spend most nights together, anyway. Why not take the next step and get a flat of our own?"

I couldn't think clearly. This was not what I'd expected at all.

"Isn't it a bit soon?" I said tentatively, not wanting to hurt his feelings.

Si squeezed my fingers. "Is it? There are no rules, Han. Who says we have to do what everyone else does?"

I scrunched up my face, trying to put into words how I felt. Scared, for one thing. Out of control, for another. This wasn't how things went for me. People loved me and then they left me, that was how it had always been. And now here was Si telling me how serious he was about me, how he saw a future for the two of us. Part of me couldn't quite accept that he meant it.

"We're still getting to know each other, aren't we?" I explained. "Won't you get bored if you have to see me every day? Once you discover all my bad habits. How messy I am. How I leave dishes in the sink. All that."

He'd laughed, kissing me hard on the forehead. "I love everything about you, Han, messy bits and all."

I brushed the tip of my nose against his. "Are you sure?" I whispered.

"Yes, I'm sure. So what do you say?" he asked, looking hopefully into my eyes.

I hesitated, not quite believing it. "I say yes."

* * *

The waiter came bustling over to take our order. I went for the posh *croque*, and Léo chose some sort of *brioche* and goat cheese combo involving several ingredients I'd never heard of, at least not in French.

"Six months is very fast," said Léo, once the waiter had whirled off to the kitchen. "Why were you in such a rush?"

I looked down at my nails, inspecting them for more chipped varnish. "When you know, you know."

He gave me a cynical look, picking up his beer. "Right."

I was sure I saw him shaking his head to himself. Who was he to question the relationship Si and I had? It *was* right, I knew it was. And I certainly didn't need Léo putting doubt in my mind. Because the only thing was, I felt a little as though things had shifted between us lately. Si hadn't seemed himself for a few weeks now and had been especially snappy whenever the topic of his job came up, although of course he refused to talk about it. He'd even done it in front of John and Ellie the week before we left for Venice.

"How's work?" John had asked.

He and Ellie had been round at ours, leaning on the counter, watching Si cook, like they always did.

"Same as ever," said Si breezily, tipping a tin of tomatoes into the pan.

"What's happened to that arsehole new boss of yours?" asked John.

Si flinched. "Still an arsehole."

"He's awful," I said to John. "Si's been working late almost every night this week, haven't you, Si, because of his ridiculous demands? Comes home exhausted half the time," I said to Ellie.

"Yeah, all right, Hannah," said Si, glaring round at me. "You don't need to keep going on about it."

I looked at Ellie, who raised her eyebrows.

Si stopped stirring the pan and took the Prosecco out of the fridge, topping up each of our glasses, although we'd only had a couple of sips each. He spilled some over the top of mine, sending creamy bubbles cascading all over the table.

"Fucking hell," he groaned, grabbing a paper towel and mopping it up.

"I've been thinking," said John, who was not the most intuitive person I'd ever met and was therefore apparently oblivious to the change in atmosphere. "I reckon I'll take your advice and call your HR department about that head of marketing position you told me about. I might not have enough experience. They might laugh me out of the interview room. But if I don't try, I'll never know, right?"

Si turned back to the chopping board, slicing some black olives into quarters.

"You know what, mate? I'm not sure that job is going after all," he said, flipping a tea towel over his shoulder and catching John's eye. "I hate to have given you the wrong idea, but I reckon the guy's staying put."

"Really?" said John, looking surprised. "Because you said—"

"If I were you, I'd sack that one off and look for something else," said Si, well and truly killing the conversation. Even John gave me a funny look that time.

•   •   •

The waiter brought our food, which in my case was a deliciously chunky piece of toasted bread topped with a layer each of ham and bubbling, squidgy cheese, with a side of fresh mixed salad drizzled with olive oil. My mouth immediately began to water.

"This looks great," I said.

Léo picked up his fork. "Perhaps you do not like me saying that I find it too quick to live together."

"It's fine, I'm used to people being judgmental about it," I said, digging into my lunch. "Pretty much everyone thought it was too soon. I got all the: *Why don't you wait? What's the hurry? Enjoy the fun of dating each other while you still can!* Everyone except my mum, that was, who was positively ecstatic."

"Why is your mother so happy about this?" asked Léo, lifting a huge forkful of avocado and arugula into his mouth and chewing enthusiastically.

"She thinks I'm a bit of a failure," I said, taking a slug of my coffee. "My career has never really taken off, for example. The boyfriends I've had up until now have all been useless. I think she'd given up on the idea that I could make something of myself."

Léo put his fork down on the side of his plate, wiping his mouth with a napkin.

"How is moving in with your boyfriend making something of yourself?" he asked, looking genuinely confused.

Wasn't it obvious?

"Well, it's about becoming an adult, isn't it? That's what you do. You find someone and you fall in love and you start making plans for the future. That's what people expect, isn't it?"

Léo looked skeptical. "So we must all conform to what society expects of us, is that what you mean?"

God, this was coming out all wrong.

"Si has a good job," I said, feeling like I needed to justify myself but having the sneaking suspicion I was making things ten times worse. "He earns three times as much as I do. The reality is that without him, I'd still be renting a bedsit in a shabby house share at the dodgy end of Green Lanes."

Léo rubbed at his temple as though he couldn't believe what he was hearing. "You consider yourself a success or a failure based on what kind of job your boyfriend has?"

Seriously, this guy was unbelievable. For some reason he seemed to think he was well within his rights to comment on every single decision I'd ever made.

"I didn't say that," I said.

Admittedly, though, I had sort of said that and now I felt stupid, because it wasn't what I really thought at all. I didn't care about Si's money. It was just that I knew my mum did.

We sat in silence for a minute or two, the first real one we'd had. It was busy in the café now, full of locals coming in for coffee and respite, and Parisian yummy mummies. They looked so happy and relaxed, with their gorgeous, gap-toothed kids, feeding them mushed-up butternut squash out of glass jars and wiping their mouths with pristine white muslin cloths. It was another world, all of that, one that I still didn't feel quite ready for. Should I be, now I'd turned thirty? If I heeded what I'd read in the press about fertility dropping dramatically after the age of thirty-five, I should by rights be feeling broody by now, or at least be getting used to the idea, even if I wasn't quite yet.

It was something Si talked about a lot. All his mates at work were married with kids, he said, and it was what he wanted, too, and soon. He said he'd like three children, two boys and a girl. I'd laughed at this idyllic, middle-class fantasy of his. Where would we put three kids in a one-bedroom rented flat? And more to the point, did I really want to spend the next twenty-five years raising children when there was still so much I wanted to do myself? He never pushed the point, and I was sure I'd feel differently in the future, but right now, it was one more thing that we weren't on the same page about: he was ready to start a family and I wasn't. And sitting in a café in Paris, miles away from him, it felt like a major thing to disagree over.

Léo nudged my foot under the table. "You are quiet, Hannah. I have said too much?"

"You noticed," I said, making light of the fact that he'd really hit a nerve.

"Sometimes I say what is in my head and I do not think about whether it is right to say it out loud. Whether I might upset somebody with my opinions."

I looked him right in the eye. "Is that an apology?"

"Not exactly," he said, swirling *brioche* around his plate to soak up the oil. "Because I believe it is better to be truthful, even when it is difficult. Even when somebody does not want to hear it."

I put my arms on the table, leaning forward. "So you're telling me you've never pretended that you like something when you don't? Or lied to spare someone's feelings? Or because you're scared of the consequences?"

"Never. Have you?"

"Yes. I do it all the time," I said, laughing softly.

"You do?"

I took another mouthful of coffee.

"I take it you don't mind people being honest with you, either, then?" I said.

He shook his head. "Of course not. I like it."

I narrowed my eyes. "Do you, though?"

He smiled at me. "Let us try."

"What do you mean?"

"Do you still think I am rude, Hannah?"

"Absolutely," I said. And then I smiled, too. "Did you see that? I just told you exactly what I thought of you."

He nodded. "See? It really is not that difficult."

I watched other customers coming in and out, one holding a tiny fluffy dog under her arm, and a ridiculously gorgeous couple draped all over each other as though they'd actually morphed into one exceptionally esthetically pleasing human.

"What is it like, then, this place you have together that you could not wait to move into?" asked Léo, pressing remnants of goat cheese onto his fork.

"We've got a one-bedroom flat," I said, pleased to be back on familiar territory. "Small, but it has a little balcony, which I love. Any outdoor space in London is a massive bonus, by the way."

We had the best view over other people's back gardens and of high-rises, and the shops across the road that never seemed to close, their colorful stripy awnings permanently extended out onto the street. I loved sitting out there, watching the world go by, listening to the sounds of the city, the honking and the police sirens and the jumbo jets coming in to land at Heathrow; the odd fight outside the dodgy pub a couple of blocks away.

"I sit out there sometimes and I drink tea and watch people down on street level. Try to work out where they're going, or who they might be meeting. You can see all sorts from up there."

"Like what?"

"People chatting with their neighbors. Drunk blokes staggering home from the pub. Arguments."

"What are they arguing about?" he asked.

"I can't really make it out. There's a load of shouting and finger-pointing and then the next minute someone's crying and they're hugging it out. Occasionally there's a really bad one, though. I hate that, seeing people screaming at each other, saying things they don't mean."

"Perhaps they do mean it," he said.

He took a mouthful of beer, leaving a trail of froth on his upper lip. I watched him lick it off.

"I don't know. When I say things in anger, I always regret it," I said.

He frowned. "Why?"

"I suppose I'm worried I've pushed them too far. That they'll give up on me altogether. Walk away."

Léo pushed his plate to the side, looking around for the waiter to clear our table.

"What makes you think that people will walk away?" he asked.

"Well, my dad did."

He cocked his head to the side. "What do you mean?"

"He left us, me and my mum."

"When you were how old?"

"Seven."

"That is tough," he said. "But it was your mother he left, Hannah, not you."

I still remembered little details about the day he'd gone. My dad had been packing his tatty old suitcase and I'd run into his room and jumped on his back, wrapping my arms around his neck; my legs around his waist. I'd begged him not to go. *I'll be good*, I'd told him. *I won't be naughty again.* And when I'd looked up, panicked, Mum had been crying quietly in the corner, blowing her nose into a soggy tissue.

"So your parents divorced?" he said.

"Yeah. Eventually."

"You are close to your mother?"

I shook my head. "Not really. We don't talk much. Not about anything important, anyway."

"It was difficult, for the two of you, when your father left?"

I nodded. Talking about Dad was usually something I avoided at all costs. But oddly, with Léo sitting across from me, the words didn't get stuck in my throat the way they usually did. "Once a month he'd arrange to take me out somewhere. For lunch, or to the park or whatever. I'd be there at the window, waiting for him, all dressed up. Every time a man turned the corner into our street my heart would thump hard in my chest. I'd watch as they got closer and closer, crossing my fingers, standing on tiptoes, straining my neck to get a better view, but it would never be him."

Léo finished his drink, tipping his head back to reach the last dregs. He placed his glass back on the table. "He did not show up?"

"Never. Not once. I'd be there for hours sometimes, hovering about like an idiot. Eventually my mum would tell me to forget it, to go and do something else. She took great delight in it, actually, as though she'd got one up on him. As though she was delighted that he'd finally exposed himself for what he really was."

"You really think that is what she thought?" asked Léo, looking dubious.

I traced a fingernail over a swirly floral logo on the front of the menu. "I think so, yeah."

A waiter came to clear our plates, gathering up crumbs and sweeping them efficiently into his free hand.

"Do you want more to eat, Hannah?" asked Léo. "A glass of wine?"

I shook my head. "I'm fine."

"Do you find it hard to talk about your dad?" asked Léo once the waiter had gone.

I shrugged. "There's not much to say, is there? I haven't seen him for years."

"You never tried to contact him?"

I inspected a strand of my hair, pulling it taut across my face. "Once."

"You want to tell me about it?"

He had lovely eyes, I thought, almond-shaped and so dark that I couldn't make out his pupils in this light.

I shook my head. "Thanks, though."

I rubbed my arms, trying to warm them through, listening to the melodic beat of the music.

"Anyway, it's your turn now," I said.

He sat back, crossing his arms. "My turn for what?"

"To tell me something I don't know about you."

He laughed dismissively. "That is not so interesting."

"I'll be the judge of that," I said, ramping up the drama, drumming my fingertips on my chin. "Now . . . what do I want to know . . . ?"

He shifted in his seat.

"You know what? I'm just going to go for the jugular," I said.

"This sounds ominous," he said, asking a passing waiter for the bill. *"L'addition, s'il vous plaît?"*

"We've talked about my relationships, but what about yours?"

He shook his head. "What about them?"

"Are you seeing anyone?" I asked.

He pushed his hand through his hair, ruffling the back of his head.

"Not at this moment, no," he said.

"How come?"

"Because I am busy with my work. My friends. I have no time for a relationship."

I laughed. "Living up to the Parisian stereotype, then, I see."

"That is not it, Hannah."

"What is it, then?"

"It is more complicated than you think."

I slurped the last of my coffee, bashing the cup on the saucer as I put it down. "Well, I don't know what to think, do I?"

"It is just how things are, Hannah," he said. "To me, there are more important things in life than being in the 'perfect' relation-ship."

He used imaginary quote marks to make his point.

"You really don't like talking about yourself, do you?" I said, searching his eyes, trying to figure out what was going on. "You said we were strangers. That it doesn't matter what we say to each other because we'll only know each other for this one morning. So why don't you try me?"

"I do not get close to people like that," he said, pushing his chair back from the table and getting up. "It is easier that way."

I watched him walk through the restaurant in the direction of the bathrooms, weaving between tables, his T-shirt riding up to show a strip of brown skin on his back. For all his gruffness and bad attitude, I was beginning to think that there was more to him than met the eye.

13

By the time we'd made it back to the bike my clothes had
dried out a little, but I still felt grimy and damp all over. I missed
my clothes, I missed my makeup, and even though I'd spruced my
hair up the best I could in the loos at the café, I felt far from my
best. I'd caught a couple of people glancing at me as we'd walked
along and I'd convinced myself it was because they were wondering what somebody who looked as good as Léo was doing with
someone who looked like me. I'd rationalized it in my head, told
myself they probably weren't thinking any such thing, but the
feeling had stuck with me.

He'd suggested we call in to see a friend of his, a girl called
Sylvie, who had an apartment right on the Canal Saint-Martin. It
was her boyfriend's bike he'd borrowed, apparently, and he needed
to drop it back. I'd insisted that I needed to get to the station, that
I was perfectly capable of finding my own way to Gare du Nord,
but as always, he'd known just the right thing to say to talk me into
it. He said we could dry off before getting on the train, that I could

borrow some of his friend's clothes. The offer had been too tempting to refuse, given I was currently wearing wet denim that smelled
like a dog who'd been swimming in a stagnant pond, and he'd
promised we'd only stay a few minutes. I wondered, though, whether
his friends were all as generous as him, whether she, too, would be
prepared to hand over her possessions to a complete stranger. I
thought she might not be.

The door to Sylvie's apartment was sandwiched between a ce-
ramics shop and a *fromagerie*. She buzzed us in and we climbed the
stairs to the second floor. When we reached the landing she was
standing in the doorway, the epitome of esthetic perfection, a Clé-
mence Poésy lookalike dressed in skinny jeans and an expensive-
looking pale gray sweater, wearing no makeup, her hair scraped up
into a messy bun, like an off-duty ballet dancer. She was everything I wished I was.

Sylvie and Léo kissed four times on alternate cheeks (it was
very time-consuming, I'd noticed, this ritual the Parisians had)
and then reeled off into fast and furious French. He nodded his
head in my direction every so often and Sylvie looked at me with
a sort of insouciant suspicion, like she didn't trust me but also as
though she couldn't care less who I was. Why would I, a mud-
stained, curly-haired British girl, have any bearing on her seemingly perfect life?

"Come, Hannah," said Léo, beckoning me inside.

I slipped off my shoes, bending to wipe the soles of my feet
with a crumpled-up tissue I'd found in the bottom of my bag. It
was one of those apartments that felt like a show home, like a
piece of art that you'd be strung up for getting a speck of dirt on.

"Hi," I said, waving at Sylvie in an embarrassingly child-
like way.

She ignored me completely, anyway, preferring to talk to Léo as though I wasn't there, using words I had no hope of comprehending. I followed them into the living room, a parquet-floored, minimalistic, French-windowed delight. Whatever she did (modeling, probably, or something equally as glamorous), she was obviously very successful at it because her apartment was huge and bright and in the most unbelievable location, overlooking the boutiques and restaurants on the quayside. Through the leafy sweet chestnut trees, which created a gorgeous shady canopy for the hundreds of people who were now meandering up and down both sides of the canal, I could see the teal façade and blue parasols of the Hôtel du Nord, which I was pretty sure there had been a film about.

"Sylvie will give you some clothes," called Léo over his shoulder, disappearing off into another room.

I unzipped the wet hoodie, draping it limply over my arm.

"You have a lovely apartment, Sylvie," I said, wishing I could have come up with something more original to say.

It was true, though. The details were perfect: the quirky leaf-print cushion on the mustard velvet armchair, the framed black-and-white prints of Sylvie posing with her boyfriend. The stack of magazines on the table: American *Vogue*, *Vanity Fair*, *W.* The shiny black upright piano with sheets of music placed neatly on top of it. I wanted to take some photos of my own, some close-ups of light falling on the burnished-copper fruit bowl or of the rail in the corner hung with clothes arranged like a rainbow, going from whites and pastels at the far end to brightest nearest me.

"*Merci*, Hannah," she said, brushing imaginary dust off a bookshelf with her finger and then wafting off in the direction of the kitchen. Léo reappeared in a completely different set of clothes— dark blue jeans this time, with a pale gray T-shirt and no socks.

"They belong to Sylvie's boyfriend, Hugo," said Léo, noticing my confusion. "Luckily we are the same size."

He threw himself on the sofa, sticking his feet up on the coffee table.

"Sit," he said to me, patting the seat next to him. "Relax."

I could not relax. I perched awkwardly next to him.

Sylvie reappeared carrying a retro tray containing a stainless-steel pot of something hot and steaming and three oversized cups and saucers. She padded barefoot across the floor, revealing perfectly pedicured plum-colored toenails.

"You want tea, Hannah?" she asked.

I nodded. "Sure. Thanks."

She filled each of our cups. I didn't dare ask for milk, and dropped a lemon slice on top instead.

"It is your first time in Paris?" she asked, looking bored before I'd even thought about how to answer.

"I've been once before," I said. It would have been rude not to respond, even though I knew she couldn't care less what I said. "Years ago."

"*Sucre?*" asked Sylvie, offering me a delicate china bowl of pale brown sugar.

I shook my head. "No, thanks."

I took a sip of tea too soon and burned my lips, making my eyes water. I put down the cup, blinking frantically and dabbing the corner of my eyes with my fingertips, hoping they hadn't noticed.

"So how do you two know each other?" I asked, looking from one to the other.

"Hugo and I were at music college together," said Léo. "He is a brilliant musician, *oui*, Sylvie?"

Sylvie almost smiled. "He plays the saxophone," she said to me. "He is in a very well-known jazz band here in Paris."

Léo put his hands behind his head, as though he was sunning himself on the beach. I noticed that his feet were tanned, too, just like the rest of him.

"They have just this month signed a recording deal with one of the biggest labels in France," he said. I could tell he was impressed but trying to play it cool.

"You must be so proud of him," I said, turning to Sylvie.

She shrugged.

Léo laughed. "That is Sylvie's way of saying that yes, she is very proud."

"Oh, right," I said, pretending to understand why she couldn't just say it.

"You are not doing so badly yourself, eh, Léo?" said Sylvie.

"Really?" I said, perking up, wondering why he was so reluctant to talk about his job, then, if things were going so well.

He didn't look pleased and said something to Sylvie in French. I glared at him, annoyed that he'd done it purposely so that I couldn't understand.

"You want to come and look in my closet?" said Sylvie. "What size are you, Hannah?"

"A twelve," I said. "Sometimes a ten on the top."

"Come, then," she said.

I shot off the sofa, following her, determined to keep out the negative thoughts that were threatening to start nagging away in the back of my mind. So what if she was at least two dress sizes smaller than me and about four inches taller? In general, I was happy with the way my body looked. I'd long ago come to terms with what it was and what it would not be; my stomach would never be flat; my thighs would never have a gap between them, and that was okay. But there was something about Sylvie that brought back all the insecurities I'd had when I was younger, when I'd never felt good enough, when I'd longed to be like the pale, thin, popular girls that the boys from round our way had seemed to prefer.

Sylvie's bedroom was awash with color, from the pop art propped casually against the walls to the deep purple rug and the red velvet armchair. Her bed was unmade, as though she'd only just rolled out of it, fresh from a romantic tryst with her musician lover.

"Nice room," I said.

She threw open the doors of an antique wooden wardrobe and began to flick through the hangers with a frightening intensity.

"What do you want, a dress? Some jeans?" She glanced at me. "*Non.* My trousers are too small for you. I have some skirts that are stretchy here."

She made a circular movement around her waist.

"Great," I said, trying not to feel deflated.

She threw a black elastic-waistbanded miniskirt and a white oversized T-shirt in my direction.

"Léo said you met on the train," said Sylvie, putting the things I wouldn't have a hope of squeezing into back in the wardrobe.

"Yeah," I said, stroking the satin label on the inside collar of the T-shirt. It was from Sandro, the chic French clothing line I'd only ever peered longingly at through a shop window because I wasn't into torturing myself by trying on things I couldn't afford. I'd looked on the website once and even a pair of socks had been over my budget.

"You two seem very—how do you say?—cozy," said Sylvie, folding a pair of indigo jeans and placing them on a shelf full of other tiny, skinny trousers.

"Hardly," I said, leaning against the foot of her bed. "We've been at each other's throats all day. I think he's only sticking around because he felt too guilty to leave me at Gare du Nord after I fell over his stupid bag."

Sylvie turned to look at me, nodding knowingly. "He felt responsible for you. He is like that."

She swanned over to her bedside table, where she straightened yet another stunning photo of her and Hugo, this time on a beach, the pair of them sitting cross-legged under a palm tree. Sylvie was actually smiling in this one.

"Do you need anything else?" she asked, going over to a shabby-chic chest of drawers and opening the top one. "You want underwear?"

"Um . . ."

"Here," she said, lobbing a pair of pristine white briefs in my direction. "Do not worry, I have not worn them."

I wondered what kind of person owned a drawer full of knickers they didn't wear. I was lucky if I could find a clean pair with the elastic intact.

"I will leave you to dress. There are things in the bathroom, soap and perfume, makeup. There is a towel you can use, the blue one. Take whatever you need."

I nodded. "Thanks, Sylvie, I really appreciate this," I called after her as she marched out of the room looking all sulky. I'd thought Léo was hard work, but she stormed around as though she was constantly on the brink of having an almighty meltdown. That all it might take would be for someone to say the wrong thing, or even look at her in the wrong way. There must be many advantages to being beautiful, but I imagined that being able to behave badly and get away with it was probably one of them.

I went into the bathroom, where Sylvie's huge collection of products were placed artfully around the sink. Careful not to knock anything over, I peered at labels, trying to work out what was what. I had a quick wash, never having enjoyed the feel of warm, soapy water on my face quite as much. Then I picked through Sylvie's toiletries bag and applied some of her makeup; her foundation was too pale for me, but the powder was fine. I was ecstatic to find a bottle of detangling serum that looked like it cost a fortune and used a ton of it to give my curls some definition, pulling the front off my face so that my hair was half up, half down. I squeezed toothpaste onto my middle finger and scrubbed at my teeth. And then I dressed in the outfit Sylvie had selected for me, tying the hoodie around my waist, because I'd got quite used to wearing it and thought I might need it later, when the weather inevitably turned chilly again. I examined myself in the full-length free-standing mirror at the end of her bed, relieved that I was looking halfway decent for the first time since leaving Venice. Before I went to find Léo, I doused myself in Sylvie's Diptyque Eau des Sens, leaving a trail of orange and patchouli behind me in the room.

I couldn't see them immediately, but I could hear someone playing the piano, a slow, romantic piece I wasn't familiar with. I followed the sound into Sylvie's living room, stopping dead in the doorway when I saw Léo sitting at the piano. He was curved over the keys with his back to me, his elbows rising and falling as he moved them from the lower register to the higher one. When he'd said he played the piano, I hadn't imagined him to be anywhere near this good. How could such an insensitive guy produce a sound as tender and beautiful as this? I leaned against the door frame, closing my eyes, enjoying the music, wondering why he hadn't told me how talented he was. He ended the piece on an exquisite run of notes that actually sounded the tiniest bit familiar, pausing with his hands on the keys before swiveling round on the stool.

He almost jumped when he saw me. "Fuck, Hannah. I thought you were still getting changed."

I shrugged.

"You're really good," I said, reluctant to rub his ego even more, but feeling the need to say something. How could I not?

He slammed the lid on the keys and shot out of his seat.

"What was that piece of music?" I said. "I feel like I've heard it before."

He flung himself onto the sofa, refusing to look at me. "It is something I wrote."

"Tell her more, Léo," said Sylvie, appearing in the room and sitting cross-legged on her exquisite duck-egg-blue chaise longue. She looked all neat and compact, like a curled-up cat.

"It is for the project I am working on in Amsterdam," he said, pretending there was something on his phone that urgently needed attending to.

"He has written a song for an up-and-coming Dutch pop singer," said Sylvie, jumping in. "And that piece you heard was sampled for the track."

It dawned on me then, where I'd heard it before.

"That's what you were listening to on the train, wasn't it?" I said to Léo, who was now looking to be in a darker mood than ever.

"Terrible dance music, I think you called it," he said, glancing up at me.

I grimaced. "Sorry. I could only hear the bass, and in my defense I was so tired, the slightest noise would have set me off."

"No, Hannah. You are right. Terrible is exactly what it is."

"I know nothing about music, anyway," I added, looking nervously at Sylvie, who started speaking French to him again and then, as though remembering I was there, switched to English.

"It is not the decision of that silly girl, it is for the record company to decide," she was saying. "She is a teenager, Léo. What does she know?"

This was too intriguing, I had to know what they were talking about. "What's going on?" I asked, as casually as I could manage.

Léo waved his hand dismissively. "They hate it, Hannah, that is all."

Sylvie rolled her eyes and looked at me. "They do not hate it. The pop star, who is a brat, by the way, performed Léo's song on television in Amsterdam and she did not feel it went well. The record company has asked Léo to make some small changes, that is all."

"And that's what your meeting was about?" I asked.

"Exactly. Now I have missed the meeting and instead must go straight to the concert of this girl tonight."

"Maybe it's one of those songs that grows on you," I suggested, terrified of saying the wrong thing and still mortified that I'd called his work terrible. "I bet she'll love it eventually."

"Can we talk about something else?" he asked, rubbing his face with both hands. "You want to use the computer?" he said, turning to me.

"I guess I could check my e-mails, if that would be okay?"

"Of course," said Sylvie.

Léo moved over to make room for me on the sofa. "Here, let me write my phone number down for you. In case there is somebody you would like to give it to."

"Thanks," I said, admiring his twirly handwriting, which was neater and more ornate than I would have expected. Did this mean we'd be sticking together for the entire journey, then? I hadn't thought that far ahead. And I had to admit, I didn't *hate* the idea. It was handy to have a translator on tap, and I was kind of enjoying winding him up about being so closed off. Time was passing more quickly, anyway, so that had to be a good thing.

I opened Sylvie's laptop. It didn't seem right that I was sitting in a gorgeous Parisian apartment drinking tea out of a ceramic mug that probably cost more than all our crockery put together while Si's family flew around the wedding venue covering all the jobs that I should have been doing. Catherine would be a nervous wreck, I knew that. She had her bridesmaids with her, but still; we'd spent a lot of time together lately, and I thought she'd quite liked using me as a sounding board for all her anxieties about the wedding. Despite everything, I wanted her wedding day to be everything she'd dreamed of. I wondered whether I should send her an e-mail, tell her I was thinking about her, that I would get there as soon as I could. I supposed she wouldn't get around to reading it, anyway.

I finished my lemon tea and half listened to Léo and Sylvie, who had moved into the kitchen and were chatting away animatedly about something in lyrical French, his voice low and melodic, Sylvie's soft and breathy. I could listen to the way they rolled their *r*'s all day. I logged into my e-mail account and scrolled through my in-box. I probably wouldn't bother messaging Si, because I was basically doing everything he'd told me not to do: I *had* left the station, despite his warnings not to. I'd got on the back of a motorbike, I'd had lunch with a stranger and had told him stuff about our lives. He'd be livid if he knew the half of it. So instead I e-mailed Ellie, struggling to explain what had happened. I told her briefly how Léo and I had met, about everything that had gone wrong. How a terrible start to the day had turned into something quite different: I was starting to see Paris in a different light, I told her. It was beginning to feel cathartic being here again, seeing it through the eyes of someone who loved his city and who could show me places and tell me facts about it that made it come alive. I gave Ellie Léo's number, playing it down, mentioning Sylvie. It felt strange putting it into words, even though theoretically I hadn't done anything wrong. So why did it feel like I had?

I briefly messaged Mum, leaving out any mention of Léo, and just letting her know that I was all right and heading to Amsterdam in a matter of hours. And then, before I could overthink it and talk myself out of it, I opened a new tab and logged in to Si's Gmail account. As soon as his in-box appeared on the screen, I felt bad. I'd never done anything like this before, partly because I'd always assumed I couldn't trust people anyway, so why bother to check? But it was different with Si; I trusted him more than anyone I'd ever met. Except that suddenly I'd started not to. We were both in our thirties now and living together. It would be marriage next, and then possibly a baby. I didn't think I'd be able to do any of that until I was completely sure he meant it when he told me that he wanted us to be together forever. And if snooping in his e-mails put my mind at rest, then surely it was worth the guilt I'd probably feel once I realized I had absolutely nothing to worry about.

The only reason I knew his password was that just after we'd moved in to the flat, when the weather was still all over the place and had been mild one minute and freezing the next, he'd called me from a conference and had instructed me to go into his e-mails to look for some details about a boiler service. I'd had the day off work and had been lying on the sofa watching Netflix when what I should have been doing was polishing my CV so that I could start looking for a new job. He'd told me his password was Gameofthrones. I'd wound him up about that for weeks afterward and as a result had never forgotten it. I was surprised he hadn't changed it, actually. Proof, perhaps, that there was nothing untoward going on—he wouldn't be that stupid, surely.

I took a deep breath and scrolled through his e-mails, scanning them for names I recognized. I was terrified about getting caught—was there any way he would know what I'd done? Did he have it alarmed or something, so that he'd get a message alerting him to the fact that somebody had hacked his e-mail account? It wouldn't surprise me; he was very good with technology. I carried on scrolling, my hand shaking slightly as I rolled the dial on the mouse. There were loads of messages from Catherine, tons from work, a couple from his mum with wedding-related subject headers. I didn't bother to open any of them, just whizzed through, looking for anything out of the ordinary. And then I stopped, leaving the cursor hovering ominously over a group of messages to and from somebody called Alison. Wedding Alison. I swallowed, but it felt difficult, as though my throat had sealed itself up. I clicked into them.

The most recent had been sent the night before we'd flown to Venice.

Alison Clarke
Sat, Jun 29, 8:17 PM

Si,

I know you said not to text, so I thought I'd let
you know I've got some news. Let's talk at the
wedding.

A x

I bit my lip and scrolled down. The previous message had been
sent a few weeks before, on the night of my birthday dinner.

Simon Woodburn
Sat, Jun 8, 9:52 PM

Dear Al,

Thank you—again!—for everything. Can meet on Tuesday
evening if that suits? I'll tell Hannah I'm pulling a late one
at the gym.

S x

Her initial e-mail was underneath it.

Alison Clarke
Fri, Jun 7, 11:31 AM

Dear Si,

Good to see you last night. Hope your hangover's not as
bad as mine!

Listen, I think it's best to keep our e-mail correspondence
to a minimum for now, while we're working out the
logistics of everything. Might be safer to arrange a time to
meet? Let me know how you're fixed next week.

Stay strong, Si, I believe we can find you a way out of this.

A x

I snapped the laptop shut, closed my eyes for a second or two
and then opened it again, rereading the messages in case I'd missed
something the first time. Fucking hell. I didn't know what I'd been
expecting, but it hadn't been this. I supposed that was the problem with snooping: there was a chance you'd find something that
was even worse than the thing you'd imagined. At worst, I'd expected a couple of flirty messages. But they'd actually been meeting up. They'd got drunk together. And what hurt more than
anything was that they'd conspired to dupe me by pretending he
was going to the gym. We'd only been living together for six
months, surely that was too soon for him to be looking elsewhere.
Why wouldn't he just end things? Leave me and move on. He
didn't share everything with me, I already knew that, but this was
a whole other level of secrecy. I could still picture the moment it
had dawned on me, what a shock it had been when I'd realized

that our relationship wasn't quite as straightforward as I'd thought it was going to be. It had been the weekend I'd met his family for the first time. We'd been together six months by then and were spending pretty much every day together, about to move into the flat. Catherine had whisked me up to her room to talk weddings.

"So . . . ," Catherine had said ominously. "Tell me everything."

She was even more well-spoken than Si, and more direct. I seemed to remember they'd been at different schools: he'd gone to a nearby boys' school, but they'd "had" to educate Catherine privately, apparently.

"Um . . . what about?" I asked, as if I didn't know.

She elbowed me in the ribs. "How's it going with Si? It must be serious if he's asked you to move in with him so soon. He's not usually one for doing anything without months of meticulous planning."

I smiled. "I had noticed that."

"You're very different from his ex," she said, looking at me thoughtfully. "In a good way, obviously," she added quickly.

I tried not to let myself feel threatened by the idea of an ex-girlfriend who was nothing like me. The truth was, he'd barely mentioned her, or any of the other relationships he'd had. On the odd occasion I'd tried to start a conversation about it, Si had fobbed me off with some charming sentiment about not caring about the past now that he'd met me. And in some ways that suited me perfectly: he wasn't interested in hearing about my past relationships, either, and since they were pretty much a disaster across the board, I wasn't exactly eager to volunteer the information.

"Has he told you much about what happened?" asked Catherine, opening a plastic folder entitled *Wedding Ideas* and flicking through it until she got to what looked like the invitations section.

I shook my head. "He hasn't really talked about her."

Catherine looked surprised. "Not at all?"

"Not really." And then curiosity got the better of me. "Why, what was she like?"

Catherine looked at me earnestly. "What she did to him was horrendous. For Si especially, but it hit all of us hard, the entire family."

This was more interesting than I'd thought. What was this terrible, very dramatic thing that had happened to Si that he hadn't told me about?

"They were together for three years," said Catherine in a hushed tone. "And he did everything for her, Hannah. Absolutely everything. He drove her around, he picked her up from here, there and everywhere. Took her on romantic city breaks every five minutes. He helped her buy a flat, he found her a new job. He basically organized her entire life for her."

"Right," I said, thinking that the dynamic sounded very familiar. It sometimes felt as though Si was the parent in our relationship and I was the wanton child who needed pulling into line.

"They were basically the golden couple of Berkhamsted," said Catherine, on a roll now. "We'd known her for years. Her dad played golf with my dad. It was almost inevitable they'd end up together."

"Sounds like it," I said, starting to feel uncomfortable. I could just picture the perfection of it.

"So you can imagine the devastation all round when it turned out she'd been shagging Si's best friend, Will. For months. And nobody had had a clue, least of all Si, of course."

"Blimey," I said, shocked. I hadn't expected that.

"He was in bits," said Catherine. "We were all really worried about him."

I was confused, though. Why on earth hadn't he told me? He'd given me the impression that he'd breezed through life without a hitch and I would have much preferred to have known that things hadn't run altogether smoothly for him, either.

Catherine put her hand on my arm.

"Anyway, that's all in the past now, Hannah. I can see how much he adores you, it's practically radiating out of him," she said.

I smiled politely at her, my mind ticking over. I wondered, suddenly, how wise it was to move in with someone I clearly knew very little about.

"I'm serious, Hannah," said Catherine, taking my hand. "I honestly can't thank you enough for making my brother happy again. You're just what he needs. You're a tonic. A new lease on life. No wonder he's grabbing it with both hands."

I smiled at her, attempting to radiate calm, but really feeling the beginnings of panic. My chest felt tight and sweat prickled at my hairline. I pushed up the sleeves of my jumper, wishing I'd worn something lighter. It was just that this was all a bit much to take in. I'd only known Catherine about half an hour and already I'd had more of an insight into Si's history than I'd had from him since we'd met.

"I think we're going to get along brilliantly," she said triumphantly, although I wasn't sure what she'd based that assumption upon.

"Hope so," I said, sort of meaning it. I wasn't sure what to think right at that moment, about this or anything else.

"Now," said Catherine, spreading out the folder across both of our laps. "Have a look at these invitations, will you, and tell me whether you prefer the pink trim or the blue? My fiancé likes blue, but Mum's keen on the pink."

I immediately felt under an unbelievable amount of pressure to conjure up a list of wanky adjectives about how amazing they both were, and what a bind it must be for her, having to choose.

· · ·

I logged out of Si's account and sat with my hands underneath my thighs. I wanted desperately to give him the benefit of the doubt, but my mind wouldn't settle and my stomach was flipping about all over the place. I got up and moved across to the window, leaning into the pane. It was even busier down on the quayside now, full of kids from a local school out on their lunch hour. I watched them, milling about in their cliques, smoking and shouting to each other.

"Hey," said Léo, appearing next to me, his hip bones resting against the glass. He was slightly shorter than Si, I noticed. The top of my head was level with the tip of his shoulder.

"Hey," I replied, trying to sound normal.

The messages had been very vague. They didn't smack of an affair exactly, but it was clear there was something going on, something they didn't want me to know about. Surely if he was sleeping with her, he would have covered his tracks, would have had the sense to delete the evidence. Unless, of course, he thought me too stupid to suspect anything. He might have imagined that he'd done such a great job of persuading me that he loved me that it wouldn't cross my mind to go searching through his things.

I felt stung by the betrayal. He'd e-mailed her on the night of my birthday, then. When had he done it? Before the presents or after? Had it been when he'd disappeared off to get the cake? How could it be that one minute he was entertaining my friends, spoiling me with extravagant presents, being so attentive, so loving, the perfect partner, and the next he'd sloped off to message another woman? It didn't make any sense. I shook my head, wanting to get rid of the images of that night, of how happy I'd been. Had it all been a lie? Wasn't I enough for him after all?

"So, I must go to meet some friends," said Léo. "Would you like me to drive you back to the station?"

I nodded wildly. "Sure." I'd obviously got it wrong when I thought we'd be traveling together. What had been the point in giving me his number to hand out, then?

"What will you do at the station?" he asked, looking at his watch. "It is not even 12:00."

"I'll read for a bit," I said, giving him the impression I'd like nothing more. "Channel my inner trainspotter, note down how many different types of train I can see. I don't know."

"You certainly know how to have a good time, Hannah," said Léo mock-seriously.

I glanced round at Sylvie, who was putting things away in the kitchen. She flitted in and out of sight, stretching up to reach a cupboard and then bending down to the dishwasher.

"I suppose you have had enough of Paris for one day," he said, laying the palm of his hand on the glass.

I laughed softly. "Funnily enough, Paris has turned out to be the least of my worries."

"Ah, so you love it after all!"

"I wouldn't say love, exactly."

"Enough to come and meet some more Parisians?"

I rested my forehead on the glass to try to stop my mind from racing. It was full of lots of things, but mostly Si and his stupid fucking e-mails.

"You mean come with you now?" I said.

"It is okay. I understand. You think we are all arrogant and rude and you would rather spot trains."

"You know I was joking about the trains, right?"

"Yes, Hannah, I know you were joking."

If I could clear my head, I might be able to work out what to do. Figure out how I was going to get through this wedding knowing what I now knew.

"Let's go, then," I said, turning to look for my bag. "Before I change my mind."

Léo watched me. "There are always surprises when I am with you, Hannah."

"Oh, I'm full of them," I said, thinking that clearly, I wasn't the only one.

14

I looked wistfully at the restaurants lining the quay, each table packed with people on their lunch hour, the mouthwatering aromas of garlic and freshly baked bread and fragrant herbs wafting tantalizingly out of every doorway.

The three of us plus a motorbike straddled the pavement for a while as we set off, which was most inconvenient for everyone walking in the opposite direction, until Sylvie took a call and strutted off ahead.

"Where are we going?" I asked Léo, who was wheeling the bike along beside me with his bag slung over his shoulder again.

"A place on the Quai de Valmy. It is a bar we visit all the time," said Léo. "Like a second home for me. We will only stay a little while. I will not make us late, okay?"

"It's okay," I said. "I believe you."

He stopped to dab his face on the shoulder of his T-shirt. The sun was shining again, glittering on the surface of the canals, its reflection disturbed only by the odd boat drifting quietly by. The cobbled quayside was scattered with groups of teenagers sitting cross-legged in circles and lovers curled into each other, one's head in the other's lap as they looked out across the water.

"Do you still think about this wedding?" asked Léo.

"Yeah," I said, laughing lightly. "Because if I don't make it on time and I manage to upset my future in-laws before I've even begun, they'll never let me forget it."

Léo looked at me, frowning. "What do you mean by future in-laws?"

The thought of saying it out loud made me feel self-conscious. After all, until now I hadn't told a soul.

"I found an engagement ring in Si's bag," I said, crossing my arms and then uncrossing them again.

It had been our second day in Venice and we'd gone back to the hotel for a nap. I'd had the beginnings of a headache, a dull throb at the front of my skull, and I remembered Si had packed some paracetamol. I glanced across at him; he was sleeping, his eyelids flickering, his breath soft and rhythmic. Not wanting to disturb him, I knelt down on the floor, pulling his bag out from under the bed, unzipping it as quietly as I could, searching for the medical kit he'd told me he'd brought with him in case of emergencies. He was always very prepared, a holdover from his Boy Scout days, perhaps—according to Catherine, he'd been a very diligent one. I searched hesitantly through the contents of his bag, pulling aside the perfectly packed, neatly ironed selection of top-end high-street clothing. His was the polar opposite of my own suitcase, which was already in disarray, with dirty clothes mixing with clean, and everything requiring a second round of ironing. I felt around for a bottle of pills, my fist eventually closing over something small and square. I wiggled around in some sort of pocket, assuming it was the packet of tablets I needed. Instead I pulled out a little red velvet box.

I squinted at it, pulling it close to me so that my nose was almost touching it, then holding it as far away from me as my arm would stretch. My first thought was that it might be an early Christmas present, a necklace he'd seen me looking at in one of the markets and had sneakily gone back to buy. There'd been that time he'd said he needed the loo and I'd waited for what felt like ages in the sun, sitting on the wall outside the Peggy Guggenheim museum. But then when I flipped open the lid, my mouth literally fell open. Inside was the most beautiful engagement ring I'd ever seen—an exquisite vintage square-cut diamond in an art deco mount. God, he knew me so well already, and after just a year together. The ring could not have been more perfect. Was he seriously going to ask me to marry him? I gazed at it for ages, my eyes straining in their sockets, my heart fluttering high in my chest, until I heard the rustle of bedsheets and panicked and snapped the box shut and flung it back almost exactly where I'd found it, smoothing out the clothes on top. When I looked up, Si was hanging off the edge of the bed, staring wide-eyed at me.

"What are you doing?" he asked, his voice unusually high.

"Looking for painkillers," I said, wishing I was a better actor. "Sorry, I should have waited for you to wake up, but my head is pounding."

"Here," said Si, rolling naked off the bed and nudging me gently aside, looking sideways at me. "Let me."

• • •

Léo looked almost as shell-shocked as I'd been.

"That is huge, Hannah."

I nodded. "Tell me about it."

"What happened after you saw it in his bag?"

"I was worried he'd notice something was up," I said, "so I babbled away, banging on about food and boat trips and what I'd seen out the window earlier. And the whole time this funny, kind of uncomfortable feeling was rippling through me. Disbelief, I suppose."

"You could not believe that your boyfriend would want to marry somebody as preoccupied with dying as you are?"

I rolled my eyes at him. "Do you want to hear the rest of the story or not?"

"Yes," he said, although the look on his face said the opposite. He probably thought I was going to tell him some soppy tale about the proposal itself. In his mind, it might have taken place on a gondola. At midnight, while we were gliding under one of those romantic little bridges.

"I wouldn't want to bore you," I said.

"You are not particularly boring."

"That's the nicest thing you've said to me all day."

As we walked past a vegan café, I noticed a woman of about my age wearing a white camisole with pale gray jeans and a camel cardigan. Somehow it looked exquisite and neat and expensive, in a way it never would on me. She had a bowlful of green salad in front of her, therefore embodying not only the style esthetic I aspired to, but the clean eating habits, too.

"So tell me: How did he ask you?" said Léo.

"He didn't."

"What do you mean?"

"What I just said. He didn't propose."

I'd been flustered and nervy all night when I'd found the ring, with every conversation appearing to be a lead-up to "the big question." But he hadn't asked me over a candlelit dinner in Santa Croce, or when we'd strolled hand in hand across the Piazza San Marco afterward. I'd constantly been on edge, my heart pounding with anticipation every time he'd paused to take a picture or point out something of interest. It had been excruciating.

"Why not?" asked Léo.

I watched Sylvie, who looked like she was berating someone on the other end of the line.

"I don't know."

It was like he could see inside my head. Why *hadn't* Si done it? And, more to the point, was he still planning to? Venice would have been the perfect place. The two of us, standing on the Rialto Bridge (somehow there wouldn't be a million other tourists doing the same thing), the churning waters of the Grand Canal below. The palazzos lining the shores painted in gorgeous shades of burned peach and faded gold with forest-green shutters. The pleasant aroma of fresh fish from the market mixed with sweet, fruity gelato. It occurred to me—and this was absolutely the worst-case scenario—that perhaps the ring hadn't even been for me.

"Anyway, enough about proposals," I said, casting about for a change of topic. "What were *you* doing in Venice?"

"Not proposing to people?"

He threw his jacket over the handlebars of the bike when I gave him a dark look.

"Why did you take the train, by the way?" I asked. "Correct me if I'm wrong, but if you were in such a hurry, wouldn't flying have been a more reliable option?"

"Ah, yes."

"Yes what?"

"Do I have to tell you?"

"Absolutely."

He sighed, his hair flopping over his forehead. "I am not a big fan of flying."

"You're scared of it, you mean?" I said, ecstatic to have found something else to wind him up about. "Who's scared of dying, now?"

He swept his hair back, looking faintly embarrassed. "You do not need to sound so happy about it, Hannah."

"So you do have feelings . . . ," I said, gleefully rubbing it in.

He tutted, pretending to fiddle with a dial on the bike.

"Okay, carry on," I said. "Was your Venice trip something to do with work?"

"No."

I looked at him quizzically, using my hand to shield my eyes from the sun, thinking longingly of my sunglasses, which I'd packed in my suitcase because I'd assumed I wouldn't need them until we got to Amsterdam.

"Can you elaborate?"

"I went to visit my father," he said.

"He's Italian?"

He shook his head. "No, but my stepmother is. They just had a baby together, a boy."

So his dad had remarried. "How do you feel about having a baby brother?"

He laughed. "It makes a nice change. I also have four sisters."

"Four?" I said, smiling. It was nice to finally get some personal information out of him.

We passed the shop I'd seen earlier—Antoine et Lili—which

was made up of three separate sections painted in glorious shades of sunshine yellow, mint green and rose pink. I stopped for a second to have a peek through the window at the most gorgeous Parisian homewares inside, cushions and linens and ceramic teapots and pretty candleholders. If I'd had the time and money, I would have bought a little something to take home—a bowl or a tea towel or something—so that our kitchen would always remind me of Paris.

I jogged back across to Léo. "How did your dad cope with all these women in the house when you were growing up?"

"To put it simply: he did not," said Léo, looking out across the water.

So he hadn't had it easy, either, then. When I'd first met Si, and had told him what life had been like for me, he'd tried to empathize, but I'd known he was struggling with it, because he only had his own near-perfect upbringing to compare it to. A memory flashed into my mind, of the two of us at Mum and Tony's. I'd dragged him out into the hall to show him the "photo gallery," as Mum called it, the eclectic set of photographs she'd had blown up, framed and hung on the wall by the stairs. There were a couple of the two of them, a nice one of them all dressed up for one of the post office's Christmas parties. One of them walking hand in hand on Torbay beach at sunset. When it came to the pictures of me, I cringed. Mum had chosen a horrific sequence of unflattering shots, as though purposely displaying me in the worst possible light.

"This one's my favorite," I'd said, pointing to the school photograph taken when I was eleven, when I'd had a very attractive braces-and-monobrow combo, having not yet worked out that plucking my eyebrows was an actual thing. I recalled deciding, at the time, that I hated my thick curls and in the absence of straighteners and products (those would come later) they had felt almost impossible to manage.

Si had run his finger over it. "You look adorable," he said, trying to be nice.

We walked up a couple of steps to look at another standout shot, taken on Mum and Tony's wedding day: it was of Mum, a grim-faced, slightly chubby seventeen-year-old me, and Mum's sister, my auntie Sinead, who had come over from Ireland and who was wearing a black-and-white psychedelic-print jumpsuit that would have looked less out of place at Studio 54. Despite there being hundreds of much better pictures to choose from, Mum had thought the one of me looking away from the camera and sporting a double chin would be the best one to stick on the wall for all to see.

"You make a lovely bridesmaid," said Si, putting his arm around me.

"Shame about the turquoise satin meringue," I said, grimacing.

Si laughed and followed me up to the landing. I ran my fingertip around the gold frame of the only photo I did like. It was of me aged about six months; I was lying on the living room floor, on the swirly-brown-and-orange rug I still remembered because we had it for years afterward, my legs kicking up into the air, a colorful rattle clutched in my right hand. We stared at the photo for some time.

"My dad took that," I said.

"He's got a good eye," said Si, nudging me in the ribs. "Now I know where you get it from."

• • •

Sylvie finished her call and turned to hand Léo a cigarette; she lit it for him, cupping her hands around his. They were both so beautiful, the canals shining behind them, the blue sky, the treetops, that I moved to put my camera to my eye and then thought better of it.

"You smoke?" she said to me as an afterthought.

I shook my head, although I could have done with one after what I'd just read.

"Here we are," said Léo, coming to a stop outside a restaurant. The windows were opened up at the front so that most of the clientele were sitting outside, drinking beer in the warm July sun. When I realized the intimidating bunch of people gathered around a wooden trellis table were Léo's friends, I wanted to turn round and run in the opposite direction.

"This is Hannah," he announced, although I didn't know why he'd bothered, since we weren't planning to stay. I smiled weakly. They mostly looked up. I'd assumed it was a cliché, but they really were all dressed in black, with odd colorful details—a belt, a scarf—thrown in for good measure. A skateboard was propped against the window frame. It wasn't fair to make assumptions, but on first impressions, they seemed very caught up with themselves and how good they looked.

Léo parked the bike and pulled three chairs across from a neighboring table. He beckoned me into the seat next to him.

"How long are you planning to stay?" I asked him quietly, reluctantly lowering myself onto the chair and wishing I'd gone straight to the station. I was feeling unsettled after reading Si's e-mails and telling Léo about the ring and didn't think I had the energy to make small talk, which I found difficult at the best of times. It would likely turn into one of those occasions when I silently retreated into the background, observing the conversation rather than participating in it, until eventually people began to talk over me, forgetting I was there at all.

"It is boring for you, all this French?" he said, after a few minutes had passed and I'd had a fixed smile on my face as they'd all chattered around me.

I shook my head. "'Course not."

Actually, being here in Paris had kind of reignited my love of the language, although I'd been too shy to say much myself. Maybe I'd think about doing a beginners' French course sometime; they were bound to have them all over London. It was one of those things, like photography, that I'd always liked and had naturally been quite good at but had never known what to do with. It wasn't like there were many French-speaking photographers round our way.

I watched him turn to say something to Sylvie, his shoulders sloping forward, his feet crossed at the ankle. There was an easiness between them, despite her thunderous exterior, and I could tell they were close, that they knew each other well. With the guys across the table, the ones wearing a uniform of black on black who had barely glanced in my direction, he leaned forward, elbows on the table, hands gesticulating madly about something. With them he was more forthright, more direct. And then I noticed that when we talked, he swiveled toward me, his back turned completely to Sylvie. I caught her eye over his shoulder a few times and, feeling awkward, drew her back into the conversation.

To my left was a girl called Clarice, the girlfriend of one of the guys in black. She was only twenty-two and lived above a club in the apparently very trendy Oberkampf area. She was nocturnal, she told me, and rarely ventured out of her flat while it was still light, which probably explained why her skin was so pale it was practically luminous. She had a long, slim neck and several piercings in each ear.

"How long have you been with your boyfriend?" I asked, hoping she spoke good English and feeling as though I ought to make an effort to talk to someone. I didn't want Léo thinking I was socially inept; he'd only say something sarcastic about it later.

"Two months. Three, perhaps," said Clarice.

"Still quite new, then?" I said.

"Do you think?" To her, three months probably felt like an age.

"What's he like?" I asked.

Personally, I thought he loved the sound of his own voice a bit too much; I hadn't seen him talk to her once, not that it seemed to faze her. I admired that about her, her self-assuredness, the fact that she didn't appear to need anything from him, and I was envious that she'd cultivated an attitude like that at such a young age. I imagined Si and Catherine had been like that, too, when they were in their early twenties, full of bravado and the belief that they could do anything they wanted. I didn't know about Léo. I felt like my first impressions of him were changing. Were the snippiness and the disparaging comments hiding something else, a part of him that was more sensitive, that perhaps hadn't had it as easy as I'd thought?

"He is sweet," said Clarice, twirling a stud in her ear. "Otherwise I would leave him, *non*?"

I was in awe of this girl, who seemed to have it all together.

"And how is it with Léo?" asked Clarice. "Where did you meet each other?"

"Hannah, try some of this," said Léo, passing me a plate of cold meats and pâté and olives. *"Une assiette de charcuterie."*

I picked up a delicate, thinly sliced piece of prosciutto and dropped it into my mouth.

"Mmm," I said to him in between chews. "Good."

I passed the plate to Clarice.

"We met this morning," I said, grabbing a napkin to wipe my hands. "At Gare du Nord."

She looked confused and I laughed. "I managed to trip over his bag and twist my ankle, and then we both missed the train to Amsterdam. He blamed me and I blamed him, but we've had to agree to disagree on that one. He's been showing me around Paris, persuading me that it's not the awful place I thought it was."

"You do not like Paris?" said Clarice, visibly shocked at the idea that someone was less than enamored of it.

"I had a bad experience here before," I said. "Nothing to do with the city itself." Although perhaps it had taken me until today to realize that.

"You and Léo seem like you have known each other for longer than a day."

I glanced over at him. He was getting something out of his bag, a record, handing it across the table to Clarice's boyfriend.

I took a sip of the wine somebody had poured me. "Do we?"

Léo shouted something to one of the guys across the table and then turned to me.

"I want to show you one more place," he whispered into my ear. "Before we leave for the station."

"What is it?"

"Montmartre," he said, beaming. "You cannot come to Paris and not see Montmartre, and it is very close. You will get a tiny glimpse of how it was in Paris a hundred years ago. Parts of it are like taking a step back in time."

I smoothed out imaginary creases on Sylvie's skirt.

"This has to be the absolutely last thing you show me," I said. I'd seen pictures of Montmartre: the Moulin Rouge, the Sacré-Coeur; it would be a shame not to see it if it was as close as he said. "And then I'm going straight to the station."

He nodded, standing up. "Of course. It will be worth it, you will see."

"Give me a second, okay?" I said, making my way through the bar, hugging the wall to avoid the bar staff with their white shirts and their black aprons, who were twirling about with huge trays of drinks. I used the loo and then stood by the sink, turning on the tap and letting ice-cold water cascade through my fingers. I barely registered the door opening, or Sylvie coming in.

"There you are, Hannah," she said. "I wanted to see you before you go."

"Me too. I was going to come and thank you for everything," I said, turning to face her. "If you let me have your address, I'll have your clothes dry cleaned and posted back to you."

"There is no need. You can keep them if you like."

I shook my head. "I couldn't do that."

She shrugged. "Léo has my details, he can give them to you. You are getting the train to Amsterdam together, yes?" She leaned her hip against the sink next to mine.

"Probably."

"You know, he is usually very guarded around people. He does not let them get too close, not at first," she said, turning on a tap, splashing her face with water.

"Yep, I can see that," I said, thinking about his mood when we'd first met, how I'd passed him off as yet another arrogant Parisian. It was only now I was beginning to see a sweeter, softer side.

"With you it is different," she said. "Hardly ever do I see him this relaxed."

"That's what you call relaxed?" I joked, but I noticed my heart was beating high in my chest. Surely she wasn't suggesting what I thought she was suggesting.

"You know I have a boyfriend," I said, throwing it nonchalantly out there. I'd probably got the wrong end of the stick, anyway.

"Yes. Léo told me," she said, taking a paper towel and dabbing at her face. "It is fine, with this boyfriend?"

I shrugged. "Sure."

"Léo seems very confident, *non*? Very sure of himself."

"You can say that again," I said.

"But really he is very scared of getting hurt. And so he begins these relationships with women who are not right for him."

My eyes flickered across to the reflection of Sylvie's face in the mirror.

"They are always very beautiful," she continued, "but they are not a challenge to him. They are happy for him to be the fun Léo we all see and love, and they do not care about anything more, what might be happening underneath. And after a few months I say to him: How is it going, Léo? And it is always over."

I swallowed. "Why?"

"He believes he can go through life on his own, that it is simpler that way. But I do not think this is true. We all need someone, *non*?" she said, screwing the paper towel into a ball and dropping it into the bin.

I tucked a loose strand of hair behind my ear. "I think so, yeah."

"I do not think he would be like that with you," said Sylvie, reapplying her lipstick and then offering me some.

I took it gratefully, smearing some onto my lips with my thumb so that they had a sort of berry-colored stain.

"But of course, you have a boyfriend, so it does not matter," she said.

"No," I said, bracing myself on the sink. "I don't suppose it does."

I brushed past Sylvie to open the door. "I should get back," I said.

"Enjoy Montmartre, Hannah," she said, leaning closer to the mirror to apply mascara.

I walked out into the main bar, disoriented for a second, thrown by everything Sylvie had said. She was being dramatic, that was all. It wasn't like she was a mind reader: how would she have any idea what was going on in Léo's head? After today, we'd never see each other again, so what did it matter how well we got on? He was good company, a bit of fun, an excellent interpreter when I needed him to be.

And yet, I knew that at any point I could have gone back to the station, done what I was supposed to do. Put Si and his feelings first. Been the good girl, the good girlfriend. But had I been in denial all along? Did I like Léo more than I was letting on, even to myself? All day we'd been finding excuses to spend more time together, and part of that was about seeing Paris, of course it was. But it was seeing Paris with him that had made it so special. And it dawned on me that, for whatever reason, I didn't want our day together to end.

"Hannah!" called Léo, waving me over to the bike.

I waved back, putting aside the revelation I'd just had. I liked Léo more than I should. And if that was the case, what did that mean for me and Si?

15

I'll be glad when I don't have to get on this thing again," I said, wandering over to join him.

"You have not enjoyed the bike?" said Léo, giving me a suspicious look. "Because I think you have started to love it, just a little bit, but that you are too proud to admit it."

"See, you can read people," I said, suppressing a smile.

I put the helmet on and did up the strap. After today, I didn't think I'd ever get the chance to fly around a city on the back of a motorbike again. I wouldn't have the guts to do it somewhere else, with somebody else. And even if I did, it wouldn't be the same. There was something about the idea of Léo and me, cruising around Paris, the small window of time we had, the way his leather jacket flapped in the wind, the way he made me feel like Audrey Hepburn in *Roman Holiday*.

We set off, juddering at first, the engine revving. His bag was slung across his lap, which I wasn't too happy about, but he'd assured me it would be fine. Léo shouted something to his friends as we drove past and some of them waved in a cool, dismissive way, as though they couldn't care less if we returned or not. I turned away from them and looked out across the canal instead, at the tourists streaming up and down across the iron bridges. And then we were moving faster, more smoothly, down a street I remembered from earlier, the one with all the Indian restaurants, and then a sharp left onto the busy main road with the exotic fruits. I braced myself as we pulled out into the traffic again and squeezed my knees tighter, burying my face into Léo's back. When I next looked up, we'd stopped at some lights on a picturesque cobbled side street that climbed steeply upward. I dug my fingers into Léo's waist. He turned to look at me.

"What is it?" he asked.

"Where are we?" I shouted.

The sun was high in the sky now, its rays beating against the bare skin on my shoulders.

"Montmartre, already. *Tres jolie, non?*"

I nodded. "It's lovely!"

Although that didn't quite do justice to the quaint Parisian perfection I was seeing. When the lights changed we set off again, flying past trendy *patisseries* with windows full of tarts and *éclairs* and steep, winding staircases sandwiched between whitewashed, shuttered houses, which I would have loved to explore if we'd had the time. Cafés spilled out onto the pavement and locals chatted animatedly outside the supermarket, sheltering under the shade of its candy-striped awning. I looked longingly at a row of beautiful shops, the kind I'd like to spend hours browsing in if only I had the money: Aesop, Comptoir des Cotonniers, a gorgeous-looking concept store. Every corner seemed to house a cute wooden hut selling snow globes of the Sacré-Coeur and Eiffel Tower key rings and bottles of cold, crisp water.

Léo pulled over, pointing to a leafy square on our left.

"Look," he said. "See? It is a famous mural called *Le Mur des Je T'Aime*. The I Love You Wall."

The wall itself was obscured by a swath of heads and selfie sticks, but I strained my neck to see. I noticed the color first—a glistening, midnight blue. White calligraphy was etched across the tiles, although I couldn't make out the words from this distance.

"Could we stop for a sec?" I asked.

"Sure."

I slid off the bike and took off my helmet. A man wearing the quintessential black-and-white-striped T-shirt and beret combo was playing "Non, Je Ne Regrette Rien" on the accordion and somehow it wasn't clichéd, like I might have imagined it would be in this scenario; instead it created the perfect atmosphere as I followed Léo through a tiny, fragrant garden. We worked our way to the front of the crowd.

"What's the story behind it?" I asked, my eyes darting everywhere, wanting to remember this moment; how I'd felt standing in front of it.

"The artist went around to all of his neighbors in the suburbs of Paris, where he lived. There are people from many, many different countries and cultures living there, and he asked them to write down the words *I love you* in their own language," Léo told me.

I dabbed my face with a tissue and fanned myself fruitlessly with my hand. "How many are there?"

"Two hundred and fifty different languages and over three hundred declarations of love. There is every language you can imagine, from English and French to Navajo and Bambara, which is the national language of Mali."

"Is there anything you don't know about Paris?"

He looked up at the wall. "There is always more to learn."

I took a close-up of the wording on one of the tiles, which I thought might be in Arabic. "Anyway, I didn't think you believed in the idea of love," I said.

He took a step back, tipping his head to look at it from a different angle. "I do not believe in it for myself," he said. "I cannot speak for other people."

I peered at the details of the wall, the different fonts the artist had used, the shapes of the letters, the splashes of red.

"The red is to show how the world is turning on each other. That the wall is trying to bring everyone together again," he said.

I ran my fingertips over it.

"Sylvie seems to know you pretty well," I said.

"Why, what has she been saying?" he asked, crouching down. "You know, the tiles are made from enameled lava," he said, placing his hand on one.

I bent down to touch it, too, my fingertips centimeters from his.

"She told me you don't have long-term relationships. It seems like she's worried about you."

He whistled through his teeth. "She thinks that everybody must be the same. I have many friends. I have my music. There is nothing a relationship would bring to my life that I don't already have."

I looked at him quizzically. "Do you really think that?"

"Yes, otherwise why would I say it?"

"What about companionship? The joy of falling in love? Sex with somebody you have genuine feelings for?"

"Come on, Hannah. We all know that disappears over time, *non*? You can honestly tell me you experience these things, still? With your boyfriend? This joy you talk of, the excitement?"

"You're afraid of getting hurt, aren't you? That's what it is."

He groaned. "This is what Sylvie told you?"

"She didn't," I said, not wanting to throw her under the bus. "It's obvious, that's all."

"I am fine as I am, Hannah. If people paid more attention to their own love stories, perhaps they would be less concerned with mine."

I pressed my lips together, taking another series of shots.

"Don't your feelings ever just take over, though?" I asked him. "Don't you ever find yourself falling for someone, even though it's the last thing you want?"

"Yes," he said, looking sideways at me. "Sometimes."

I stood up and walked the length of the wall, dusting my fingers across the tiles, which were smooth like glass.

"Look," I said, "there are symbols, too. There's a heart, see?"

"And a peace sign," he said, reaching out to touch it.

I put my camera to my eye and took three or four more close-up shots.

"Have you always been looking for it, Hannah? This idyllic, romantic love, like we see in the movies, or read about in books?"

I shielded my eyes from the sun to look at him. "I think I always knew it wasn't like that."

"See, you are just as cynical as I am after all."

I laughed. "Let's just say my love life didn't get off to the best start," I said.

"Come," said Léo, picking up his bag and beckoning me out of the gate. "Let us take a little walk around Abbesses. You can tell me how it was for you when you were a teenager. Were you very cool, all in black? A goth?" he asked.

"Ha! Hardly. Have you seen the film *Clueless*? My friend Ellie and I would try to re-create that preppy American high school look using a terrible array of charity shop items."

"I am sure you both looked *très agréable*."

"We did not. Rest assured, boys weren't exactly breaking down the door to ask me out."

Léo smiled. "Hannah. You are too hard on yourself."

I told him about the moment Gus Davidson from my class had asked me out to the cinema, and about how my first thought had been: *Who put him up to this? Is it some kind of cruel joke?*

"I was fifteen. He was the brainiest boy in our year."

He'd been tipped to go to Oxford or Cambridge, I recalled, a mysterious and exotic notion for the rest of us who were struggling to get good enough grades to stay on in sixth form, never mind considering Oxbridge.

"How did he do it?" asked Léo.

"He ran up behind me when I was walking home one afternoon," I said. "I couldn't work out what the hell he was doing. I imagined he would have been holed up in the library, or off doing some sort of extracurricular activity for the very gifted."

"You were not used to the attention," said Léo.

"Maybe," I said. "I think I must have had confusion written all over my face."

Léo laughed. "You should have played it very cool."

"Were you listening when I told you what I looked like?"

The accordion was still playing softly. As we walked along the curved streets of Montmartre, I began to daydream. I saw myself in a gorgeous cream-colored building with the shutters of an apartment thrown open and a window box hanging off the ledge and on the cobbled street down below, somebody would be playing some mournful tune. Léo would be next to me and we would be laughing about something, the sweet smell of waffles and cherry blossoms wafting up into the air. I snapped myself out of it. What was I doing?

"I must know about the date with this . . . Gus?" said Léo. "Was it good?"

"I mean, I looked great. I'd slathered myself in my mum's blue and lilac eyeshadow and had put my hair up into a high ponytail, like this," I said, showing him how I could pull my hair off my face so tightly that it looked as though I'd had a face-lift. He raised his eyebrows and smirked, and I elbowed him playfully in the side.

"And what was he wearing, can you remember?"

I thought back. "A checked shirt. Under a navy V-neck jumper."

"Classique."

"When he saw me, he shook my hand."

"Too formal?"

"The film was terrifying, I remember that."

"You do not like scary movies?"

I shook my head. "Not at all. And he didn't put his arm around me or anything. I had my hands over my eyes most of the time."

"He did not kiss you?" he said, looking shocked. I didn't imagine Léo had ever held back in that department.

"Not that night."

"How long did it last, this romance?" he asked, pointing to a beautiful entrance to a Metro station I was sure I'd seen in a film. I took a photo of its romantic mint-green railings and glass-covered canopy. The classic green-and-yellow *Metropolitain* sign hung from its apex.

"Oh, about three weeks."

He looked impressed. "That long?"

"He stopped talking to me one day, completely out of the blue. I cornered him in the science lab to find out why and he dumped me, right there, wearing a white coat and safety goggles."

It was all so long ago, but I could still recall how I'd felt that day, how much it had hurt. How rejected I'd felt. Because I obviously wasn't good enough for a straight-A student like Gus. How could I be, I remembered thinking, when I wasn't even good enough to make my own father stick around? The two had felt linked in my mind, and it was always the same: I didn't seem to be able to get over things the way other people could. Each little glitch, every little mistake, was another reminder that I was a girl that nobody wanted. Even if Dad hadn't loved Mum anymore, he could have carried on seeing me. That feeling of being discarded, or abandoned, had continued throughout my entire life. And I was sick of feeling that way; I didn't want it to be like that anymore.

"Let me take a photo of you here," I said, shooing Léo back. "I want you right under the *Metropolitain* sign."

"There are only two original entrances like these in the whole of Paris," he said. "They are called 'the dragonfly,' for some reason. Perhaps they are modeled on their wings."

This time he didn't do a silly pose, he just put his hands in his pockets and hung his head and then looked up at me through his fringe, and when I looked at him through the viewfinder, I honestly thought it might be one of the loveliest images I'd ever seen.

He checked his watch. "Come. If we run up this staircase we will see a secret square, one of my favorites in the city. *Très artistique.* Very nice views."

"What time is it now?" I said, catching up, watching his bag bob up and down on his shoulder.

"It is 12:45," he said.

"Only one hour left," I said, to myself more than anything. Funny how when the day had started, all I wanted was for the hours to pass so that I could get to the wedding and be with Si again. And now, suddenly, what I wanted was for the hours to stand still. For us to be paused, right here in this moment.

"Hurry," he said. "Up here."

We walked up some steps to a cobbled, leafy square. To both sides, restaurants had their heaving tables spilling out onto the pavement, full of people enjoying a spritzer with their lunch in the midday sun. There was a quaint-looking hotel on the far side, and another building called the Bateau-Lavoir.

"What's that?" I asked, pointing to it.

"I will show you," he said, steering me across the square.

As we passed diagonally across the cobbles, a small group of family and friends and well-wishers were gathered around a couple who had presumably just got married. She was simply dressed in a cream shift and sling-back heels; he was in a white shirt, open at the neck. Everyone laughed as someone threw confetti and there was a flurry of camera flashes as they tried to capture the snow-storm of pastel paper.

"Now, that's my kind of wedding," I said, surreptitiously taking a photo of them myself. "If I ever get married, I'd like it to be something like that."

"*When* you get married, don't you mean?" he corrected, walking off.

I joined him and we stood outside the window of the Bateau-Lavoir, which up close was not much more than a black shop front with the somber air of a funeral parlor. A few seemingly unrelated paintings and sketches were displayed in the window.

"This was a very famous artists' residence in the late 1800s and early 1900s," he said.

"Am I right in thinking Picasso painted one of his famous paintings here?" I said.

He nodded. *"Les Demoiselles d'Avignon."*

I put my hand on the glass. "All that history."

"An exciting time to be an artist, *non?* To live and paint and drink with Modigliani and Matisse and Cocteau, can you imagine?"

"How do you know so much about Paris, anyway?" I asked him. "If you're like this with other subjects, you should definitely go on a game show. Or do pub quizzes, or something."

"What is a pub quiz?" he asked, screwing up his nose.

"It's like a general knowledge quiz. In a pub," I said, laughing. "The winning team gets money. If you ever come to London, you should try one."

"You will be on my team?" he asked.

"Absolutely."

It was impossible to imagine him in England, to picture what he'd be like out of context. Everything seemed so muddled together in my head: Paris itself, my worries about Si, the feelings I was developing for Léo, which I hadn't yet made sense of.

"Ah!" he said. "I almost forgot. You have to try the best crêperie in the world."

I tutted. "There are other places with great cuisine, you know."

"I challenge you to name somewhere with more delicious food than Paris."

I waved him away, reluctantly following him over to a hut carved into the wall, which in all honesty looked like one of the tatty pizza joints at the cheap end of Oxford Street. Léo was already scouring through a blackboard with a list of about twenty varieties of *crêpe* on it. Who knew you could do so many things with batter?

"Which one would you like, Hannah?" said Léo, ridiculously excited.

"Um, lemon and sugar?"

"No. *Absolument pas.* You must have something you have never tried before."

"Why?"

He looked at me. "That is what today is all about, *non?*"

"But what if I make the wrong choice and I don't like it?"

"Then what is the worst thing that could happen?"

I sighed, crouching down to look at the menu, trying to decipher what everything was so that I didn't choose something with snails in it, or something equally revolting.

"I'll take a *Denise,*" I said finally, which I thought was apple, salted caramel and vanilla ice cream. What wasn't to like about that?

"*Bon,*" he said, "good choice."

He made our order, and while we waited, we sat on a bench in the square, under the shade of a tree, resting our feet on his bag. Next to us was a working water fountain, which was getting lots of use today, with people holding their bottles underneath to fill them and kids running around its base. In front of us, peeping between buildings, was a charming view of the rooftops of Paris.

"You know, whenever I travel somewhere new, I always stamp

a picture of it in my mind's eye, something really colorful and evocative," I said. "So that I can conjure up the feeling of being there when I'm back home."

I took a photo, adjusting the brightness because the sun was right over our heads and making everything look blanched and hazy. It had started when I was a kid. One year, Mum had rented us a caravan near Bournemouth and what I always went back to was an image of me walking out onto the wooden pier, holding a warm pink candy floss in my hand, the tinkling music from the carousel and Mum—relaxed for once—with her sunglasses on, smiling down at me.

"I think this might be it," I said. "The image I'll think of when I want to remember Paris." I hoped it would replace the one from before, which leaped into my mind's eye occasionally when I least expected it to. I'd get this flashback, this fuzzy-edged image of me walking by the Seine, the point at which I'd realized that coming to Paris had all been for nothing. And now maybe I would have this moment instead.

Léo nudged me in the ribs. "So I have convinced you after all."

I slipped off my shoes, wiggling my toes around. "I suppose exploring Paris with you hasn't been *quite* as bad as I'd thought it would be."

"I knew it."

I laughed. "You're really annoying, do you know that?"

"Yes," he said, grinning at me.

I closed my eyes, breathing in the aroma of sweet batter and molten chocolate drifting across the square.

"What happened before?" he asked. "Last time you came here?" And then, when he saw my face, he added: "You do not have to tell me if you do not want to."

My throat felt tight. It wasn't so much the thought of telling him as it was the fear of the feelings that might come with it. I knew that if I kept them buried, never talked about them, I could bear it. It was how I'd always dealt with the things I didn't like. I had no idea what would happen if I actually addressed the past, said the words out loud. I'd never tried it before.

"I came here alone," I told him tentatively. "I'd just turned nineteen and I was in a bit of a state. I'd fucked up my A levels and all my mates had gone off to college or university. I was still living at home and working on the till at a clothes shop in my hometown. I had no idea what I wanted to do with my life."

"So you came traveling? To Paris?"

I shook my head. "Not exactly. It wasn't some nice trip, some gap-year adventure. I came looking for my dad."

Léo leaned forward, his hands clasped together on his thighs. "He was here, in the city?"

I looked down at my fingernails, examining them one by one. "I'd thought so. He'd sent me a birthday card, the first one I'd had in years. Except that it didn't reach me on my birthday. He'd put the wrong house number on it, and the postcode wasn't quite right. My birthday is in June, and I hadn't got it until that September."

"You and your mother had moved house?"

"Nope. It was the same house he used to live in. He couldn't even remember where his own daughter lived, so that was nice."

I became aware that Léo's knee was pressing against mine. Without thinking too much about it, I pressed back.

"I'd had some money saved. I was going to buy myself an old camera, funnily enough, and had been saving little bits here and there. I had just enough for a day return on the Eurostar."

"You had his address?"

"He'd scrawled it on the back of the envelope. He must want me to find him, I thought, otherwise why would he have bothered? It was the sign I'd been waiting for all those years, proof that he missed me as much as I missed him. I went to Paris the following week. He was living in an apartment in Belleville, I can't remember the name of the street."

A yappy dog walked past us, jangling my already jangled nerves. We heard someone calling and when we turned round, it was the man from the *crêperie*, waving our order around, one in each hand, our *crêpes* wrapped in white paper napkins. Léo ran over to get them.

"Here," he said, slouching back down next to me, passing me my *Denise*.

I bit into it, closing my eyes for a second or two. "You're right," I said. "I have to admit it. I declare this the absolute best pancake I have ever had in my life."

"I am desperate to say 'I told you so.'"

"Please don't."

"Want to try mine?" asked Léo.

"What's in it?"

"It is a *Spéciale Bretonne*," he said. "Chocolate, pear, vanilla ice cream, Grand Marnier, possibly something else I cannot remember."

He held it out to me and as I went to steady it, I put my hand over his. I held it tight, taking a bite. He was so close now that I could see my own reflection in his pupils.

"Mmm," I said, breaking eye contact, licking my lips. "It's delicious."

"So continue, about your father," he said.

"Damn. I thought I'd got away with it."

"You know I am the master at asking questions," he said.

I took another mouthful of *crêpe*, giving myself a few moments to think. To imagine myself back there.

"I got the early train. I thought I'd sleep most of the way, but I couldn't, I was too wound up. When I got to Gare du Nord I walked to Belleville, because I didn't have any money for the Metro, never mind a taxi."

"What happened, when you arrived at his apartment?"

I shook my head. This was the difficult part. The part that seemed unbelievable, looking back on it. The sort of thing that happened to characters in soap operas, but not to actual people in real life. Not the people I knew, anyway.

"A woman answered the door. She was very French, older, dressed all in black. She told me there had been a couple living there, a Portuguese man and a Frenchwoman, but that they'd moved out a few weeks before. Apparently they'd had to leave in a hurry, she didn't know why, or at least, she wasn't telling me."

"Had they left a forwarding address?"

"Nope. Nothing. She had no idea where they'd gone, or whether they were even still in Paris. She said they'd kept to themselves, that she knew nothing about them, except that they'd paid their rent on time, which was all she'd appeared to care about."

I watched a little girl swinging herself round and round a lamp-post, one of those old-fashioned ones that made me think of Paris late at night. It must be even more romantic, I thought, by moonlight, the streetlamps glowing, the shafts of light from the windows of the apartments above filtering through once everyone had closed their shutters.

"So your trip had been for nothing," he said quietly.

"I hung around the streets for a bit, sat on a bench in a little square, hoping I'd catch a glimpse of him strolling past if I looked hard enough. I wasn't even sure I'd recognize him after all that time. Eventually I gave up and walked into the center of the city. I had hours to wait for my train. I walked down to the Seine, all the way along to the islands. Saw Notre-Dame, which is the one thing I'm glad about now, of course. That's all I did all day, walk and walk and think. I realized, later, that perhaps my dad had sent the birthday card as a sort of goodbye."

"Why would he do that?"

"And that he hadn't meant to put his address on the back."

"No, Hannah."

"I never heard from him again. So he couldn't have wanted to see me that much, could he?"

I looked away, because the air suddenly felt charged with something and it scared me. Léo made me feel as though he was really with me when I told him about my life. It might have been the way his eyes were so wide and bright, or his melancholy voice, made all the more evocative by his lilting Parisian accent. The magic of Paris and being in this gorgeous square. It was funny how you could meet a perfect stranger, be thrown together and begin to share things that you hadn't told your closest friends and probably never would.

"You cannot control how people behave," said Léo softly. "Perhaps your father had his reasons for not getting in touch, and you might never know what they were. But what you must remember is that you did not do anything wrong. You know that, *oui*, Hannah?"

I shrugged, trying to dislodge the image of my dad that was now firmly imprinted in my mind's eye.

"It was a long time ago. About time I got over it, don't you think?"

He stood up, shielding his eyes from the sun. "There are some things we will never get over."

I hugged my arms around myself, closing my eyes for a second or two, letting the sun's rays turn the insides of my eyelids orange.

"For example, I cannot get over the fact that you made me miss my very important meeting in Amsterdam."

I looked up at him sharply, relieved when I saw him smiling.

He hesitated, looking sideways at me. "There is one more thing I must show you."

I shook my head. "Come on, Léo, there's no way we can fit anything else in."

"True, we do not have long. But I want to end your second—and far superior—trip to Paris on a high. Literally."

"What are you suggesting?"

"We need to go to the Sacré-Coeur. I insist. You cannot come to Paris without seeing it."

"If we miss the next Amsterdam train, you do know I'll kill you," I warned him.

"Oh yes," he said. "I know."

16

I rested my chin against his shoulder as we headed uphill, his hoodie, which was still tied around my waist, flapping about behind me.

"You see the basilica?" called Léo over his shoulder.

"I see it!" I shouted. It was right in front of us, looming between buildings, as spectacular as it looked in all the pictures.

We wound our way up the hill in front of it, the curving, cobbled street flanked by more of the pretty, old-fashioned lampposts I'd seen in the square, their yellow bulbs encased in clear glass. A fairground carousel tinkled out a sweet version of "Twinkle, Twinkle" and tourists swarmed across the gardens leading up to the church, being drawn to the summit by the promise of views. We flew past them all, skimming the start of the funicular railway that ran tourists up and down the hill all day. Montmartre's sloped roofs and chimney pots tumbled down the hill below us, and to our left—and looking tiny now—the Eiffel Tower.

When we reached the top, we parked and stood next to each

other, our heads thrown back in a sort of silent reverence for the huge, brilliant white domes of the Sacré-Coeur. I imagined how grand and mysterious it would look at the beginning of the day, before the tourists arrived; if we'd had it all to ourselves.

"I come up here sometimes to write," he said, as if reading my mind. "When it is quiet. In the winter, or first thing in the morning. I find the words come easier here than almost anywhere else."

I nodded, wishing we had time to go inside the church itself.

"Shall we sit?" he said. "Just for a moment?"

"It would be rude not to," I said, not ready to walk away from the view just yet.

We found a little spot on the main steps that led down through the gardens back into the village. He wedged his bag between his feet. I pulled the bottle of wine he'd bought at the Eiffel Tower out of my bag, brandishing it between us like a magician holding a rabbit.

"A quick glass each before we leave?"

"What you said before. About it being rude not to," he said.

I poured us each a cup and we sipped it silently, taking in what seemed like the whole of Paris spread out before us. It was mostly flat and low-rise, I noticed, much more so than London, and almost all one color, that lovely cream, topped with the ubiquitous slate-gray roofs.

"We are at the highest point in the whole of Paris," he said. "Something like one hundred thirty meters above the level of the sea."

"What's that?" I asked, pointing to a colorful building in the distance with bobbles on top, like a child's toy.

"The Centre Pompidou," he said. "It is a very cool art gallery with a sort of inside-out architecture. And from there—from the bar on the roof—you can see beautiful views of where we are now, of the hills of Montmartre, and the basilica."

A little boy ran past us up the steps, giggling wildly, his mother panting, trying to catch up. I laughed.

"Do you get on well with your mum?" I asked him. "You haven't really spoken about her. You must be sick of hearing me moan about mine, so go on: your turn."

He shifted position, sticking his legs out in front of him, ruffling his hair. "Actually, my mother died," he said. "When I was seventeen years old."

I looked down at my feet, mortified. How stupid of me not to know this already; how self-obsessed of me not to have asked until now.

"I'm so sorry," I said. "I had no idea."

"How could you have done? There is a difference between reading people and reading minds, Hannah," he said.

"I know, but—"

"I do not ever talk about it. That is not what I do. For me it is better if nobody knows and then they will not think differently of me afterward."

"How do you mean?"

"They will not feel sorry for me."

I tried to act as though I didn't feel sorry for him, when I did; desperately sorry.

"What's so bad about that?" I asked.

He shrugged. "It is not who I am. I have always been the strong one. The fun guy, the party boy. After it happened all I did was go out drinking with my friends and get into fights and not bother going home until it was already daylight, and everybody thought it was my way of dealing with it, that I was young and out there having a good time, despite my mother being dead. But I was drinking, and I remember it clearly, only so I could numb the pain."

"Did it work?"

"For a while. And then I thought: fuck, I cannot do this for the rest of my life. My mother would be mad! I had already been offered the place at music college, it was something she had been very proud of. So I packed up and came to Paris, as soon as I could."

A group of Japanese tourists came streaming up the steps toward us, following a guide waving a yellow flag. I shuffled closer to Léo to let them pass.

"Is that why Paris means such a lot to you?"

He nodded. "My mother was from here, so immediately I felt closer to her, more so than I had in my town."

"Where is that?"

"Limoges. It is a small city in southwest central France."

"Why did your mum leave Paris?"

"She met my father and he was not a big-city person. We had a beautiful house near the river, and everything that we could need, but she missed the excitement of Paris. We would sometimes take a trip here together, the six of us, my mother, my sisters and me. We came only once to the Sacré-Coeur. I remember we each had an ice cream and we sat on the steps over there and my mother told us stories about what it was like for her when she was a kid."

"Do you still miss her?"

"Every day. And every day, too, I think about that I did not say goodbye to her. And I still feel very bad about it."

"What happened?"

"I knew that she did not have long left, but I could not bear to see her like that, so ill and on all these different types of medication so that she was hardly ever awake. She had always been so full of life, and so it was very difficult for me to see her like this, lying in a bed, so small and sad."

"Of course," I said. "I can imagine."

"So I went out all the time, hanging around the town center, leaving it as long as possible before I had to go home. And then one day, I arrived at our house and my father was in the kitchen crying, and my sisters, too. I had heard them from the end of the street and I knew, before I set foot inside, that she had gone and that I had missed my chance."

I swallowed hard. "You feel bad that you weren't with her," I said.

He nodded. "It has stayed with me ever since. The truth is, in some small way, it is why I came back for you," he said.

I looked at him, confused. "At Gare du Nord?"

"I cannot bear to feel guilty or to let anybody down. I cannot stand it, and I do everything I can not to feel that way. Because it takes me right back to that time. And even though I know it is a different situation, a different set of circumstances, I feel almost as bad as I did then."

"Is this finally an apology for tripping me with your bag?" I said, touching his knee with my little finger.

He smiled weakly. "Nice try, Hannah."

A cheer broke out from the bottom of the steps where a street performer was blowing giant bubbles into the air, sending all the children whirling around in a frenzy as they tried desperately to catch one. Léo looked at his watch.

"We have to go," he said, standing up. "It is 1:15 already. I will have to park the bike at the station and telephone Hugo to tell him where it is. He will be mad, of course. Sylvie will go crazy with all her shouting."

"I bet she will," I said, not moving.

"Hannah?" he said, holding out his hand.

I took it and he pulled me up. Except that as we walked back to the bike, he didn't release me, and I didn't wriggle free. We let our hands trail between us, mine inside his, his fingers linked through mine. I could tell myself that it was because of what he had just told me, that I was offering him comfort and nothing more. But that wasn't how it felt. He had turned a terrible day, the worst day, into a series of moments that I would always remember. I'd started to see things more clearly at last, and I thought that part of that might be because of him. We passed a busker playing "La Vie en Rose" on the saxophone. The moment felt surreal, filmic: the Sacré-Coeur behind us, the warm sun on my skin, the music and now Léo not letting me go.

17

Cutting it dangerously fine, we'd arrived back at Gare du Nord at just after 1:30, with ten minutes to spare before the Amsterdam train left the station.

"I can't believe we were that close to missing it," I grumbled, striding along the platform and getting on a carriage toward the back of the train.

"Relax, Hannah. We made it, didn't we?" he said, dragging his bag up the steps behind him.

"Just," I said, although I knew I shouldn't be taking my bad mood out on him. He hadn't forced me to go to any of these places, to keep wandering from one pretty location to another. I had to be responsible for my own actions: I'd made a choice to go with him and now I was more confused than ever. I had nobody to blame but myself.

"You can sit near the window," said Léo, stretching up to stuff his bag in the overhead rack.

"Thanks," I said, squeezing past him, sitting down.

The air-conditioning hadn't kicked in yet and I fanned myself with a walking map I'd picked up in Venice; I'd wanted to keep it as a memento. Léo was rustling about, as though he couldn't sit still. He took off his jacket, went back to his bag to get out a magazine and then zipped it back up noisily, finally throwing himself down next to me. I rested my head against the window, watching men in fluorescent jackets scuttle up and down the platform.

"What time did they say the train gets in?" I asked.

I'd barely thought about Si for the past couple of hours, which was worrying, given that when I arrived in Amsterdam, there was a chance he could propose to me at any second. Reality was edging ever closer and this bubble I'd been in, here with Léo, the two of us meandering across Paris as though we were extras in a remake of *Amélie*, was about to pop.

"At 4:57. The wedding is at 5:30, right?" he said.

"Yep," I said, feeling sick at the thought of it.

A whistle blew and somebody in a blue uniform waved a placard and the train began to move, juddering to life, slipping out from underneath the glass canopy of Gare du Nord, carving its way through the outskirts of the city. I dug my thumbnail into the fleshy part of my palm. Soon, Paris would be behind us, and the last few hours would feel like nothing more than a glitch in my otherwise very ordinary life. I wondered whether I would forget about Léo, eventually. Whether I'd struggle to remember the timbre of his voice, the exact features of his face. How happy he'd made me, how frequently he'd made me laugh.

"Need to look at anything?" said Léo, offering me his phone.

I shrugged, lost in thought, holding out my palm for the phone and then nearly dropping it. We went to save it at the same time, our heads clashing together.

"Ow," I said, rubbing my forehead.

"And you tell me you are not clumsy," he said.

He rubbed his thumb across the exact spot near my temple where it hurt. "I hope you do not have a bruise there tomorrow," he said, stroking my skin for what felt like ages. When he stopped, I wanted to take his hand and press it back there again.

"Right," I said, trying to pull myself together and focus as I searched directions from Centraal station to the Lux Hotel, which apparently would take approximately nineteen minutes by car. I'd be lucky if I made the ceremony, then; there would have to be absolutely no holdups. Then I logged into my e-mail account to see whether either Mum or Ellie had responded to my messages. I was pretty sure that Mum wouldn't have done, because whenever I sent her an e-mail, I would first have to prompt her with a text saying *Check your e-mails*, which usually caused great excitement, even though the content of the message was almost always very dull.

I scrolled through my in-box, only half concentrating. There was an article about how to lose an inch of belly fat in four weeks; a 40 percent off Gap offer that was useless because I couldn't afford the remaining 60 percent. And then I noticed an e-mail from Central Saint Martins. My finger hovered over the open button and I pressed it. It was a reminder about the pre-degree course. A prompt to upload my portfolio and get my application form in by the following Wednesday, which was less than a week away now. I knew exactly why I'd left it this late: I'd been going back and forth with it, wondering whether I could commit to the time, whether I'd be good enough to be accepted, worrying about how I'd feel if I didn't get a place.

"What is that?" asked Léo, looking over my shoulder.

I showed him.

"This is your course, the one you will apply for?" he asked.

I nodded. "If I can get the application together in time, that is."

"Why would you not get it ready on time?" he asked.

I ran my thumbnail backward and forward across my bottom lip.

"I'd need to get all my film processed and digitized when I'm back in London. Think really carefully about which images to upload," I said, his hair tickling my cheek as we read the e-mail again together.

"You have taken lots of photographs, Hannah. I do not believe that it will be difficult to find the right ones to send."

"But now I'm doubting that they're good enough."

I could feel my heart starting to race. It felt as if I had this narrow window of opportunity to change things. That this was it, the moment I'd been waiting for. I'd just taken two rolls of film in Paris: there was bound to be a story there, a theme to base my portfolio around. I gave him back his phone and rummaged under my seat for my bag, pulling out the wine and the plastic cups.

"Let's finish this," I said.

He pulled down our tables and poured us a glass each. "See? I did not get you drunk before the wedding."

"I feel as though I need to be drunk now, as it happens," I said, trying to restrain myself from gulping the whole thing down in one.

I'd been dreaming of becoming a photographer for years. What if somebody now came along, rejected my application, told me my photos were terrible and shattered my dreams? What would I do then? And going to the open house hadn't helped. I mean, it had sounded amazing, and their facilities were out of this world, but I'd been massively out of my comfort zone in their high-concept building in Kings Cross, which was full of trendy, very young artists looking serious and creative in the foyer. But then, I'd been out of my comfort zone in Paris at first, and now look.

"Did you go through any of this, with your music?" I asked him. "This insecurity. This constant feeling that you'd been kidding yourself the whole time?"

"I still go through it," he said. "Tonight, in Amsterdam, I must convince them that my song is good enough, that my track is worthy of launching someone's career. And in the back of my mind I am starting to doubt myself, too, but I do not let it take over. I must continue to believe in myself and my work, because if I do not, then who else will do it for me?"

"I wish I had half your confidence," I said.

"You do have it. It is hidden somewhere, that is all, because of all these different experiences that you have had. But it will be there, you just need to find it."

"How do I do that?"

"Throw yourself off the edge," he said, making a diving motion with his hand. "Take a chance on something."

Or somebody, I thought. I propped my chin on the heel of my hand, looking out the window. I remembered how Ellie had said the same thing to me the day I'd met Si, when I'd told her what had happened at the Tube station and had been bemoaning the fact that he probably wouldn't call.

"Let me get this straight," Ellie had said. "He ran after you. He asked you to go for a drink. And then he took your number. Why on earth would he bother with all that if he wasn't interested, Han?"

She'd flung open the freezer, pulling out a shocking-pink tray of ice, each "cube" shaped like a flamingo.

"Hmm," I'd replied, "the eternal question."

"You need to believe in yourself a bit more," said Ellie, shoving several heaped teaspoons of sugar into her NutriBullet.

I shrugged.

"And when he calls, you'll say yes, right?" she said.

"Maybe, but he won't," I said, sliding onto a stool, watching Ellie frenetically chop a bunch of mint.

"But if he does?"

She flung the mint into the blender, followed by an entire trayful of ice.

I sighed. "I don't know. He's not really my type."

Ellie went to the fridge, retrieved a large bottle of white rum and poured at least a third of it into the blender. "You mean he's not monosyllabic, unemployed and completely clueless about how to navigate an actual grown-up relationship?"

I knew she was joking, but there was also the tiniest grain of truth in what she'd said. My track record with men was atrocious. It was as though I purposely sought out guys who had a huge amount of baggage and an aversion to monogamous relationships. There was something about the inevitability of it that felt familiar and safe. Like, it obviously had to end, so it made it less devastating if I knew that from the beginning. Letting myself believe that someone like Si might like me did not feel safe.

I heard my phone buzz. My heart skipped a beat. There was no way it could be him already, was there? I pulled it out of my pocket, sliding my thumb across the screen. I had a text from a number I didn't recognize.

Hey, it's Si. Really nice to meet you just now.
Wondering if you're free for drinks next Thursday?

I squinted at the screen to see whether I'd misread something, or misconstrued its meaning.

"Is it him?" asked Ellie, her eager face looming at me. "It is, isn't it?"

She started up the blender, sending vibrations rattling through my body. A few seconds later, she took the jug off the base, gave it a shake and split the icy liquid between the two ruby-red cocktail glasses I'd bought her for her twenty-fifth birthday.

"All right, calm down. Yes, it's him," I said, unsure now what to do. I'd done such a good job of convincing myself that he wouldn't get in touch that I hadn't considered what I'd do if he actually did.

"What did he say?" asked Ellie. "Come on, spill."

I read the text to her. It sounded even stranger when I said the words out loud.

"Well, I think he sounds great," she said, sliding a cocktail in my direction. "*Voilà!*"

I took a sip and gave her a thumbs-up.

She would think that, because he was much more her type. She'd always gone for the good guys, shunning excitement for stability, which was almost certainly why her relationships had been infinitely more successful than mine.

"I'm not sure what to do," I said, turning the phone over so that I wouldn't have to keep looking at the screen.

"Don't, Han," said Ellie, suddenly all serious.

"Don't what?"

"Don't do what you always do, lately. Talk yourself out of it before you've given it a chance."

I frowned. "Do I?"

Ellie leaned on the counter, looking uncomfortable. "Well, you've become a lot more wary of people, haven't you, over the last few years? Sort of given up a bit. It feels like you expect the worst all the time."

I laughed hollowly. She'd never mentioned anything before.

"What do you mean?" I asked, gulping down my cocktail, not sure if I really wanted to know.

"You used to take risks all the time, Han. Don't you remember? You'd be the one with all the chat, getting us into clubs when we were underage. Gate-crashing parties we hadn't been invited to. Buying cigarettes from the corner shop because you weren't the tallest, but you were the only one who had the balls to try. And then, I don't know . . . something happened. Just before I started uni. You changed, and I never really understood why."

"I didn't," I protested. "I'm exactly the same person I always was."

"Prove it, then. Say yes, you'd love to go out with him. What have you got to lose?"

. . .

There had been something different about Si. A sort of intoxicating stability; just the right amount of self-assuredness. I'd imagined what it would be like to have someone like that in my life, and now I knew. In the space of a year, my life had changed beyond recognition. But I wondered, suddenly, what his motives were for moving so fast. If he'd been hurt before, by his ex, then perhaps he was looking for something easier this time around. Someone who wouldn't present a challenge, who would never leave him because she needed him too much. Had he chosen me because with my low self-esteem and my inability to do anything productive with my life, I was the ultimate safe bet?

We'd stopped at a station, which I thought must be somewhere in Belgium. I watched passengers getting on and off the train, thinking about cameras and portfolios and what my fellow students might be like if I did get a place on the course and how I was going to cobble together the money for fees. And then I wondered what Si would say when I told him I was definitely going to apply. And I thought that perhaps I wouldn't let him influence me so much anymore. That it was about time I put my stamp on things; made my own decisions, did things without him, things he didn't approve of, if I felt passionately enough about it.

Ten or twelve people joined our carriage and there was a flurry of seat-finding and the ramming of luggage into already-full racks and the sliding of laptops out of bags. The train pulled off again, its wheels squealing on the track, the usual run of flat green fields coming into view. Léo had been scrolling through his phone for a while and, like a child, I wanted his full attention again. I wanted to listen to him talk. I wanted to know everything I could about him in the short space of time that we had left.

I nudged him. "What are you thinking about?"

He put his phone on his lap.

"I was thinking," he said, clasping his hands in front of his mouth, "about many things. But one of them was about whether we will remember this day. In five years' time, or in ten. Do you think we will, Hannah?"

I tucked a loose curl behind my ear. "I think so," I said, turning to look out the window.

The train plunged into a tunnel. I took a mouthful of wine. I could see my reflection very clearly because of the darkness. My eyes were bright and alert, even though I'd had very little sleep. I could see Léo's arm resting on his thigh. And then he leaned forward, and I could see that he was looking at me. He reached out to brush my hair off my shoulder with his hand, trailing his fingers across the back of my neck. When we emerged on the other side, and the carriage became bright again, he dropped his hand away, settling back in his seat.

"Want something from the buffet car?" he asked.

I nodded overenthusiastically. "Sure. Anything."

I watched him making his way along the aisle, his jeans hanging loosely on his hips, his Calvin Klein boxers on show. I was relieved when he disappeared through to the next carriage and I didn't have to look at him anymore. I might be able to think more clearly now he was out of sight. But then my mind drifted back to him, another vivid daydream, an extension of my Paris apartment one. This time, we'd moved away from the window. We could still hear the accordion playing, feel the soft breeze. He pressed me up against a wall, his hands on my waist, his face close to mine, his lips parted, and I knew he was going to kiss me and that I wanted him to more than anything.

"*Ça va?*" he said, appearing beside me, putting an end to my daydream.

"That was quick," I said, taking a sip of wine and then spluttering it all over my lap when it went down the wrong way.

It was as though I suddenly had no control over what was going on in my head. Si was the one I cared about, the man I loved and wanted to spend the rest of my life with, wasn't he? Had my head really been turned by Léo and all his French charm, just because I felt listened to, because I thought he already understood me more than anyone ever really had, after less than a day together?

He passed me a paper cup of tea.

"You have it black, right?" he said, offering me a little sealed pot of milk.

"Actually, I don't," I said with a wry smile. "I was just too scared to ask Sylvie for some."

He tutted. "She is very softhearted underneath. She is not as tough as she makes out."

I nodded. "Your friends are important to you, aren't they?"

He thought about it for a second or two. "You know, in a way they saved me. When I first came to Paris, my head was all over the place. I could not play my instruments, I could not apply myself to anything. My father was falling apart, already dating other women only a month after my mother had died."

"That must have been tough."

He shrugged. "But then I met Hugo and some of the others and we had the same interests, the same outlook on life. Similar hopes for the future. And I know what you might think of them, that they are very cool, a little too Parisian, not very welcoming, perhaps. And that is true. But these friends became my family, at a time when that was what I needed in my life."

I nodded, concentrating on my now-empty wine cup, putting my finger inside the rim and twirling it around and around. I could feel his eyes on me. We thought we had a connection, but we couldn't have, how could we? Of course it had been lovely, the two of us wandering around Paris in the sun, with hours to kill and nothing to do but talk and walk. I felt excited about life again, had been reminded of how much fun it could be, and some of that was because of him and the risk-taking part of myself he'd tapped into. But in reality, Léo was exactly the sort of person I went out of my way to avoid. He was too good-looking and overconfident (on the outside, at least) and—most worrying of all—afraid of commitment. I'd never let myself fall in love with a man like that; it was the polar opposite of what was good for me. Until yesterday, I'd been reassured by Si's stability and straightforwardness, by the fact he didn't care about the past, and had concrete plans for our future. But now I wasn't so sure.

I pulled off the top of the milk, spraying it everywhere, all over the table, on the knees of Léo's jeans. He laughed, wiping it off with his hand. I sipped at my tea and borrowed his phone again to check whether Catherine had posted any pictures of the wedding preparations on Instagram. Since I was going to this wedding whether I liked it or not, I had to find some way to feel invested in it again.

"You are on Instagram?" said Léo, craning his neck to see.

"Mmm," I said.

"You like it? All these showy photographs that people share?"

"God, no," I said.

I felt him looking at me.

"I know, I know, then why do I bother?" I sighed and promptly carried on scrolling.

Three or four posts in there was a shot of Catherine. She was admiring herself in a full-length mirror, all wistful and serene in her white cotton robe, her hair up in curlers, and her three bridesmaids—her cousin Nancy, Jasper's sister Sophie, and an ethereal-looking Alison—were gathered around her, one of them crouched next to her, another with her hand on Catherine's shoulder. It was such a picture of female solidarity, of friendship, that I almost forgot myself and smiled. I zoomed in on Alison, looking for clues. I managed to deduce absolutely nothing, except that she looked lovely. That was the thing about weddings: everybody was at their very best, as though you were observing them through a rose-tinted filter. And Catherine had chosen the most gorgeous bridesmaids' dresses. She'd described them to me in great detail on numerous occasions, but they looked even better than I'd imagined. I liked the way the magenta fabric pulled Alison in at the waist and then billowed out in romantic drapes down to her ankles.

I refreshed the page, and Catherine's most recent post came up.

"Who is that?" asked Léo, his face so close to mine that I could feel the warmth of his breath on the nape of my neck.

"Si's sister, Catherine."

"This is the wedding you go to?"

I nodded.

Catherine had captioned the shot with the title: *The calm before the storm.*

I had butterflies in my stomach for some reason, as though I knew it was going to reveal something to prove that I'd been right to have all these suspicions about Si and his secret messages. I clicked on the photo anyway, enlarging it, sliding my fingers across the screen, zooming in. It was a wide shot of the hotel room: the tiara laid out on the bed, the white satin heels by the door. The bridesmaids.

"You know these girls?" he asked.

"Sort of."

In the bottom corner was Catherine with her back to the camera, a teaser of the yet-to-be-revealed gown. Jasper's sister was arranging the veil with the sort of soft, dutiful look in her eyes that only the most selfless of bridesmaids could achieve. Nancy was flopped on the sofa holding a glass of champagne aloft and looking altogether less interested. And by the door, leaning against the wall, were Alison and Si. She was looking directly at the camera, her hands clasping her bouquet. But Si was not looking at the camera, he was looking at her. His arms were crossed in front of him and he was all grim-faced, as if they'd had a row. Or he was upset about something. I couldn't tell. They had some sort of history, I could see it in his eyes. She'd needed to speak to him at the wedding for a reason, and by the looks of it, he hadn't liked what she'd had to say.

Léo stopped fiddling around with the plastic lid of his tea. "What is it?"

"Nothing," I said, shaking my head.

"Hannah?"

"Yes."

"Why has the photo upset you?"

I put the phone in his hand.

"It hasn't."

And it was true: I wasn't upset. I was angry and I wanted answers, but I wasn't upset. I didn't feel gutted about it. I wasn't panicking about losing him. And what that meant about him and me, about the future we'd planned together, I couldn't even begin to think about now.

"Is that your boyfriend?" he asked, looking at the photo.

"Yeah," I said, laughing lightly.

"And who is he with, this blond-haired girl?"

"Alison."

It was hard to imagine that Si would throw away everything we had to start something with her. And then, for the first time, I thought: Would I consider it? Would I ever be the one to leave him?

"Alison," said Léo, as though he was mulling the name over. "And you do not like that they talk?"

I nibbled on my thumbnail. "I wouldn't usually care. Except that he got a text from her. Last night on the train, before I moved seats."

He put his phone in his pocket. "What did it say?"

"Something about needing to talk to him."

"Well, they are at a wedding, *non*? There are things to organize."

"That's what I'd thought, too, initially. But then when we were at Sylvie's, I hacked his e-mail account and read his messages," I said, visibly cringing.

He raised his eyebrows at me, surprised. "Hannah! I did not imagine you to be the jealous type."

"I'm not usually. And I know I shouldn't have read his stupid messages; he'll go mad when he finds out."

"So why did you do it?"

I put my head back, looking up at the ceiling, as though I was going to find the answers up there. "You'd be amazed what the prospect of marrying someone can do to you. Everything becomes much more urgent. There's things you need answers to. I found myself thinking: Can I really spend the rest of my life with this person I'm not sure I trust?"

He glanced across at me. "You know I am never going to trust *you* with my phone again, right?"

I rolled my eyes. "Don't worry, my French wouldn't be good enough to decipher your messages, anyway."

He tidied up his table, putting the plastic wine cup inside the paper cup containing the remnants of tea. "Are you really going to marry this guy, Hannah?" he asked.

It was bizarre how my feelings about our relationship had changed in such a short space of time. Yesterday Si and I were wandering hand in hand across the Rialto Bridge and today I was crossing my fingers that he wouldn't propose to me before I'd had a chance to work out if I still wanted him to.

"I don't know," I said, looking down at my hands. It felt too dangerous to look at him, somehow, as though if we made eye contact, that would be the end of it. There would be no going back.

"Hannah?" he said.

I bit my lip. "Yes?"

"Before we get to Amsterdam, and you rush off to your wedding, there is something I wanted to say."

He lifted my chin with the crook of his finger. My breath caught in my throat. I looked at the floor, the walls of the train, anywhere but at him.

"What is it?" I said, my voice barely audible.

"I cannot say this to the side of your head."

I looked at him, suppressing a smile.

"Better," he said, reaching out to smooth his thumb across my cheek.

I swallowed so hard I was sure he must have heard me.

"I wanted to say that some of the things I have told you today, I have never spoken to anyone about. Not a single person."

I nodded, the smallest of movements. "I know. Me too."

There was hardly any space between us. I could move my head the tiniest bit and we would be kissing, just like we had in my daydream.

"And that I have been thinking, for a little while now, that . . . that we might—"

His phone rang, filling the space.

He pulled back, sighing. "Good timing, *non?*"

I dabbed my forehead with the cuff of his hoodie, relieved, in a way, because I thought I knew what he was going to say and I wouldn't have known how to reply. What I wanted to do and what I *should* do were two completely different things.

He fumbled around for his phone, blocking his other ear with his finger.

"*Oui?*"

There was a moment or two of confusion on his face before he raised his eyebrows at me.

"One moment, please," he said.

He held the phone out for me to take. "It is for you, Hannah. Your friend Ellie."

18

I staggered down the aisle, Léo's phone in one hand, my other gripping hold of whichever seat back I could grab.

"One second, Ells, I'm just finding somewhere quieter," I said, making it to the area by the doors. I took a deep breath.

"Hey, Ells," I said as loudly as I could without actually shouting, trying to regulate the sound of my voice. "Everything okay?"

"Never mind me, what on earth is happening?" she said, sounding overexcited, the way she always did when there was some sort of drama she could get behind.

"You read my e-mail, then."

"'Course I read your bloody e-mail. What's going on, Han?"

I slid down the wall so that I was crouching, my elbows resting on my thighs, my knees pressed tightly together.

"I'm on my way to Amsterdam now. Nearly there, in fact. Should just about make it in time for the wedding."

"Jesus," said Ellie. "How's Si taking it? I bet he's livid that one of his meticulously planned schedules has gone to pot."

"You could say that."

"Who's this guy, then? The one with the phone?"

I made a concerted effort to sound casual. "Just someone I spoke to briefly on the train. He was supposed to be going to Amsterdam earlier, too."

The sun came out from behind a cloud and light flooded the corridor, changing the way everything looked; the way it felt. The door to the next carriage slid open and a man wearing a gray suit came lurching through.

"And what, you've been hanging out with him all day?" said Ellie.

"Kind of."

"Is he hot?"

I chewed my thumbnail. "He's nice, yeah."

Strips of light moved around, bending this way and that as the train rocked us from one side to the other. Somebody else stumbled past on their way back from the buffet car and I stood up, flattening my back against the wall.

"Good for you, Han. Sounds a lot more fun than running around after nutty brides. Does Si know?"

"Si does not know."

Not a single part of me wanted to tell her what was really going on. I couldn't even make sense of it myself yet, so there was no way I could put it into words. One day I would; when we got back to London, I supposed. She was quick to give advice and always told me, in no uncertain terms, exactly what she thought. Sometimes I listened, nodded, agreed with her and then did the complete opposite, but there was always some value to what she had to say. I just wasn't ready to hear it yet.

"I'm so glad you're okay, Han, I actually screamed out loud when I read your e-mail."

I laughed. Trust her to be over-the-top about it.

"But, um, before I go, I just wanted to . . . I felt I ought to tell you about something strange that happened earlier today," she said, her tone turning serious.

I frowned. "Go on."

She cleared her throat. "I've gone back and forth about whether to say anything, whether to wait until you got home. But when I saw your e-mail, I don't know . . . I just got this feeling that it might all be connected somehow."

"What might be connected?"

It felt as though my heart was beating in my temples. When Ellie didn't answer, I knew it must be something bad, because there wasn't much that rendered her speechless.

"Ellie! What is it? Just tell me."

"Okay, okay." Another nervous cough. "Do you remember that John's thinking of moving jobs and Si had told him the head of marketing was leaving at his place, and that there might be a position coming up? And then, at dinner, Si told us the job wasn't available anymore?"

I didn't like the babbling sound of her voice. Surely there couldn't be anything else?

"Yep, I remember," I said, covering my mouth with my fingers.

"Well, John bit the bullet and called the HR department, anyway. Said he was a friend of Si's and that he knew they weren't recruiting for the head of marketing position but was there anything else on the horizon that he might be able to apply for? And when he mentioned Si's name, the guy said—now, I don't want to jump to conclusions here, Han—that Si no longer works for the company."

I swallowed hard.

"That's ridiculous," I said. "The HR guy was probably new."

"I know," she said, her voice sheepish. "That's what I thought. But John said . . . he said he spelled out Si's name, his surname, everything. Gave him the department name, even the floor number. But the guy was adamant. Said he'd left several weeks ago."

I paced up and down the corridor, a few steps this way, a few steps the other. The suited guy came back and I moved to the side to let him pass. Léo's phone was clamped to my ear, the screen slicked with sweat. I couldn't think of a thing to say. I didn't know where to begin, how to articulate to Ellie that this was just the latest in a long line of things that didn't make any sense.

"Are you still there, Han?"

"Just about," I said.

"What do you make of it?" asked Ellie gently.

I covered my eyes with my free hand. This was too much, after everything.

"I'm sorry if I did the wrong thing," said Ellie, just as a train came shooting past in the opposite direction and the windows shuddered, the roar of its engine drowning out every other sound. We rocketed into a tunnel and it was suddenly very dark and very noisy. The line instantly went dead and I was relieved, because it meant I didn't have to find an excuse to end the call.

I walked back through the carriages, concentrating on putting one foot in front of the other. It felt as though the world was spinning, as though I couldn't center myself. What had Si been doing, then, these past few weeks, if he hadn't been at work? And if something had happened, if he'd left his job, why hadn't he told me?

"Hannah?" said Léo, touching my elbow as I drifted straight past our seats.

"Oh," I said, turning round. "I was miles away."

He got up to let me sit down. I fished his phone out of my pocket and gave it back to him.

"Is everything all right with your friend?" he asked.

"Yes," I said, taking a sip of tea, not caring that it was stone cold. "Fine."

"Has something happened, Hannah?" he asked.

"No."

"But you are drinking cold tea."

I shook my head. "We'll be arriving soon. I can't think about it now."

He watched me carefully. "What did your friend say?"

I covered my mouth and nose, my hands in the prayer position. "Her boyfriend called Si's work, something about a job. They said Si left weeks ago, that he doesn't work there anymore."

Léo frowned. "So he has changed jobs and not told you?"

"Maybe." Maybe. I hadn't thought of that. I'd jumped to the conclusion that he was without a job altogether, but perhaps he had just taken another one. But then I was pretty sure he wouldn't have hidden that from me.

"You will see him soon, *non*? You can ask him then."

I folded my arms around myself, feeling as though all the good feelings I'd built up over the course of the day had been sucked out of me and I was left with nothing but a cold, hard, hopeless shell. I pressed my temple against the window. We were in a built-up area now, the endless fields replaced by houses and roads and traffic. I was finally in the same city as Si and I'd never felt farther apart from him.

"We should get our things together," said Léo quietly, standing up, pulling down his stuff.

I grabbed my bag, throwing everything haphazardly into it, stuffing the empty wine bottle into the nearest bin in case it fell out at the hotel and everyone thought I'd drunk it all myself. The aisle was already full of passengers dragging luggage down from the racks, flooding toward the doors, eager to be the first to get off. I felt like staying where I was, welding myself to my seat, refusing to leave the train. What if I just didn't go? I supposed that would mean I was running away from my problems and I was determined not to do that anymore. I had to be strong. Face the truth and deal with whatever life threw at me.

"Are we coming in on time?" I asked Léo.

"Two minutes early. It is five minutes to five."

I put my palm on my chest, feeling it rise and fall. Everything felt wrong again. Léo would be gone soon, and in less than half an hour I would see Si again. And then, one way or another, I'd know.

"Are you ready?" said Léo.

I nodded. When the doors opened, we were among the first to step onto the platform. We hurried along, sandwiched between our train and a yellow double-decker on the opposite platform. Above us was a curved glass roof letting in a soft, mustardy light.

"I don't have any money for the taxi," I realized with a panic.

Why hadn't I thought of it sooner? I'd have to find a cashpoint now and hope I could remember the PIN for my card. I whirled around, looking for one.

"Take this," said Léo, fishing around in his pockets, pulling out a note.

"No," I said, shaking my head. "You've done enough already."

"Just take it." He thrust a twenty-euro note into my hand.

"There is no time to argue with me." He hauled his bag onto his shoulder. "Come. Let us go, quickly."

We sprinted down an escalator and into the bowels of the station.

"Taxis that way," I said, pointing to a sign.

We ran, my twisted ankle forgotten, past brightly lit sandwich shops and someone playing a piano and a place selling clog-shaped doormats and bunches of wooden tulips. Once outside we joined the end of the queue, and when I stood on tiptoes I saw at least four or five taxis snaking into the station. It shouldn't be long.

I took a deep breath, glad of the fresh air.

"So," said Léo. "This is it."

My eyes flickered over his shoulder, keeping an eye on the taxis coming in, feeling sick at the idea of saying goodbye, of never seeing him again.

"You didn't get to finish whatever it was you wanted to say."

"No," he said, pushing his fringe back off his face. "And now the moment has passed, *non?*"

We took a step forward, the queue moving faster than I'd expected. My mind was full of contrasts. It would have been easier if I'd never met Léo; it was unthinkable that I might not have done.

"What are you going to do about your boyfriend?" he asked.

I ran my fingers up and down the length of my camera strap. "I haven't decided."

A family of four got into a car, leaving only one studenty-looking guy in front of us.

"Do you want to share?" I asked. "God, I don't even know where you're going, where your gig is."

He shook his head. "It is fine. I must go in a different direction."

I put my hand on my forehead. "I don't want to leave you," I told him, not quite believing that I'd said it out loud. But then again, if not now, when?

"You know, you turned out to be quite good company after all, Hannah."

"I'll take that as a compliment," I said.

He brushed a hair out of my eye. "I had a good time," he whispered.

I nodded. "Me too." In a few seconds he would be gone, out of my life forever.

We reached the front of the queue and a cab pulled up to the curb. It was cooler in Amsterdam than it had been in Paris. The wind rippled through Sylvie's T-shirt, the fabric flapping around my waist, his hoodie still tied there.

"Oh," I said, pulling at the knot, "you should take this."

"*Non*," he said, putting his hand on top of mine. "Keep it. Then you will not forget me."

I lifted my camera and took a quick photo of him, his dark eyes burning into me through the lens.

"Now I never will," I said.

He took my head between his hands, smoothing his thumbs across my temples. "I will miss you, Hannah," he said.

I wanted to run my hands through his hair, to know what it felt like, but if I started something, if I touched him at all, I might not be able to stop.

The taxi driver beeped his horn.

"I have to go," I said, pulling away, opening the car door. "The Lux Hotel, please," I shouted over the noise of the engine.

Léo slammed the door behind me.

"I hope everything works out for you, Hannah," he said, bend-

ing down to look through the window, his face right there, centimeters from mine.

I smiled at him as the taxi screeched away from the curb, following the U-shaped driveway out of the station.

"Good luck tonight!" I shouted out the window.

He waved and I waved back and within seconds we'd pulled
out onto the main road. Just like that, I couldn't see him anymore.
I sat back in my seat, finding my belt, doing it up, swallowing hard
to try to dislodge the lump in my throat.

19

We were driving so quickly through Amsterdam that it was impossible to take everything in. It felt like a riot of color and sound after the relative silence of the train, with trams squealing past on their tracks everywhere you looked, and huge squares teeming with tourists. If I looked down the side streets, I caught the odd glimpse of the bridges I'd seen so many pictures of, and the heaving bike racks housing hundreds of bikes that looked as though they could tumble over like dominoes with one wrong move. It wasn't as pretty as Paris, I thought. I already missed its grandness, the sweeping boulevards. Léo.

According to the clock on the driver's dashboard, it was 5:17 p.m. when we pulled into the driveway of the hotel, coming to a stop in a cobbled courtyard. Even from the outside it looked just as chic and upmarket as Catherine had described. *It's where all the Dutch celebrities stay*, she'd told us. *All the models.* I'd pretended to be impressed, but since I didn't actually know any famous Dutch people, I would be none the wiser, anyway.

A porter in a sleek black suit rushed over, flinging open the taxi door.

"Madam?" he said, looking for my bags.

"No luggage," I explained, handing the driver the money Léo had given me. It seemed wrong that I had no way of paying him back.

I followed the porter into the lobby, which was completely encased in glass and exposed brickwork, with huge wooden candelabras hanging from the ceiling. And there were actual trees. Inside. It was like entering a different world, which explained why it had cost a small fortune to stay here. I was suddenly hyperaware of feeling like an impostor, which happened whenever I mixed with people with money. I didn't imagine their usual clientele arrived with a tatty straw bag and mud-stained ballet pumps.

Si must have spoken to them because the front desk seemed to be expecting me. Room 305, the receptionist told me. He already had my passport, he said, and all my details. I asked him to point me in the direction of the stairs, keeping my head down in the hope that I wouldn't bump into anyone I knew. There were wedding guests milling about everywhere. I could spot them out of the corner of my eye, lounging on the leather sofas, all dressed up in heels and fascinators, champagne clasped in their hands. I loosened my hair from its bun, pulling it across my face in a pathetic attempt at disguise.

"Hannah!"

I pretended to be oblivious to the fact that somebody had called my name, but then there was a tap on my shoulder that I couldn't ignore. I turned round, plastering the requisite smile on my face.

"You made it, then."

It was Si's dad. I didn't know him as well as the other members of the family. He was rarely at home when I was over there for dinner, or was late to the table, citing an extended round at the golf club or work drinks with some visiting vice president from the Boston office. Mind you, if I'd lived with Catherine and Pauline at the height of wedding fever, I'd have made excuses to be out most of the time, too.

"Hi, Roger," I said, dredging up as much enthusiasm as I could manage. "Good to see you."

He'd been drinking. I could tell by the way he was rocking back and forth on his heels. His lips were stained red with wine and he kept licking them with a fat pink tongue.

"Hear you've had a bit of bother with the trains," said Roger, leaning against the metal staircase for support. It zigzagged upward, with glass sides as you went farther up. Apparently there was a floating meeting room somewhere, Catherine had told us.

"You could say that," I said. "How's the bride doing?"

"Oh, she's all right. Ordering everyone about as usual."

He pulled a hankie from the pocket of his (admittedly beautiful) charcoal-gray suit, which Catherine had harangued him into buying from Paul Smith so that it would match the suit she'd also harangued Jasper into buying from Paul Smith. The poor guy hadn't even been allowed to choose an outfit for his own wedding, which if I were him, would have set alarm bells ringing.

"Roger, I really have to go and get changed. See you back down here in a minute, okay?"

"Yes, fine, fine," he said, dabbing sweat off his face. "You go, make yourself beautiful, I know what you ladies are like."

When I reached the third floor, huffing and puffing and wishing I'd got the lift, I strode down the corridor to our room and let myself in. Inside, it smelled like Si, which made me feel lots of

different things: sad, scared, angry, nostalgic for how uncompli-
cated things had been before. For now, he was still my boyfriend.
As far as he knew, nothing had changed, that was the strange thing.
He was still the man I lived with, whose face I woke up to every
morning, who stroked my head while I fell asleep next to him at
night. He was the boyfriend who had treated me to a trip to Venice, because he knew I'd always wanted to go and because he could
be romantic when he wanted to be. I wondered now about his job,
whether that was why he'd put his foot down about the water taxi
to the station, because he'd run out of money. Was that why he'd
seemed so stressed lately, why he'd been so tired all the time? And
I wouldn't have had a clue about our finances, because he managed our joint account. He'd set up the direct debits, he paid the
bills. Because he was on the ball with all that stuff and I wasn't
particularly, which was crap of me, because now look. It was pathetic that it had taken me until now to realize that I had to start
taking control of my own life, my own money, my career and lots
of other things. I'd simply paid half my salary into the joint account each month and had trusted him to take care of it.

My suitcase was on the floor next to the huge king-sized bed,
which was made up with pristine white cotton sheets with a cozy-
looking gray blanket draped across the bottom of it. If I could have,
I would have got in it and pulled the covers over my head and
stayed there. I knelt down on the wooden floor and unzipped the
suitcase, rooting through my stuff, relieved to have it all back,
picking out bits I needed: my wedding shoes, my clutch bag. And
then, glancing over my shoulder, I opened up Si's bag, which he'd
placed on the floor at the end of the bed. I dug gingerly around
inside, not really knowing what I was looking for. A note? A second phone, because wasn't that what people carried around with

them when they were having an affair? All I had to go on was my imagination and what I'd seen on *Doctor Foster*, which hardly prepared me for the reality of working out whether my boyfriend was cheating on me or not.

I put everything back and stood up, looking around for more clues as to what might be going on. His things were strewn across the bed—his iPad, a pair of socks, a can of deodorant. My wedding outfit, a light blue sleeveless prom dress with delicate sprigs of white flowers embroidered onto it, had been ironed and was hanging on the back of the door. Si was thoughtful like that. Good at the detail, which was probably why I felt like I needed him so much. He remembered to do stuff that hadn't even occurred to me. But today I'd started to think that that wasn't what relationships were all about. It shouldn't be about them filling a hole, replacing something that was missing from your life. It was about connection. Trust. Attraction. God, even having fun, which Si and I hadn't been having much of lately.

I thought briefly of Léo, wondered where he was, whether I was already firmly relegated to the back of his mind. Part of me assumed he'd consider our day together a sweet, funny little interlude that meant nothing in the scheme of things and that had no effect on his already very interesting life. I also held on to the tiniest bit of hope that what we'd had had been genuine. That he'd meant it when he said he'd miss me. Not that I'd ever know now.

I washed and dressed in a matter of minutes, dabbing on some of my makeup, brushing my hair, dousing myself in perfume. I slipped on my heels and left the room. Out in the corridor I passed a porter and asked him the time: it was 5:28. I'd made it, then, against the odds. I half ran down the staircase, clattering on the metal steps, very aware of everything I did, the sharp pain that occasionally spiked in my ankle, the way my breath was coming in quick, light bursts, how my shoes were already pinching at the toe. A concierge directed me to the terrace.

When I ran down the steps into the atrium, Catherine and her bridesmaids were standing at the bottom. Roger was there, too, wild-eyed, busy propping up the wall with his hand. There was a sort of loaded silence, the way there always seemed to be before a wedding ceremony. The bridesmaids were fussing about. One of them was straightening Catherine's veil and another was on the floor rearranging the hem of her dress. Alison was holding the bride's bouquet as well as her own. Catherine looked stunning, just as I'd known she would. Her body was encased in swaths of cream lace, cinched in at the waist to show off her amazing figure, her makeup dewy and discreet. As I moved closer, my eyes flickered across to Alison and the diamond-drop earrings she was wearing that sparkled in the light. Was she the kind of woman Si would fall for? Would he like her enough to give up on everything we'd built together?

"Hello, Catherine," I said, in the soft voice I always used when conversing with brides. For some reason, I found it impossible to talk normally to someone on their wedding day, no matter how well I knew them. What were you supposed to chat about, when really nothing else mattered except the huge, life-changing journey they were about to embark on?

"You look stunning. What a gorgeous dress," I said, settling for clichés, although I meant them, too. She had the same features as Si, with nothing too big or too small, and perfectly aligned white teeth and the same light green eyes. Her hair was a darker blond than his and usually swished between her shoulder blades with just the right amount of volume courtesy of regular and very expensive blow-dries. Today, though, it was pulled back off her face in a complicated, twisty bun.

"I'm glad you're here, Hannah," she said, smiling at me.

"Sorry I'm late," I said, wincing.

"You made it, that's the main thing," she said, taking my hands and squeezing them. And then she whispered in my ear, "I'm so nervous."

Her fingers felt quivery and cold.

"We're all here, rooting for you," I told her. "And you look amazing. Really beautiful. Just try and enjoy it, okay?"

And then, with a quick glance at Alison, who smiled at me in a friendly way, as though she hadn't been secretly messaging my boyfriend, I ran out onto the terrace. Eva Cassidy's version of "Over the Rainbow" started up the second I stepped through the door and I scooted into the first empty chair I saw, at the end of the back row. Seconds later everyone stood up and I followed suit, tucking my hair behind my ears, wishing I'd had time to put it up in the more sophisticated style I'd intended. I strained my neck, looking for Si, who would be up at the front. I wondered if he'd seen me come in. I wanted him to know that I was here, that I'd made it after all, like I'd promised. That, at least, felt important.

He eventually turned round and caught my eye. I half waved and he smiled and then he looked away again, focusing on watching his sister glide down the aisle. I noticed that she had a tight hold on Roger's arm, possibly so that he didn't fall over, and perhaps so that she didn't, either. Jasper was waiting for her underneath a wooden pergola covered in yellow roses, resplendent and watery-eyed. What with the music and the dress and the beautiful setting, I almost forgot that anything was wrong. The woman in front of me was dabbing her eyes with a tissue, which made me feel tearful again, myself. I couldn't pinpoint what it was, whether it was the emotion of the day, the rousing violin on the track or the fact that it could have been me, next. If he'd proposed to me in Venice, if I hadn't moved seats, if I'd never met Léo, then it could have been me and Si walking down the aisle in a year's time and I'd never have known any different.

The music faded out and everyone except Catherine, Jasper and the registrar sat down. My stomach flipped as we waited for the ceremony to begin.

20

Catherine was officially married. The ceremony had been short and very sweet with lots of tears and much laughter. Jasper's sister had read a Shakespearean sonnet and Si had recited an extract from *Captain Corelli's Mandolin*, which he'd been practicing obsessively, of course, and had duly delivered to perfection, like one of his work presentations. Catherine had arranged for candles housed in lanterns to cover every available surface, and Pauline's suggestion that ivy and gypsophila be twisted around the tree trunks lining the perimeter of the terrace had made the area all dreamy and romantic. Léo's face popped into my head and I pushed it out again as quickly as it had arrived. I couldn't think about him now.

Once Catherine and Jasper had walked back down the aisle to rapturous applause (and a more upbeat piece of music), the guests began to stream out after them, peeling off from the front, row by row. First came Si, Roger and Pauline, who was in the Max Mara royal-blue dress and jacket she'd been banging on about for weeks, her short, flicky hair coiffed to within an inch of its life, a fascinator placed precariously on top. Si winked at me as he went past before turning to shake the hand of a man I didn't know on the other side of the aisle. Behind him were Jasper's parents, who were very blond and very elegant, and then the bridesmaids.

The reception was taking place in the hotel's swanky restaurant, which, handily enough, was about two feet away. By the time I stepped inside, the photographs were already in full swing, with Catherine and Jasper standing underneath one of the indoor trees, kissing for the camera.

I spotted Si immediately and made my way over, grabbing a glass of champagne on the way. How things had changed in the space of a day. Yesterday I was happily wandering around Italy imagining my future with the man I loved, and now I wasn't so sure that I really knew him at all. The more I thought about it, the more I realized he'd taken on the "caring father" role with me and that I'd let him. He did the same thing with Catherine. He liked being relied upon, the go-to person for problem-solving and disaster-averting. It was what made him tick, what made him feel powerful, I supposed, and honestly, I thought it might have been what had drawn me to him in the first place. I'd loved having someone to care about me, who wanted to look after me in a way my dad never had. But what would be better, I was starting to realize, would be to find out who I was, and what I wanted, first.

Si had his back to me and didn't see me coming, so I touched his arm, sliding up next to him.

"Hello," I said.

He was talking to a man who I seemed to remember was an

uncle on his mum's side. I'd met him once at Pauline and Roger's house.

"Hello, gorgeous. You made it, then," said Si, kissing me lightly on the lips.

His uncle gave me a hug and I made him laugh with my account of the disastrous journey and after a while he went off to find another drink, leaving the two of us alone. I looked around. It was perfect, just as Catherine had wanted. The restaurant was decorated with flowers and candles, and the tables were all set up with the marshmallow favors and the place cards that somebody else had written out.

"Ceremony went well, didn't it?" said Si.

"It was lovely," I said, shifting my weight from one foot to the other, my feet already aching.

"I'm glad you're here, Han," he said.

He looked smart in his suit. Catherine had tried to strong-arm him into wearing Paul Smith, too, but once he'd seen the price tag, he'd swiftly declined. He'd chosen the navy French Connection one he wore to work instead, with a white shirt and a red tie.

"How was Paris?" he asked.

I looked down at my glass, swirling the liquid around. "Fine."

He grabbed a flute of champagne from a passing waiter and necked half of it in seconds.

"You're drinking?" I said, surprised.

He nodded. "Just this once. As it's a special occasion."

I sipped slowly at mine; I didn't think getting drunk was the best idea, given the circumstances. The room was full of chatter and the low rumble of laughter and the photographer shouting instructions and the celebratory clinking of glasses all around us.

"You were better off out of it," he said. "I never want to see another napkin ring as long as I live."

I looked sympathetic. "That bad?"

He nodded. "Afraid so."

"She seems to have chilled out now it's all over," I said.

I could see them over Si's shoulder, Jasper's hands on her waist, the photographer snapping away, leaping about, trying to get the right angle, clambering on top of an ornamental rock garden.

Alison walked past us with a glass of champagne in each hand, holding them precariously above her head as she made her way through the crowds.

"The bridesmaids look stunning," I said, thinking this might be an opportunity to weave her organically into the conversation. We didn't have to have it out right now, that would be inappropriate, but if I could just test the waters. Get a feel for what had been going on. He might even volunteer the information.

He grabbed another two glasses of champagne and handed me one. He was drinking much too quickly. At this rate he'd be out of it before the meal started.

"It must have been a help having them around," I said. "Alison is maid of honor, isn't she? Hope she managed to keep Catherine calm."

"Not sure," he said, sounding vague.

"How well do you know her?" I asked, watching her stop to whisper something in Catherine's ear.

He shrugged. "Not very. She's an old school friend of Cath's."

He was lying to me again. My heart began to thump. "You must have had a lot to catch up on, then," I said.

He looked at me strangely. "I've barely seen any of them this morning, Han. I was busy doing all your jobs, remember?"

He was on the defensive. He did that when he felt under pressure, I'd seen it before.

There was a whoop as the photographer took a group shot of Catherine and the bridesmaids. They all threw their bouquets in the air and caught them, except Alison, who dropped hers.

"Relax, Hannah," he said, trying to laugh it off. "I know what you're like when you haven't had much sleep."

I finished my drink, placing my empty glass on a nearby table and starting on my next. He was hiding something from me—I could see it in his eyes, in the sweat slicked across his upper lip. And then, because he could have been nicer about it all, and because I was too exhausted to pretend anymore, my resolve to wait and hash it out later, in private, seemed to dissolve in the blink of an eye.

"I read your texts," I said, very quietly, so that nobody but him could hear.

I saw him swallow, watched his left eye twitch.

"What texts?"

"The ones from Alison," I said. "What was she trying to get hold of you for?"

He rubbed at his eyebrow nervously. "It was nothing, Han. Something about the wedding, that was all. She was getting fed up with Cath and needed some advice."

"That's all it was?"

He put his hands on my shoulders, pressing down too hard, looking into my eyes in what he probably thought was an earnest and sincere manner but really felt like the opposite of that. "You're being silly. Jumping to conclusions."

"You're hurting me," I said quietly.

He let go, dragging his hands through his hair.

"It's my sister's wedding, for God's sake," he hissed. "I'm not having this ridiculous conversation with you here."

And then there was the tinny chiming of metal on glass, signaling it was time for the speeches. Si took a step back so that there was half a meter between us, but really it felt like much more.

21

I headed back to the terrace for the speeches. The last thing I wanted to do was make a scene, and it was becoming increasingly difficult not to tell him everything I knew and to demand an explanation. If I kept my distance, talked to other people, spent some time up in the room if I needed to, there was a chance I could do the right thing and keep it together until we got the opportunity to be alone.

I edged through the throng of guests, stopping to say hello to one of Si's cousins, his aunt Patricia, the group of Catherine's mates from work I'd met on the hen weekend. I managed to hold perfectly normal conversations with them, made polite small talk about the dress, about the weather, about how long we were all staying in Amsterdam. And then I edged toward the microphone that had been set up in front of the pergola, where the speakers would be framed by the beautifully fragrant roses that Catherine had chosen from Amsterdam's most exclusive florist. I found a spot behind Pauline, who was whispering urgently into Roger's ear before ripping a drink out of his hand and then beaming around at us all as though nobody had noticed that (a) he was wasted and (b) she was fuming about it. Léo flashed into my mind. I imagined his smirk, the funny remarks he might make, and since he clearly wasn't a fan of weddings, I was pretty sure he'd have plenty to say on the subject. From my new position I could see Alison sitting at a table with the other bridesmaids. I watched her run her fingertips absentmindedly around the rim of a glass of Buck's fizz. How did she fit into this puzzle that was now surrounding Si and the relationship I'd thought we had?

"Hannah!"

Catherine was beckoning me over, pulling me close to her, linking her arm through mine.

"Congratulations," I whispered to her, kissing her lightly on the cheek. "It was a beautiful ceremony."

"My dad's drunk," she said out of the corner of her mouth. "What should I do?"

I suppressed a smile. "He is a bit. It'll be fine, though. He'll say a few words, we'll all do a toast and job done."

I stood on tiptoes, keeping Alison in my eyeline.

"What if he says something awful?" asked Catherine, widening her eyes. "Something to embarrass me?"

"He won't," I reassured her, although I wasn't so sure. Roger was a liability when he'd been drinking, from what Si had told me.

I looked over my shoulder for Si, but he was nowhere to be seen. The best man's speech had begun and was being delivered by some dry, charmless friend of Jasper's from university. When it came to an end we all clapped politely. I imagined Léo making some funny and perfectly observed comment about it. A passing waiter topped up my glass. I wanted to take the edge off, but I also had to keep my focus. Roger took to the stage, knocking a chair over in the process. He'd managed to get his hands on another drink and was swinging it precariously around, holding the glass by its stem.

"Hello? Hello? Testing, testing?" he said, a squeal ringing out because his mouth was too close to the mike.

"Oh God," said Catherine under her breath.

She turned to say something to Jasper and I scanned the room for Si. He was usually easy to spot, but because we were in Holland, there were more blond guys than usual. Where was he?

Roger started his speech, reading from a crumpled piece of paper that looked as though it had been retrieved from the bin. His words were slurred but, when you could make them out, very lovely. He told us about the moment he and Pauline had brought their beautiful daughter home from the hospital and how she'd been the most precious thing they'd ever seen. And about how Catherine's face had lit up when she'd first told them about Jasper, how she'd insisted immediately that she'd met "the One."

"See? He's doing fine," I whispered to Catherine.

"I suppose," she said, sighing and shaking her head. "Because I don't need anything else going wrong."

"Oh yeah, I heard about the makeup artist not turning up on time. Just what you didn't need," I said.

Catherine frowned, as though she didn't know what I was talking about.

"Was she not late?" I asked. Surely Si hadn't been telling more lies.

"Not as far as I know," she said. "But loads of other stuff went tits up. I had to get the deputy manager from the hotel to write out the place cards and she did a terrible job." She reached over and swiped one from the table behind us. "Look. She rushed them and her handwriting looks crap. It's all spiky."

I glanced down. "Yeah," I said, feeling bad. "It's not great, is it?"

"I'm not blaming you, I know you had a tough time getting here, but I've been running around all morning making sure that everyone had done what I asked them to do. It wasn't the best."

The words *hotel*, *wedding* and *planner* were on the tip of my tongue.

"Sorry," I said.

"I know you are," she said, giving her dad a thumbs-up and making a circular motion with her finger, indicating that she would like him to wind it up now, please. "And then to top it off, I had to deal with a bridesmaid who didn't fit into her dress," said Catherine, keeping her voice low while simultaneously fake-smiling at her dad. "She only just squeezed into it; it took two of us to yank the zip up."

"But you had so many fittings! Had she put on weight or something?"

Pauline threw me a look over her shoulder.

"You could say that. She's pregnant," said Catherine, rolling her eyes at me.

I suddenly felt burning hot and I picked up a drinks menu, fanning myself with it. Roger was still blathering on, his voice sounding muffled, as though he was underwater. I heard the clashing of glasses as everyone raised a toast to the bride and groom.

"Which bridesmaid?" I asked, my voice high and light. I thought: *Please don't let it be her.*

Catherine didn't hear me at first, because of course she'd been caught up with the toast and had turned away from me to kiss

Jasper. There was a minute or so of unbearable uncertainty. Perhaps it was one of the others. Even if it was Alison, it could be anybody's baby, it didn't mean it had anything to do with Si.

"Cath," I hissed. "Which one is pregnant?"

She looked around, scanning the terrace, then said conspiratorially in my ear: "Alison. You know, my friend from school."

My brain went all fuzzy, like when there was interference on the TV. It was too much of a coincidence, surely: Si's moods, his refusal to come clean about being in touch with her, his inability to reassure me that I had nothing to worry about. The fact she'd been so keen to talk to him, seemingly as a matter of urgency.

"Are you okay?" asked Catherine, looking concerned.

I nodded, smiling tightly. "Back in a sec," I said, touching her elbow, stumbling away.

I rushed to the nearest bathroom and locked myself in a cubicle, taking huge breaths, gulping in as much air as I could, willing myself not to throw up. I leaned my forehead against the door of the cubicle, trying to cool my skin, desperately trying to hold it together. Once my stomach had settled, I went out to the sinks and dabbed my forehead with a tissue, trying not to ruin my makeup, although I supposed that was the least of my worries. My pale, clammy, crumpled face was reflected back at me in the mirror. I thought back to that moment on the train with Léo, when I'd seen the two of us so clearly in the window as we went through a tunnel. I'd looked relaxed and happy then. At peace. Nothing like the way I felt now. It was no good, I was going to have to find Si and confront him, and there was no way it could wait.

I headed straight for Alison, for the table she'd been sitting at, but she wasn't there anymore. I changed direction, whirling around, looking for Si. I thought about the engagement ring hidden somewhere in his bag. If he'd been sleeping with her, and she was pregnant, it was perfectly possible that it wasn't meant for me at all. How naive of me to presume it was; I should have put two and two together when we left Venice and he still hadn't done it. Who took a ring to Venice and didn't propose?

I went back out into the atrium, smiling at people as I passed them, trying to act like my normal, sane self. Somebody called my name but I pretended not to hear; I didn't think I'd be able to string a sentence together, anyway. Distracted by the music starting up, I knocked clumsily into a waitress carrying a tray of canapés, all the while looking for a flash of magenta chiffon and Si's navy suit. I couldn't see them anywhere, but I had a feeling they were together.

I knew I should wait until I'd calmed down, that I ought to consider Catherine's feelings, my own dignity, but I suspected I wouldn't be able to contain myself once I'd found them. I marched around the perimeter of the atrium, opening doors, peering behind them. It wasn't until I started out toward the bedrooms that I saw them: Alison and Si, standing together at the bottom of the stairs, having some sort of heated conversation. I flattened myself against the wall, tipping my head so that my right ear was angled toward them. I could hear snatches of what they were saying, words that I couldn't fit together. I heard her mention my name. I heard Si say that he couldn't do something. He was trying to keep her calm, I thought, but in that passive-aggressive, hissy tone he often adopted with me. I thought of Léo, about what he would do if it were him, and I took some kind of strength from that. From the way in which he was honest with everyone, how he said exactly what was on his mind no matter what the consequences, because it made sense to me now. Honesty suddenly seemed like the only thing I wanted.

And then Roger weaved toward me and blew my cover.

"Hannah! What are you doing lurking about up here?" he shouted. I peeled myself away from the wall, brushing down my skirt, straightening my hair.

"Nothing much," I said brightly.

He carried on past and I glanced casually toward the staircase, where the two of them were now standing guiltily to attention.

"Hi," said Si, pulling it together first. "You remember Alison, don't you? From the hen weekend?"

"Sure," I said. Two could play at that game. "How's it going, Alison?"

She nodded like a maniac. "Fine, fine. You?"

I kept my tone even. "Beautiful ceremony, wasn't it?"

"Um, yeah, lovely," she said, dragging her fingers through her hair, which considering the amount of hair spray that had been applied, was a feat in itself.

I crossed my arms, cold suddenly, my body temperature going from one extreme to the other. I was vaguely aware of hotel guests coming past with suitcases, the concierge bustling about, waiters scuttling past with room-service trolleys.

"Did you two manage to catch up, then?" I asked.

Now Si was hair-dragging. A dead giveaway, I would remember not to do that next time I felt the need to lie.

"I noticed you texted Si earlier, Alison, while we were on the train. Sounded like you needed to speak to him about something quite important. I hope everything was all right?" I said, taking a step toward them, trying to read their body language, looking for a flicker of something that might give them away.

Si stepped in to rescue her, of course. "Oh, that. I already told you, Hannah, it was about Cath, wasn't it, Al? She was making everyone's life a misery and you thought I might be able to help."

"Well, not exactly," she said, glaring at Si.

Because I had nothing to lose, I thought I might as well come clean about everything. Compared to what they'd done, snooping around in someone's e-mail account was hardly the crime of the century. Actually, it was pretty bad, but there wasn't much I could do about it now. I'd seen what I'd seen, and I wasn't going to be able to challenge them about it if I didn't admit to it.

"The thing is, when I was in Paris—you probably know already, Alison, but I was stuck in Paris all day with no money and no phone—I had this niggling feeling. About your texts."

Si laughed nervously. "Come on, Han, why don't we go and mingle?" he said, trying to steer me out of the stairwell. "There's loads of people you haven't spoken to yet. They've all been asking after you."

I shrugged Si off. "And so the thing is, Si," I said, turning to face him, "I checked your e-mails. While I was in Paris."

I let my words hang in the air for a second or two. I knew Si and Alison must be desperate to look at each other, I could almost feel their eyes bulging in their sockets.

"What?" said Si, seemingly incredulous. "What's got into you, Hannah? Since when do you go snooping about in my stuff?"

In a different moment, I might have felt bad. But now I was only glad that I'd done it. Because there was an engagement ring in his bag, and there was the small matter of my future happiness at stake.

"That's beside the point," I said, looking at Alison. "I'm just wondering why my boyfriend was lying about going to the gym so that he could come and see you?"

Si was now not just pale but a sickly shade of gray. "All right, Hannah, I think that's enough. Why don't we get back to the wedding, see if Cath's all right? After all, it's her day, isn't it? Wouldn't want to spoil it for her, would we?" he said through gritted teeth. "Come on, let's go. Let's all go back to the terrace."

A couple in their mid-thirties brushed past me, heading for the staircase. "Sorry, guys, can we just squeeze past?" the woman said in a plummy accent. And then, "Oh my God, Simon, is that you? It's me, Joanna. Cath's roommate from Durham?"

Si, who had begun sprouting sweat from every pore, had turned into a stuttering wreck. "Hi! Um, blimey. Long time no see, Joanna. How are you?"

"We're good, we're good," said Joanna, who was wearing a knee-length coral shift dress with a matching fascinator. "This is my husband, Daniel. And you must be . . . ," she said, extending her hand to me.

"Hannah," I said. I couldn't quite bring myself to explain that I was Si's girlfriend, because until someone told me what was going on, it didn't feel as though I was.

"Lovely to meet you, Hannah," said Joanna, shaking my hand warmly. "You're Simon's partner, aren't you? I've heard lots about you from Cath. All good," she clarified, laughing.

Alison introduced herself and if the circumstances had been different, I would have been in awe of her self-assurance. She was cool as a cucumber, and seemingly not fazed by the fact I'd just all but accused her of having an affair with my boyfriend.

Joanna and Daniel, perhaps sensing an atmosphere, shifted

awkwardly from one foot to the other, then sidled past, heading up the stairs. "Just popping up to our room," called Joanna over her shoulder. "Catch up later, yeah, Simon? And lovely to meet you both," she said, giving me a strange look.

I turned back to Alison. I thought I might as well finish what I'd started.

"Catherine tells me you're pregnant," I said, gauging her reaction.

She had the good grace to look embarrassed but also slightly smug, which I thought was very insensitive.

"Thanks. Yeah. A bit of a shock, but you know . . ."

"I didn't even know you had a boyfriend. You didn't mention him on the hen weekend," I said.

"No, no. It was a casual thing," she said, looking awkward.

I turned to Si, bracing myself. "I was wondering whether it was yours?" I asked.

"What?"

"You heard me, Si."

"No!" he said. "For fuck's sake, Hannah, of course not."

"You'll have to tell her, Si," said Alison, putting her hands on her hips. "I told you something like this would happen."

"Here we go. Tell me what?"

"Look, let's go up to our room, talk about it there," he said. He put his hand out to touch me. "Come upstairs. Please. I'll explain everything."

"Fine. But don't bother feeding me any more lies," I told him. "Oh, and I know about your job," I said, unable to stop myself now. "That you left. What have you been doing for the last few weeks, Si? Where have you been going every day, all dressed up in your shirt and tie?"

And then I pushed past him and stumbled up the stairs. My heart was beating everywhere: in my chest, in my temples, in my mouth. And as though things couldn't get any worse, when I looked up, I saw Joanna and Daniel standing on the floor above, watching me, Joanna's hand flung dramatically across her mouth.

22

He caught up with me when I was nearly on the third-floor landing. I'd had to slow my pace because I was out of breath; he'd been sprinting up behind me, taking two steps at a time.

"Hannah! Wait," he was saying.

I ignored him and carried on climbing but then he was there, next to me, trying to take my arm. I wriggled out of his grasp.

"I'm sorry," he said, his breath ragged. "I'm so, so sorry about all of this."

"You still haven't told me what you've got to be sorry about," I said.

"Stop a second," he said.

I turned to face him, catching my breath, holding my arms out in front of me to create a sort of barrier between us. He didn't look like Si anymore. Everything about him was different: his posture, the way there were lines of tension etched across his brow, the sweat rings under his arms, the flat, watery eyes. Or perhaps it was more that this was the first time I'd seen him for what he really was, imperfections and all. I'd been happy to take him at face value, was so flattered that somebody like him would want somebody like me that I hadn't thought to scratch beneath the surface.

"I love you, Han. I've made a terrible, terrible mistake and I'm truly sorry. I am. But I'll make it up to you, I promise I will."

Over his shoulder I could see faces peering up at us from the foyer—a cross-looking Alison had been joined by Pauline, whose mouth had dropped open like a sinkhole.

"Please, Han. Hear me out."

I turned my head to the side, not wanting his hot, acidic breath on my face. And yet, at the same time, I had a compulsion to know all the gory details, every one of them. Perhaps if I did, I could have some sort of closure. I'd had some experience of this, after all: I'd found it was best to know where you stood with someone, even if it hurt, so that there was no ambiguity, no back-and-forth. Like with Dad; now that I'd started to accept him for what he was and was not capable of, I was able to bear the fact that he wasn't in my life anymore and was never likely to be again.

"Let's go to our room," said Si. His voice had a tremor flecked through it. "We can talk there."

Our room. Insinuating that we were still a partnership, that we still loved each other, like I'd thought we always would. I started up the stairs again, each step an effort, my head loaded with the things I wanted to say. There were questions buzzing around in there, lots of them, but not fully formed ones. I fumbled in my clutch bag for the key card and as I swiped it in the door, I was aware of Si behind me, felt him breathing heavily on the back of my neck, inhaled the familiar scent of him, the sharp citrus shower gel he used. Was this really the end of our relationship? Could it be that simple, this fast?

I flung myself into the room and he followed me inside, closing the door quietly behind him. I went over to the window, resting my forehead against the glass. There was a view of a canal, just like the one I'd imagined when I'd pictured the idyllic morning we were supposed to have together the following day. So much for rose petals and proposals and waffles.

"I've been fired from work," Si said, coming to stand next to me, his hip inches from mine.

I turned to him, incredulous. "When?"

"Six weeks ago now."

"What for?"

He went to sit on the edge of the bed, throwing his head into his hands. I leaned against the window, too exhausted to stand.

"I hit Dave," he said.

My stomach turned. "What?"

"He's a bully, Hannah, he never let up. Every opportunity he had to belittle my work, he jumped on it. It killed me, after everything I'd put into that fucking company."

"When was this?" I said.

"There was that party, wasn't there, back in May? At that restaurant in town?"

"May? Si, that's ages ago."

"I'd had a terrible day at work. A really fucking stressful day. When I got to the party, I started drinking heavily. And I couldn't stop, even though a few people told me they thought I'd had enough."

I shook my head. "I can't believe this."

"I lost it, Han. Something just snapped. I started laying into him, telling him exactly what I thought of him, what an arsehole he was, how nobody respected him. I had to be dragged off of him, apparently, not that I can remember much about it."

I put my hands over my mouth in the prayer position. "God, Si."

"Apparently I broke his nose, or so he said."

I sank down onto the windowsill, trying to take it all in.

He sighed. "They fired me on the spot. Said it was gross misconduct, that violence in the workplace was unacceptable. They said they couldn't keep me on."

"Why didn't you tell me?" I said, shocked.

This was worse than an affair, because it was so out of character. I'd never even seen Si get properly angry; I certainly couldn't imagine him hitting anyone.

His eyes filled with tears. "I was embarrassed, Han. And devastated about it all, because now you'd know that I wasn't the nice guy you thought I was. I was so used to providing for everyone, being the strong one that everyone leans on, looking after people, that I couldn't stand the idea of people—you, mainly—feeling disgusted by me. And once I'd kept it a secret for a few days, I didn't know how to get out of it. I spiraled into a sort of panic. A depression almost, if I'm honest."

I rubbed the tops of my arms with my hands. I was shaking now that the adrenaline had worn off. What I felt was a sort of resignation, a dull, thudding pain. What kind of relationship did we have if he didn't trust me enough to share these huge life events, to show me the good and the bad parts of himself? If he thought me too fragile to bear it?

"Where were you, then, when I thought you were at work?" I asked him.

"In the library mostly. Sat trawling through the papers for jobs. I went to join some agencies, that sort of thing. I even thought about getting a bar job at one point. During the day so you'd never find out."

"They haven't been paying you, then?"

He hung his head. "No."

"The joint account," I said, remembering how the card had been refused. "There's no money in there, is there, because you haven't been putting anything into it?"

"I've been trying to keep it topped up," he said. "But, yeah. I don't know what we're going to do now, to be honest."

There was some noise outside the window. Laughter; a cork popping.

"And the Venice trip?" I said, realizing now that he must have spent a fortune on it. A fortune he clearly didn't have. "Couldn't you have canceled it?"

"I tried," he said. "I called the travel agent, but I'd got a special deal and it was all paid for in advance. They were sympathetic and all that. I lied and told them I'd been made redundant. But still . . . they wouldn't give me my money back. Since it was all paid for, I thought we might as well go."

I nodded, prying myself to my feet, walking into the bathroom, pouring myself a glass of warm, soft water from the cold tap and sipping it slowly, looking at myself in the mirror. Then I went back into the bedroom and began to gather up my things, dropping them haphazardly into my suitcase. All I knew was that I needed to get away. It would take time for it to sink in, all of this, the lies, the sham our relationship had become. I couldn't be around him, not tonight. Not any night. And not just because of what he'd told me, but also because of what I'd discovered about myself.

That I was not the person he thought I was, either. That I wanted more from life than I'd admitted to. And that clearly we weren't as "right" for each other as I'd thought.

"What about Alison?" I said. "What's she got to do with all of this?"

"The baby's not mine, Han. I don't know why you would think it could be."

"You haven't slept with her?"

"No. Of course not."

"What is it, then? Because I know there's something."

He coughed. "She was . . . in a bar one afternoon. I needed a beer, so I stopped at this pub in town, and she happened to be in there with a couple of mates, ones I didn't know. And we got talking about Catherine, the wedding, a bit about school. I hadn't seen her for years, since we were all teens."

"But you'd always had a thing for her?" I said, scooping up my camera, putting it carefully around my neck.

He shook his head. "No, there's nothing like that."

"What, then?"

He flung himself back on the bed, staring glassy-eyed at the ceiling. "We got talking. She's a corporate lawyer, isn't she, so she's got loads of contacts. She said she'd do what she could to help if it goes to court."

"Are the police involved, then? Is he pressing charges?"

"'Course he is."

I shook my head. "Bloody hell, Si."

How could he keep something that important from me? Something that affected us both.

"I asked Alison to keep it between the two of us, told her I didn't want to worry you, but she's been going mad at me. Said she didn't think it was right."

"Well, at least someone's talking sense," I said, picking up my still-damp ballet pumps from the end of the bed and shoving them into my suitcase.

There was a knock on the door.

"For fuck's sake," said Si, sitting up. "Go away!"

We waited in silence for whoever was at the door to give up and go back downstairs.

"What are you going to do?" I asked him quietly.

"I don't know," he said. "I'm waiting to hear about a court date."

I sighed, collecting the remainder of my things: the toothbrush I'd put in the glass by the sink, Sylvie's clothes, which were in a crumpled heap on the floor. The hair straighteners I hadn't had time to use. I stuffed them all inside my suitcase, zipping it up. Then I stood it upright, the handle poised in my hand.

"What are you doing?" asked Si, standing up, his eyes bulging.

"Leaving."

"Don't be ridiculous," he said, laughing hollowly. "Where would you go?"

"Back to London. I'll stay at Ellie's for a bit, until we can sort out the flat."

"What do you mean, sort out the flat?"

"I guess we'll have to give notice or something. God knows. I can't think about that now."

I felt a pang of regret about our lovely little home. We'd spent so long choosing colors together, splashing out on a Farrow & Ball cobalt blue for the hall, a matte slate gray for the kitchen. I thought about the bits of furniture we'd bought, the plant pots and rugs and picture frames we'd treated ourselves to. What would I take with me, I wondered: What was his and what was mine?

"No, Han. No. Look, don't do anything rash. Please. Nothing has to change."

"It does, Si."

"I still love you. And I know I've fucked up and I know how much I've hurt you. But you're still the person I love most in the world and I'll do anything to make things right. It's why I stopped drinking, so that nothing like this can ever happen again. I promise you, you can trust me, Han. You have to believe me."

I had one last look around the room to check I'd picked up everything that was mine. I didn't know what to make of his declarations of love and his heartfelt apologies. Were they genuine, or was it just that he couldn't stand the idea of me leaving him?

"Please, Hannah," he said, scrabbling in his bag. "There's something I've been meaning to ask you. I was going to do it in Venice but I bottled it because there was this huge thing I was keeping from you and it didn't feel right. But I want to ask you now."

I looked at him in horror as he produced the ring box and crawled in my direction, coming to a stop in front of me with one knee bent.

"Hannah, will you—"

"Don't," I said, putting my hand out to stop him.

"Please, I love you and I—"

"No, Si," I said. "You can't propose to someone like this!"

He staggered to his feet and threw himself between me and the door, holding out his arms to stop me getting past.

"Let's talk some more. See if we can't sort through this. Work something out. This can't be the end, Han, it can't."

All I could hear was our breath, the ragged ins and outs of it.

"Please, Si. Just let me go."

I couldn't believe I was actually walking out on the man I'd thought I was going to marry. But something had died inside me, I realized, almost from the moment I'd read Alison's texts on the train. I'd been left with the shell of our relationship, the superficial, external part. I could remember clearly what we'd had, how important it had been to me. But I would always be wondering when he would keep something from me again. I'd thought he'd been sitting happily in his office in Fenchurch Street like always. For weeks now I'd imagined him popping out to Pret at lunchtime, having meetings in the boardroom, writing figures on a flip chart. I'd never thought he'd be flicking through the jobs section of the paper in our local library or getting legal advice from old school friends in pubs in town.

He stood to one side, wringing his hands, not knowing what to do with himself.

"Bye, Si," I said, walking out the door and slamming it behind me.

As I walked along the corridor, I thought about Léo again. He was the first person who popped into my head, the person I wished I could talk to most. He'd have told me I should have left Si months ago. That I'd been settling for something I thought I wanted, and how it hadn't been what I'd wanted at all.

Catherine's carefully orchestrated playlist was in full swing and I could hear the dulcet tones of John Legend's "All of Me" drifting up from the dining room. The lift appeared to be stuck in the basement and I was worried that Si would come after me, so I began to pick my way down the stairs, bumping my suitcase behind me step by step, floor by floor. There were wedding guests milling about everywhere; I could see them lurking in the atrium and I couldn't wait to get out of there so that I could breathe again. I would dart past them so quickly they'd think I'd been a figment of their imagination.

I remembered to collect my passport from the front desk and handed in my room key. The concierge asked if I'd had a nice stay and I said not really but thanked him for asking. I had no real concept of time, but I guessed it must have been about 7:30. I heard a couple of people jovially calling my name but I didn't turn round. And then, as the porter opened the door for me and I stepped out into the most beautifully cool, quiet evening air, Catherine came running up behind me, her dress swishing around her ankles.

"Hannah? What are you doing?"

I closed my eyes for a second. The last thing I wanted was to ruin her big day; was there a way, I wondered, to explain myself without giving her all the facts? To make it seem less awful than it was?

"Is everything all right?" she asked, laughing nervously.

A tram came squealing past on the street at the end of the driveway. The sky had begun to darken and I could see the first few stars popping on the skyline.

"Everything's fine," I said, trying to sound as though it was.

"Why are you leaving, then?"

I looked down at my feet, flexing my foot, which only hurt very slightly now. And then, while I was stalling, trying to compile an answer that was a softer version of the truth, Si came charging through the doors behind us, his shirt open at the neck.

Catherine looked at him expectantly, crossing her arms. "Si, what's going on?"

"Go back inside, Catherine," I said gently. "There's nothing for you to worry about, honestly. Go and enjoy your day."

She put her hands on her hips. "Can somebody please tell me what is happening?"

"You know what?" said Si. "I may as well come clean. Get it all out there."

I shook my head at him. Even I could see it wasn't the time.

"I've been fired from work," said Si. "And understandably Hannah is very upset. So she's going to find a hotel for the night. That's it, that's all there is to tell."

Catherine looked at him, her forehead creased in confusion. Part of me had wondered whether she already knew, whether she'd been in on it all along. But seeing her now, I knew that she hadn't had a clue, either.

"Is this true?" Catherine asked me. I nodded.

"You've lost your job?" she said, turning to Si. "When?"

He dropped his eyes, like a child about to be scolded. "Six weeks ago," he mumbled.

"I've only just found out," I said quietly.

A silence.

"What did you do?" asked Catherine, incredulous.

"I broke my manager's nose. But he's an arsehole, Cath, you've heard me talk about him. He deserved it."

She still looked confused. "You actually hit someone?"

"I know, I know," he said. "I was drunk and I don't remember anything about it, you have to believe me. Both of you, please."

And then, out of the blue, Catherine launched herself at Si, pushing him so hard that he nearly stumbled backward onto the cobbles. Even the porter did a double take, probably of two minds about whether or not to step in.

"What is wrong with you? How could you keep this from your family, from your own girlfriend? That's not what you do in relationships, Si! And now you've lost her—look, she's walking away and I don't blame her. I don't blame her at all."

I stood watching them for a while, wondering what to do, how to make things better for Catherine, because I felt guilty now that she had to hear this stuff about her brother on her wedding day. If I'd just kept quiet, put a brave face on it, she could have enjoyed herself without all of this. My only hope was that she'd go back inside, find Jasper, forget about me, get back to her celebration.

I picked up my suitcase and walked away, down the driveway to the street beyond, bumping my suitcase over the cobbles.

"Hannah, wait!"

I sighed, turning round. Si was there, bent at the waist, his breath ragged.

"Is there anything I can do to make this up to you?" he said, looking at me with desperation in his eyes. "I'll beg if you like. Is that what you want?"

"For God's sake."

"Aren't I allowed to make a mistake?"

"It's a pretty big mistake," I said.

A tram screeched to a halt at the stop on the corner. I heard its doors hiss open.

"Anyway, it's not just that," I said, wondering how much to tell him. It didn't seem fair to make him think that he was entirely responsible for what our relationship had become. "It's more that we don't communicate. About anything, Si."

"What do you mean?" he asked.

A small crowd had gathered in the courtyard. I noticed Pauline was desperately trying to usher them inside.

"We don't really know each other, not properly," I said. "We don't tell each other anything. I think we've presented these watered-down versions of ourselves to each other. And that once we started, we couldn't stop."

He laughed. "You're not serious."

I went to walk away.

"Sorry!" he said. "Go on, I'm listening."

"Look, it's not the fact that you hit Dave that bothers me. Okay, it bothers me a bit. But it's more that you didn't feel able to tell me. That you created this web of lies to keep it from me, and for what? This can't be how you want to live your life, Si. What kind of partnership is that?"

He looked so deflated, I almost started to feel sorry for him.

"Also, I met someone," I said. I'd have to tell him sometime, it was only fair. "In Paris."

He did an exaggerated double take. "What?"

"Nothing happened, before you go mad. We just talked. We walked around Paris and we talked. About our parents, our pasts, our hopes for the future."

"I knew you weren't at the station when you called me!"

"You don't even know that I've been to Paris before, do you? That there was a whole lot of stuff to do with my dad. Because you've never asked."

"That makes it all right, then, does it, for you to go off with some French idiot as soon as my back's turned? Did you do it on purpose, then? Get on the wrong bit of the train?"

I took a deep breath. "This isn't getting us anywhere, Si."

"Well, knowing you're not perfect either is making me feel *much* better," he said nastily.

"Great. Glad I could be of service."

I turned and carried on down the driveway. "And don't follow me this time," I shouted over my shoulder.

23

I hugged the canal, which was beautifully lit by the warm, orange glow beaming out the windows of the canal houses. Bobbing on the water was a row of houseboats, some of them huge, modern structures that must have cost tens of thousands of pounds, some more traditional, painted in muted colors that I couldn't quite make out under the shadows of the trees. Groups of people sat on the edge of the water, swigging from beer bottles, hanging their feet over the edge.

I spotted a phone box and reluctantly went inside, tiptoeing over the newspapers and crisp packets covering the ground. I scrabbled in my purse for some coins and then wiped the handset on the hem of my dress. Because I didn't know who else to call, I dialed Mum and Tony's home number. My stomach turned at the prospect of explaining what had happened. She'd be disappointed in me, no doubt, would assume that I was the one to blame, because how could the wonderful Si be at fault? I'd never turned to her in a crisis before, because she'd made it clear very early on that she couldn't handle my "emotional outbursts"—i.e., any exploration of feelings at all. And on the odd occasion she did try, she'd end up saying something to make the situation worse. I'd learned to keep things from her, preferring to pretend that I was coasting happily through life, which Mum seemed easily and conveniently to accept.

While I listened to the dial tone I leaned my shoulder against the smeared glass of the phone box, realizing that for the first time in years, nobody was expecting me to be anywhere. And that might have felt terrifying once, being alone in a city I didn't know, without the safety net of Si or Ellie or any of the other people I'd leaned on over the years, but I felt strangely liberated. A bit foggy-headed, completely exhausted, but with the inner conviction that whatever happened, I would be able to cope.

"Hello?" said Mum, a touch of panic in her voice. It would be a little after 6:30 in England. She'd be having tea, watching *Britain's Got Talent* or some equally middle-of-the-road light entertainment show.

"Hi, Mum," I said, cradling the receiver between my shoulder and my chin while unzipping my suitcase and pulling out the first warm thing I could find: Léo's hoodie. I slipped it on, burying my face inside the shoulder of it, inhaling the scent of him.

"My God, we've been out of our heads with worry here," said Mum. "Why haven't you called us? I've been texting you like mad."

"My phone got stolen in Paris," I said. "Remember?"

"That explains it!" announced Mum. "I don't know how I managed to forget that."

I sighed, listening while she relayed the whole thing to Tony.

"Did you make it to the wedding, then?" she asked.

"I made it."

And then I dropped the bombshell, got it out there before I bottled it. I didn't want these filtered relationships anymore, ones where I second-guessed what people were thinking, what it was they needed. Because I had proof now that life did not work that way. Even by doing what I'd thought was the right thing, by becoming what I'd thought Si wanted me to be, it had still gone wrong in the end. I may as well show people who I really was; at least then, if nothing else, I'd be being true to myself.

"I've left Si, Mum."

There was silence for what seemed like an age. A group of lads wearing cowboy hats and T-shirts with someone's photo on them staggered past. One of them banged on the window and waved and I wiggled my fingers back.

"Mum, are you still there?"

"What do you mean, left him?"

I would have to tell her straight. There was no easy way to do it. She adored Si and she was going to be gutted, however I sugarcoated it. She, too, had thought Si was the perfect man, the answer to all my prayers and hers. But of course, the glaringly obvious fact that we'd both been missing was that nobody could ever be perfect. And also, that nobody could sort my life out for me *except* me. And that was, starting from this very moment, in this grimy phone box in the middle of Amsterdam, what I fully intended to do.

"He's been fired from work," I told her. "Weeks ago, without telling me. For punching his line manager at a party. Calling him names. Being threatening, all that."

I heard her coughing, gulping down mouthfuls of the always-stale water I knew she kept on the coffee table.

"What? No, Hannah, no. He couldn't have done all that," she said eventually.

It would have been the last thing she'd expected of him; it was the last thing any of us would have imagined.

"Are you sure you haven't got it wrong?" she asked. "You know, read too much into things? Have you actually spoken to him about it, Hannah? Because I'm sure he'd put you straight, tell you it's all been a silly mistake."

"It's true, Mum. He told me himself."

I heard Mum sniffing and wondered whether she was tearful or something, which would have been odd, since that would require her to have actual feelings on my behalf.

"We thought he was going to ask you to marry him," she said, her voice all quivery.

I pinched the top of my nose. "Honestly, Mum, I'm not entirely sure that our relationship was everything I thought it was."

I thought briefly of Léo, who I'd dismissed initially for being rude and brash and full of himself, which (apart from the rude bit) couldn't have been further from the truth. You had to get to know people. You had to open yourselves up to them, so that they could do the same.

"Si loves you, Hannah, I know he does."

"But I don't think he understands me. Not in the way I've always wanted someone to."

"It's not about that, though, is it? What's this need to know everything about each other?"

I bit my lip. This was probably the most honest conversation I'd had with Mum in years.

"Tony gets you, doesn't he?" I said gently, by way of an example. "Somehow he just knows what you need. He loves every part of you, the good bits and the bad bits. And that's what I want, Mum. Not someone like Dad, who only wanted the fun stuff and wasn't prepared to stick around when things got tough between the two of you."

"He loved you, you know," she said. "Your dad."

"Sure. But not in the way I deserved. I've wasted enough time worrying about what I might have said or done to make him go, to make him not care enough to keep in touch. And the last thing I want is to be in another relationship where I feel like being myself isn't good enough."

Mum sighed heavily. "You want to find your own version of Tony."

"I think so, yeah."

Admittedly, my version looked very different. But I was beginning to think it might be possible for me to meet someone who made me truly happy, a deeper, more honest, less idyllic kind of happy. I was only thirty, it wasn't too late yet. I could hear Tony mumbling in the background, no doubt bewildered by this unexpected turn of events. Mum and I never talked like this. Everything was brushed under the carpet, everything went unsaid, either eventually forgotten or relegated to a position of simmering resentment. And now that I'd said it, put stuff out there that I would usually have kept from her, it felt good. Like a release. And, importantly, I felt as though she was actually listening for once.

"Don't do anything rash, Hannah," she said. "Take some time to think it through."

"I will, Mum," I said, although in my heart, I already knew.

I waited while she whispered something to Tony and then she came back on the phone, sounding all businesslike.

"Where are you now?" she asked.

"In a pay phone, somewhere in the middle of Amsterdam, not far from the wedding venue."

"Let's think . . . have you got money?" she asked me.

"Not much. I've got my credit card, a few notes. Let me see," I said, opening my purse, which I was relieved to have back, totting it up. "I've got about eighty euros in cash."

"Well, if you need anything, anything at all, money or whatever, or for us to come and pick you up from somewhere, you ask us, all right? We're here, aren't we, Tony?"

I heard him mumbling in the background.

"Why don't we book you into a hotel? Let me get the laptop, we can do it from here. Tony, get your card. Quickly!"

I was amazed that she was being so helpful, and wondered whether I'd underestimated her all this time, whether I'd always looked for the worst in her and not seen the best. I was angry when Dad left. I was mad at him for going, but I was also angry with her, because if she'd been different, if he'd loved her more, then maybe they could have worked things out. I'd been unfair. I'd blamed Mum, deep down, when it should have been him I took all my disappointment and frustration out on.

I talked Mum through the bookings.com website. She originally tried to check me in to the cheapest hotel she could find, which was out near Schiphol airport, but we eventually worked out where I was (Tony was a whiz on Google Maps) and they booked me into a B&B about half a mile away. I would ask for directions, I told her.

"But how, when you don't speak Dutch, Hannah?" she said.

"I'll find it, Mum."

"Call us when you get there, all right? And then we can think about flights home and things."

I hadn't even thought that far ahead: I was booked on a flight home, the day after tomorrow, but I didn't think I could wait that long, and also, I'd left my tickets with Si. And there was the small matter of having to sit next to him for an hour on the plane.

"And if you like," said Mum, "you could move in here for a bit, couldn't she, Tony, if you need somewhere to stay? Just until you get back on your feet."

I nibbled on the nail of my little finger, suddenly very touched. "Thanks, Mum."

"Oh, and Hannah?"

"Yes?"

She cleared her throat. "Thank you for telling me. I know it can't have been easy."

I smiled, even though she couldn't see me. I didn't want to get too deep, it wasn't the time, but I felt as though something might be beginning to shift, that there could be a newfound respect for each other, one that had been bubbling away under the surface all these years but that neither of us had been able to tap into.

We ended the call and I retraced my steps, back along the canal in the direction of the Lux, looking for a street called something beginning with *H*, which should lead to the B&B we'd booked. There was music coming from somewhere, a live band, and it got louder and quieter and louder and quieter as the door to the venue opened and closed. I spotted the street I was looking for over on the other side of the canal, a quaint, curving cobbled lane lined with bikes propped in racks and with a cozy little restaurant on the corner that had candles flickering in the window. I swallowed hard. I'd been high on adrenaline, buoyed by being in Paris, and meeting Léo and the shock of finding out what Si had been up to. But now it was just me again, alone in the world. I waited for the familiar empty, thudding feeling I'd had a million times before, but it didn't come. Perhaps it hadn't quite sunk in.

Running my hand across the railings, I'd just started out across the bridge when I heard somebody calling my name.

"Hannah!"

I turned round. For a second I let myself imagine it could be Léo, but how could it, when he wouldn't know how to find me?

I squinted into the half-light. At first I couldn't see him, there was just a shadow, but then he came into view with his perfect face and his leather jacket, the jeans that were slung too low on his hips. That smile.

"It is you," he said, panting.

I laughed. "Are you all right there?"

"No," he said, clutching his chest with a grin.

"Did you run all the way here, or something?"

He nodded. "I only have a few minutes before the concert starts," he said, trying to catch his breath.

"Short on time, eh? The story of our lives," I said.

A group of girls tottered past, off their heads, singing loudly. They were eating some sort of kebab, scooping up handfuls of meat from oily paper bags clutched in their hands.

"How did you know where I was?" I asked.

"I heard what you said when you got into the taxi, so I went to the Lux. I could not see you among the wedding party, so I asked the doorman at the hotel. He thought you might have gone in this direction."

"What are you doing here, anyway?"

"I came to see whether you are all right," he said, leaning his back against the railings, crossing one foot over the other. "That you have not tripped over the bride's dress and twisted your other ankle."

I smiled. "You know, I don't think I deserve the clumsy rep."

Léo looked down at the ground, then back at me. "What happened with your boyfriend? Why are you not at the wedding?"

I pulled his hoodie tighter around my body. "I was right, he'd been lying to me."

"You knew that, *non?*"

"Sort of, I suppose. But it wasn't what I thought it was. He wasn't having an affair," I said.

"No?"

"He got fired from his job and then covered it up by pretending to go to work every day when he had no actual job to go to."

"He is an idiot," said Léo, tutting. "I knew that, without ever meeting him."

A nearby door opened, flooding the cobbles with white light, sending jazz music blasting out into the night.

"Don't you need to go?" I asked.

He glanced at his watch. "Yes."

"They're going to love your song, by the way," I said.

He shrugged. "I hope so."

"You're not going to make me do the whole sad goodbye thing all over again, are you?"

"Ah, yes. I did not think of that," he said.

"So now that you've found me . . ."

"Now that I have found you, I am not sure how to say what I want to say."

"It's not like you to be lost for words," I said, leaning on the railings next to him, our hip bones knocking together.

"I wanted to see you, again, okay?"

I bit my lip. "I thought you were a pro at walking away from things."

"I am. Very good at it, usually," he added. "But when I got to my meeting and I was talking about my work, you kept coming in and out of my mind. It was very strange. I kept thinking about how when I saw you at Gare du Nord—*non*, before that, on the train—I thought you were very beautiful. And interesting and smart and funny. Which I suppose explains why I was such an arsehole to you."

I laughed. "You certainly did an excellent job of pretending you couldn't stand me," I said.

"Why do you think I came back to Gare du Nord? Why I persuaded you to let me take you to the police station?"

"You told me already. Because you can't stand feeling guilty."

"Yes, that is true. But that rule applies only if I care what that person thinks of me," he said.

"Which must mean . . ."

"That I care what you think of me."

We turned to watch a tiny motorboat chug underneath us, leaving a trail of froth behind it.

"What will you do tonight?" he asked. "Where will you stay?"

"I've booked a hotel," I said. "Not far from here."

He nodded.

"You're being very serious," I said, looking warily across at him.

"I thought I would not see you again, that is all," he said, looking earnest. "And now that you are here in front of me, I feel I must say all the things I wanted to say to you all day but was not brave enough to."

I reached out and tucked his hair behind his ear. "I thought flying was the only thing you were scared of."

I was suddenly very aware of the sounds around me. Léo's soft, rapid breathing. The click-clack of someone's heels as they passed over the bridge. The water below us lapping against the quay. The cold, wet metal of the railings seeping through the fabric of my skirt.

"You know, there is much more of Paris to show you," he said.

"Is that an invitation?"

He nodded. "I think so."

"You don't seem sure," I said, teasing him.

He took my hands in his, linking our fingers together. "I am sure, Hannah. I would like you to come to Paris again," he said. "To see me."

"Will you buy me another *Mont Blanc*?"

"Naturally," he said, stroking my wrists with his thumbs.

"I should probably let things settle down first. Make a proper break from Si."

He nodded. "Absolutely."

I pulled him closer to me, resting his hands on my hips, noticing how the heat of his hands burned through to my skin. I was painfully aware of the rise and fall of my chest, of the way the tips of our noses almost brushed together.

"I have wanted to kiss you all day, you know," he said.

I curled my arms around him, linking them around his neck. "Well, you hid it very well."

He laughed. "I will wait for you, then," he said. "Until you are ready. And then you will come to Paris and we will eat *Monts Blancs* again."

I smiled. "It's a date."

"So. Let us see . . . you have your course, *non*?"

"Yes," I said, meaning it. I was going to write the statement for my application on the plane home, and get my images processed as soon as I got back.

He slid his phone out of his pocket, flicking his thumb across the screen. "And you will be finished by . . . Christmas?"

I shook my head. "End of February."

"Then we will meet at the Gare du Nord on the . . . *un moment* . . . February 29 next year. A little more than seven months from now. *Oui*?"

I laughed, confused. "Are you serious?"

"Of course. I will be waiting for you there, at twelve noon, at the end of Platform 19, where we had our second conversation."

"Conversation or argument?"

"Definitely a conversation."

I looked doubtful. "What if you change your mind? It's a long way to come to get stood up."

"I promise you I will be there," he said, raking his hands through my hair. "I already know that I will not change my mind. But I want you to be sure, Hannah. And if we still think about each other after seven months, we will know that we have something special, yes?"

"Are we allowed any contact at all?" I asked, not sure what the rules were.

He thought about it. "I think you should have a clean break. Focus on your course, work everything out with your boyfriend. If we text and call, it becomes more complicated, *non*?"

I had to admit, I quite liked the idea of some time to myself. I didn't want to go rushing from one relationship headlong into another.

"Platform 19, you say?"

"You will be there?" he asked.

"As long as you don't try to break my neck this time."

"Noted. I will leave my bag at home."

I cupped his cheek in my hand. "February 29 it is, then."

We looked at each other for what felt like ages and then he was gone, striding off down the street, his keys jangling in his back pocket. "See you in seven months, Hannah!" he called over his shoulder.

I stood very still, watching him, pulling at the hem of his hoodie, my heart racing, trying to tell myself that he must have meant what he'd said. He never said things he didn't mean, he'd told me that himself. I watched him until he reached a bend in the road and disappeared out of sight.

Paris, seven months later

I pressed my cheek against the window of the train, watching the bleaker, emptier outskirts of Paris transform into the more built-up center of the city. The train was already beginning to slow and the usual announcements were made, first in English, then in French. I checked my phone: 11:50. I'd booked the train without thinking it through: What if we'd been delayed? It was as though I'd left it up to fate: Would I get there in time or wouldn't I?

As we pulled into the station, I caught a glimpse of the domes of the Sacré-Coeur. It looked incongruous there, next to the more modern buildings surrounding it, a beautiful piece of history, all white and gleaming and serene like an over-the-top wedding cake. Several times over the past seven months, I'd imagined Léo sitting on the steps in the early-morning light, looking at his beloved Paris spread out in front of him, writing lyrics, or tweaking a melody for a song. And I always wondered, afterward, whether he'd had the same thoughts about me: about where I might be, or what might be going well and what might not be. Whether I'd applied for my photography course and whether I'd finished it. I'd been tempted to call him, lots of times. I wished I had now, because then at least I'd have known whether he still felt the same way about me.

The train came to a complete stop, hissing off steam. I felt actually, physically sick. Because there was a chance that I was going to come full circle, that this was going to be another disastrous trip to Paris, like my first. I'd spent one day with Léo. We hadn't spoken for over half a year; the odds of him turning up weren't great. Everything had changed for me, so I could only assume that it had been the same for him. He could have met somebody. He could have forgotten about me completely. It was impossible to know, and there was only one way to find out.

All around me there was the usual flurry of activity. People shot out of their seats and I watched them scrabbling their things together, clambering to be first off the train. Perhaps I'd just stay on board, unnoticed, until the train filled up again and we turned back to London.

The doors pinged open. The aisle full of eager passengers began to empty out. My throat felt tight; I swallowed hard to loosen it. I stood up and pulled my coat and my carry-on out of the luggage rack, light-headed now as well as nauseated.

I stepped off the train. There were only a few of us straggling behind the crowd, a woman trying desperately to strap a toddler into a buggy and a businessman on a phone call, his briefcase swinging wildly in his hand. We'd come in on Platform 4. That would buy me some time to gather my thoughts. According to the departures and arrivals screen above my head, it was 11:54. Six minutes to go.

I began to walk very slowly along the concourse, feeling as though I was dragging my suitcase through mud. I badly regretted bringing it now, but the plans we'd made were so vague that I hadn't known what to do. In hindsight, it would have looked much cooler to have come with only my shoulder bag, to have given the impression I was just breezing through Paris for the day, and that I might, *might* pop along to Platform 19 on the off chance he'd be there. At least I'd booked a hotel—there was no way I could presume I'd be staying at his. And my return journey was locked in for the following evening. Even if he was there, even if it was as lovely as the first time, I wasn't going to moon around waiting for him to dictate how long I should stay. I'd bought myself a ticket for an exhibition at the Centre Pompidou, too, just in case. So that if he didn't come, I could somehow convince myself that the trip hadn't been for nothing.

I stopped, my breath catching in my throat, fumbling around in my pocket for my phone. It was 11:58. There was no way I could be early. I killed some time waiting underneath one of the lampposts that were dotted about; I'd seen them last time, sprouting randomly out of the concourse. Passengers weaved past me, kids or suitcases in their hands, headphones on, phones clamped to their ear. Everyone looked relaxed, everyone knew where they were going and why. Nobody looked as nervous as I felt, although perhaps they were just hiding it well. I swiped at my phone again, bringing the screen to life with a shaking thumb: 12:00. I took several deep, abdominal breaths and I touched my hair, smoothing down the curls. I'd worn it like I'd had it before, half up, half down, in case he only recognized me that way, although my hair was a few inches longer than it had been.

I made my way to the platform, slowly at first and then more quickly, because now that it was time, I sort of wanted to get it over with. If he wasn't there, I'd put a brave face on it and I'd move on, just as I'd been doing my whole life. If he was? Well, then, I didn't know. My ankle boots clip-clopped on the marble flooring as I walked along. My skirt flipped against my thighs. I had a white camisole on, like I'd had before, but this time I wore a chunky knitted cardigan on top of it, my winter coat slung over my arm.

I arrived at Platform 19, placing my hand on my chest, as if that was going to stop the hammering. I stood very still for a bit, but it was too quiet and I could hear my pulse beating in my eardrums, so I turned full circle, very slowly, as casually as I could, my eyes flicking left and right. Where would he be, if he was here? Where would he stand? I did one full rotation and couldn't see him. I crossed my arms, swallowing the lump in my throat.

"Hannah?"

I was looking down the platform at the time, out at the end of the glass canopy, the way I had been when I'd missed the Amsterdam train and had been staring at it in disbelief. I turned my head, scared to look. What if my mind had been playing tricks on me? What if I'd imagined his voice, because that was what I'd wanted to hear?

"Hey," he said, smiling at me.

It was him. His hair was shorter than it had been before. He had jeans on and his leather jacket and a gray scarf and looked a little unsure of himself.

"Hi," I said.

I felt breathless, as though I could only speak in short bursts.

"You are upright, at least," he said.

318

I smiled, gripping the handle of my suitcase. "Yep. No accidents yet."

"You look beautiful, Hannah," he said.

I nodded, my eyes fixed to the floor. "You too."

He took a step closer to me. "Did you believe I would be here?"

I lifted my head. "I wouldn't have come all this way otherwise, would I?"

"You have found your confidence, I see." He reached out to touch my hair. "It is longer," he said.

"You cut yours."

An announcement blared over the loudspeaker. We both jumped and then laughed, self-conscious.

"I've missed you," I said, which felt strange to say, but I'd decided that if he was there, I was going to be completely honest about my feelings for him. Was going to share every single thought in my head.

"I think about you all of the time," he said.

I cupped his head in my hands, tugging at him to come closer.

"Oh, right. I can kiss you now, can I?" he said, teasing me.

I pretended to think about it, and then instead I kissed him. Gently at first, enjoying this moment that I'd daydreamed about every single day since I'd seen him last. Then his thumb was running across my cheek and his hands were in my hair and I dropped the handle of my suitcase and it clattered to the floor and I didn't care who could see us. I pressed myself into him.

"I am so happy to see you, Hannah," he said, kissing my neck, then my lips again.

I laughed softly. "We have so much to tell each other."

"I want to hear everything," he whispered in my ear, running his fingers up and down my spine.

"Where shall we start?"

"Your course!" he said, pulling back, full of the energy I remembered. "What is happening with your course?"

"I finished it," I told him, proud of myself for once. "I did it and I loved every second. I work in a gallery now, too. I'm surrounded by photography all day every day, so, as you can imagine, I'm in my absolute element."

He laughed. "I knew you could do it, Hannah."

"And what about you?" I asked excitedly. "Your music?"

He looked embarrassed, suddenly, his fringe too short to cover his eyes now, even when he tried to hide behind it. "The track was a hit. Number one in five countries."

I took his hands in mine and squeezed them. "I told you she'd love it in the end."

"So now you are a fortune-teller as well as a mind reader?"

A train pulled in on the platform, hissing to a stop.

He looked up. "Shall we go?"

I watched the train's doors open, passengers piling off. "Sure. Where to?"

He hesitated. "Can I buy lunch for you?"

"Hmm, that depends. What's on the menu?"

"No, you cannot only have *Monts Blancs* for lunch, Hannah."

I frowned playfully. "Anyway, I'm pretty sure it's my turn to pay."

"Ah well, in that case, I know just the place," he said, winking at me.

He picked up my suitcase and took my hand, leading me toward the exit, the same one he'd pulled up at on the motorbike all those months before.

"Now, you do know there is no bike this time?" he said mock-apologetically.

"You can imagine how disappointed I am," I joked, smiling with relief and wrapping both arms around his waist, burying my head in his chest. He smelled exactly the same. As we stepped outside, our breath just visible in the freezing February air, I noticed how easy and familiar everything felt already, as though I had never been away.

Acknowledgments

There are so many people I'd like to thank for helping and supporting me on my journey to publication.

Thank you to Claire Collison, who taught the Novel Writing module at Birkbeck, University of London, in 2011, the point at which I realized that writing a book wasn't a completely ridiculous idea. To the writing group we formed afterward—I miss our monthly sessions and your thoughtful feedback. To Connie and John for their unwavering kindness and generosity.

Thank you to the Bath Novel Award, Joanna Barnard and the Society of Authors. To everyone involved with the Penguin Random House WriteNow program, particularly Siena Parker, Molly Crawford, Sally Williamson and especially Katie Seaman—I would not have got to this point without you. To my fellow WriteNow mentees, whose encouragement has been invaluable. To the Debut 20 group, who always make me feel much better about everything.

Acknowledgments

To my brilliant agent, Hannah Ferguson—thank you for everything you've done for me, for never doubting I could do it, for being an all-round lovely person and for making my dreams come true. To the amazing Thérèse Coen for talking to people around the world about my book with such enthusiasm, and to Caroline, Jo and Nicole at Hardman & Swainson. To my talented editors Margo Lipschultz, Helen O'Hare, Victoria Oundjian and Charlotte Mursell, whose combined vision shaped the book into something much better than I'd imagined it could be—I will be forever thankful for your hard work, your insight and your belief in the story. Thanks also to the teams at Orion Fiction and G. P. Putnam's Sons, who have worked so tirelessly behind the scenes, particularly Patricja Okuniewska, Chandra Wohleber, Sandra Chiu and Claire Winecoff.

To my kind and beautiful mum and dad, who encouraged and celebrated my love of reading and who made me believe I could be anything I wanted to be. To Matthew and Helen, who had a "train incident" of their own and whose story inspired me to write this book. To Alyson and Janet, who always support me whatever I do. To my longtime friend Louise, who walked the length and breadth of Paris with me without complaint, and to Alex for being the best companion for a research trip to Amsterdam ever! And finally, thank you to my boyfriend, Robbie—my best friend and biggest supporter. And to Gabriel, the light of my life—thank you for believing that Mummy could do this.

Discussion Guide

1) At the beginning of the novel, Hannah and Si are rushing onto their train to Amsterdam. Discuss the series of events that lead to them being split up in the middle of the night.

2) Under what circumstances do Léo and Hannah first meet? What are their reactions upon discovering they're actually en route to Paris?

3) What goes wrong when Hannah arrives in Paris and tries to make her way back to Amsterdam, and what forces her to stay in the city for the morning?

4) Discuss your first impressions of Léo. In what ways is he different from Si?

5) What quintessentially Parisian things does Hannah do and see? If you had a day to spend in Paris, what activities would you plan and why?

6) How does Hannah's previous trip to Paris dictate how she feels about the city in the present of the story, and how does her time with Léo change her mind about it? What is she able to see with a fresh perspective?

7) Discuss how the trip changes Hannah's mind about her career and love life. Why does she ultimately decide to pursue photography, and how does Hannah's relationship with art mirror Léo's relationship with music?

8) An important theme in *The Paris Connection* is that the unexpected detours in life can turn out to be some of the most valuable experiences. To what extent is that true in this novel?

9) What do you think is in store for Hannah and Léo?